# MASTER OF SEDUCTION

## Marie Harte

Erotic Futuristic Romance

New Concepts             Georgia

Be sure to check out our website for the very best in fiction at fantastic prices!

When you visit our webpage, you can:

* Read excerpts of currently available books
* View cover art of upcoming books and current releases
* Find out more about the talented artists who capture the magic of the writer's imagination on the covers
* Order books from our backlist
* Find out the latest NCP and author news--including any upcoming book signings by your favorite NCP author
* Read author bios and reviews of our books
* Get NCP submission guidelines
* And so much more!

We offer a 20% discount on all new Trade Paperback releases ordered from our website!

Be sure to visit our webpage to find the best deals in e-books and paperbacks! To find out about our new releases as soon as they are available, please be sure to sign up for our newsletter (http://www.newconceptspublishing.com/newsletter.htm) or join our reader group (http://groups.yahoo.com/group/new_concepts_pub/join)!

The newsletter is available by double opt in only and our customer information is *never* shared!

Visit our webpage at:
www.newconceptspublishing.com

Master of Seduction is an original publication of NCP. This work has never before appeared in book form. This work is a novel. Any similarity to actual persons or events is purely coincidental.

New Concepts Publishing
5202 Humphreys Rd.
Lake Park, GA 31636

ISBN 1-58608-713-4
© copyright 2005, Marie Harte

Cover art (c) copyright 2005 Eliza Black

All rights reserved, which includes the right to reproduce this book or portions thereof in any form whatsoever except as provided by the U.S. Copyright Law.

If you purchased this book without a cover you should be aware this book is stolen property.

NCP books are available at special quantity discounts for bulk purchases for sales promotions, premiums, fund raising, or educational use. For details, write, email, or phone New Concepts Publishing, 5202 Humphreys Rd., Lake Park, GA 31636; Ph. 229-257-0367, Fax 229-219-1097; orders@newconceptspublishing.com.

First NCP Paperback Printing: 2005

## TABLE OF CONTENTS

Lurin's Surrender										Page 5

The Thief of Mardu										Page 102

# LURIN'S SURRENDER

### Chapter One

Captain Mara Seni swore as the ship encountered another round of hostile fire from the Melan rebels.

"Damned ex-patriots," she seethed as she fought to keep her ship in one piece. Not only had the rebels come out of nowhere in the middle of an asteroid storm, but they'd interrupted her crew's attempts to subdue her thrashing and less-than-willing captive.

She narrowly guided the ship out of a speeding asteroid's path and smiled grimly as she watched it destroy one of the three Melan ships tracking her.

"Damn it, release me, you heathen *fethra*," a deep voice bellowed angrily from the hallway. "When I get free I'm going to make you all pay for this," he roared, a deadly promise too intense to ignore.

Swearing under her breath, Mara jockeyed her ship out of the storm and quickly thrust into hyper drive. The minute her ship leapt out of the Melans' sight, she exhaled with relief and left the controls to see to her prisoner.

She encountered him with the other three of her crew. She grudgingly respected her captive's strength. He struggled under the two hulking Fas brothers and the quick-as-a-whip Catam of Mardu. She had ordered her crew to be firm and if necessary, a bit rough. After all, the prisoner had committed a ruthless crime.

"Ah, so the dark eyed woman was not a mere figment of my imagination after all," the captive purred and stared at her insolently as she approached. His light blue eyes fairly sizzled as they traced her from the top of her golden brown hair to the tips of her boots.

"That's our captain," Catam said quietly and knocked the

captive back with a hard punch to his midsection. "Show some respect."

The captive absorbed the blow but made not a sound. Again Mara studied him curiously, wondering how a man that looked like this could have turned into a murdering rapist.

He had dark blue-black hair and sun-kissed skin. His build towered over hers, and Mara considered herself a tall woman.

His muscular forearms led to thick biceps and a broad chest, visible through the sleeveless and ripped tunic he wore. His skintight rak-hide leggings suggested similar strength in his powerful thighs.

But his face. Stars, Mara thought, irritated for having noticed. With a face like that and a body to match, this man should never have to resort to rape. His straight nose and sharp chin framed an arrogant face. High cheekbones and cat-slanted eyes gave him an exotic look, made even more stunning by his thickly lashed electric-blue eyes and full, sensuous lips.

Mara watched those lips curve in sardonic amusement as she said nothing, merely studied the man before her.

"Like what you see?" His smooth voice beckoned her closer. For a startled moment she almost stepped forward. Then she mentally shook herself and stared angrily at her prisoner.

"You are Lurin Vez, are you not?" she asked throatily, suddenly conscious of her own sensuality.

His eyes lit but he said nothing, his gaze firmly on her mouth.

"He is," Nu, the elder Fas brother spoke.

"We searched his belongings earlier and found this," his brother Set remarked. He held out a system tag that clearly showed her prisoner's likeness against the name Lurin Vez.

"Good." Mara smiled and the prisoner blinked, his gaze leaving her lips to peruse the rest of her face. "Nobless Cari Elaran has a bounty on your head," she said pleasantly. She watched but could detect no recognition in his shuttered gaze at the name. "We'll have you at her estate in less than a week's time, captive Vez."

"Why are you doing this?" Lurin struggled against the Fas brothers again, his muscles straining to regain freedom from the shackles at his wrists and legs.

"Come now, captive Vez." Mara shook her head in disappointment, making a mental note to continue to address him as "captive". He didn't like it one bit. "You raped the Nobless' virgin daughter and murdered her future mate. Surely you didn't think that action would go unpunished?"

He stared at her in surprise, as if unaware of the heinous crimes he'd committed. Mara waited patiently for him to refute the accusations; she could read the denial on his face.

"That's why you're bringing me in?" he asked softly, his eyes intent on her face.

"Please, no more games." Mara felt an odd sense of disappointment. Most of her bounties protested innocence until confronted with their guilt. For some reason she thought Vez would be different. He possessed a core of strength that unfortunately went no further than the physical. "Nu, Set, take him to his new quarters. And Catam, make sure all is clear for our journey to planet Jaron."

Her crew did her bidding easily since the prisoner ceased fighting. Perhaps now that his crimes had been brought into the open, he realized he had nothing with which to bargain.

Mara smiled bitterly. She didn't believe in bargaining with men regardless. She lived a simple life, a solitary existence devoted to her career as a bounty hunter. She had no use for pleasures of the flesh or emotional attachments. And though not overly satisfied with her lot in life, she did feel content.

Though her job brought bursts of excitement, Mara preferred when the job went smoothly. Relieved that the crisis with Vez had been averted, she headed to the galley for some sustenance. Since the capture of her prisoner, she'd been awake for more than two days.

His capture had been a thing of beauty, she recalled, and grabbed a tray of food before she sat down. Staring at the unappetizing fare, she thought about Vez and the circumstances surrounding the mysterious criminal.

From one of her many sources, Mara had received word that her latest quarry had been hiding out on one of the Melan moons, a smart move considering the Melans' dislike for anything Elaran.

Disguised as a pleasurer, Mara had visited bar after bar on Sheias--the central moon to which all information funneled concerning planet Melan. Soon armed with his whereabouts, she'd easily infiltrated the rebel club where Vez had been drinking by himself in a corner. For the right price, a serving girl agreed to tamper with his next drink.

The drug had worked surprisingly well and the Fas brothers escorted him unhindered to her ship. They'd been sitting cloaked in space, waiting out the Melan rebel force's movements, when her captive had revived.

She frowned and forced herself to eat. Vez had proven himself amazingly strong, almost defeating both Fas brothers until Catam had entered the scene. The Fas brothers hailed from Ragga, a planet known for delivering inhumanly strong species due to the minerals found in the water.

For Vez to have almost defeated not one, but two Raggas meant that he was no ordinary human. His unusual good looks could be attributed to any number of planetary inhabitants, but his strength made her wonder. Then there was the matter of his intoxicating voice. Something in his tenor denoted simmering power. A telepath, maybe? His overt sensuality though, bespoke of something more. If she hadn't known better, she might have thought him a Thesha.

*A Thesha, sure.* She scoffed at her overworked imagination.

The Thesha had been a legend for as long as she could remember. No matter that the nobles in the system still searched and raged about the sensually gifted race, Mara didn't believe they existed anymore, if they had in the first place. Imagine a race of men able to pleasure a woman without cease. Obviously a tale created by deprived women.

"Captain?" Catam stepped quietly into the galley and waited for her to acknowledge him.

"Yes?"

"We're set for Jaron. I enabled the communicator should you like to inform Nobless Cari that we're on our way." His sensual, gold eyes brightened with intensity as he stared at her, and Mara had the uneasy suspicion that she would need to make at least one stop before reaching Jaron.

From the beginning of her captaincy, Mara hadn't wanted

to use a crew of men only, but her need for their strength and solidarity of warlike mindsets had made the decision to exclude females an easy one.

An unusual maiden, Mara had been trained in the arts of war since she was old enough to stand. Softness was not a part of her. When she felt such uncomfortable stirrings, she returned to her training. Unlike the men she worked with, however, she felt free of the lusts they often suffered.

She'd made sure to take on men she could trust, and though they never discussed such matters, Mara always made sure to stop at a pleasure point somewhere in space where her crew could see to their base needs. Left untended, she worried her men might grow lustful around her.

"Good work, Catam." She nodded at him. He watched her carefully while maintaining a respectful distance. Mara knew should she give him the slightest hint, Catam would take her to bed without question. Rumors of the sensual Mardu had at times made her wonder what held her back.

"I'll go talk to the Nobless." She pushed away her half-eaten food and stood. "Oh, and Catam? Set a course for Nebe6 on our way to Jaron. You and the others have performed well this week."

At mention of the pleasure planet Nebe6, Catam smiled widely. He bowed and with a mischievous wink left her to reset course.

Mara shook her head. *Males. They were so predictable.* She left the galley and moments later entered her captain's quarters. She sat down at the communicator and activated the vidscreen.

"Nobless Cari?"

She watched as the vidscreen revealed a handsome woman in her midyears. Nobless Cari had a head of dark red hair, brown eyes, and the gloriously smooth skin of a woman many years younger. Wealthy beyond belief, the Nobless had survived two past matings and now had only herself and her daughter Sara to care for.

"Yes, Mara," the Nobless answered in a voice used to being obeyed. "I'm glad you called. I trust everything is in order."

Mara ignored the Nobless' imperious tone and focused instead on the other twenty thousand beks she'd receive once she pulled off this bounty. "Everything went like clockwork, my lady. We have Lurin Vez in captivity and should arrive within the next few days."

"Splendid, Mara," the Nobless commented evenly. Mara thought the woman's satisfaction a trifle odd. If Mara had a daughter that had been raped, the rapist's capture would stir more than a cool "splendid".

"I've got plans for him," Nobless Cari murmured slyly, her face darkening with an expression akin to ... desire?

"Yes, well," Mara trailed uncomfortably. "I just wanted to let you know we've got him."

"Wonderful. I trust he's not overly harmed?"

*What does that matter? He raped your daughter.* "He's not happy, but he's in good health."

"Wonderful. We'll see you soon. And for a job well done, I'm adding another five thousand on top of the twenty awaiting your arrival."

Mara watched in consternation as the vidscreen blanked. Something about this entire situation felt wrong. Mara had met young Sara. A quiet yet pretty young woman of eighteen, she was betrothed to a wealthy, older nobleman. Though Sara appeared the proper young miss, Mara had seen something in Sara's eyes to suggest the girl had more fire under her skin than she allowed to show.

*Foolishness.* Shaking her head, Mara forced thoughts of the perplexing Nobless Cari and her daughter from her mind to focus on the present. She finished some administrative details she'd been procrastinating and decided to take some much needed rest. She paged Catam and informed him of her status, then made a last trip to ensure the security of her prisoner.

Around the corner from the crew's berthing, Mara opened a small portal at eyelevel on the secured door of Vez's cell. He lay on a narrow bed, his massive arms folded behind his head as he contemplated the ceiling. She shifted to get a better look. Sensing her movement by the door, he shot up in bed, his eyes locked on hers.

The quickness of his action startled her. He had seemed rested, half asleep, when suddenly he moved like one of Catam's people, the Mardu.

Vez leapt off the bed and approached her. Though a door separated them, she felt as if he stood directly in front of her. Her eyes narrowed and she frowned, irritated that she had to look up to see his face.

Her captive smiled down at her, the expression not reaching his icy blue eyes.

"Ah, lady, how good to see you again," he said in a low purr. "Why don't you come in and visit for a spell?"

His gaze beckoned and Mara felt an odd compulsion to do as he suggested. In his eyes she saw herself enfolded in his grasp, his large hands removing every piece of her clothing, his mouth trailing down her neck to her full breasts....

Mara shook her head, shocked to see her hand poised above the security console. She angrily moved away from the window and glared up at him.

"You, Vez, are going to receive Nobless Cari's hospitality in just under a week's time." Mara's eyes darkened to black and her mouth flattened into a grim line. "And when the Nobless takes you behind closed doors, you'll pray for mercy, something unlike that which you showed poor Sara and her mate."

"I don't think so, beauty," he rasped, his voice all the more threatening for its soft intensity. He lowered his head so that they saw eye to eye through the opened window. "I think you've made a grave mistake, one that's going to cost you." His eyes raked over her body and he licked his lips, an action that sent heat spiraling to her loins. "I'll enjoy making you pay."

Mara simply stared at him, appearing unfazed by his threats. Ignoring her racing heartbeat, she raised a brow at him and grinned as if amused, then slapped the portal shut. She congratulated herself when she heard him curse.

Having faced down her menacing prisoner, she returned to her private quarters, determined to get at least a few hours of sleep. Confused at her odd reactions to Vez, she suddenly felt as limp as a rag. Apparently her sleepless nights had caught up to her. She stumbled into bed, exhausted and fully clothed, and fell immediately asleep.

Chapter Two

Lurin swore as he collapsed back into the bed too small to

comfortably encompass his large frame. Damn, but that infuriating woman had twice now evaded his efforts to control her. He frowned in puzzlement. She looked like an average human. Average, he amended, in that she didn't seem to pose any unnatural threat.

Her looks, however, were anything but ordinary. Captain Mara's beauty was outshone only by her fierce pride and determination to meet him glare for glare. He'd been more than attracted when he'd first seen her dark brown eyes looking so distant and yet full of feminine appeal, surrounded by thick black lashes set under gracefully arched brows.

She had a classically beautiful face, a straight nose, high cheekbones and full, ripe lips practically begging to be kissed. Had he been able, he would now be sampling those sweet red petals, tasting her very essence and putting her further under his spell. But the infernal witch had rebuffed him!

If he could only understand how she did this. Human females could not refuse the Thesha. He had never heard of such a thing happening. And yet, the curvaceous captain with the dismissive stare had the ability to deny him, and had unfortunately been responsible for his capture.

He cursed the situation and his careless lack of attention. He really had no one but himself to blame. He should have known better than to imbibe so heavily that night on Melan's third moon.

With Nobless Cari and her whorish daughter Sara chasing after him, he'd had the devil's own time trying to remain discreet. How the Nobless had gotten wind of his Thesha heritage still baffled him. But somehow she'd discovered the Thesha's signature birthmark. And when her sexually charged daughter had spied on him bathing in her home, his identity was revealed.

He'd only attended Nobless Cari's birth celebration as a favor to a friend, a nobleman of good standing and utter allegiance to Lurin's kind. Yet now Denal lay dead, with his murderess accusing him of the crime. And who would contend that the Nobless and her daughter spoke lies? Hell, the only thing working in his favor right now was the sultry captain's ignorance of his bloodline.

Were Mara to learn of his true identity, she would most

likely sell him to the highest bidder. Theshas had long since existed only as legend, having been labeled extinct long ago, and his people preferred it that way. Finding a live and healthy specimen, like himself, would bring the cold little captain more beks than she could possibly think to spend in her lifetime, much more than the Nobless was surely offering for his return.

He wondered if he could use that information to his advantage and sighed, realizing that to expose himself as a Thesha could only bring him more harm than good.

He had to get out of here! He swore again and flung a hand over his face to blot out the dim light from the floor illuminations. He knew in another few hours the lights would fade, as they had the previous night.

If only she hadn't drugged him. Gathering his wits on board her ship, he'd found the large Raggas hard to defeat, and the added strength of the Mardu had been his undoing. His gift didn't work on males, so if he couldn't defeat them physically, he had to resort to weaponry. On the troublesome females he encountered, however, he employed his most valuable skill. Usually with little effort, he could make them mere slaves in both mind and body. But the captain's reaction baffled him.

He had lost precious strength due to the drug's effects, and he still hadn't fully recovered. *Perhaps that explained the captain's resistance.* He nodded, the notion pleasing him. Yes, that made sense. The woman was nothing more than a typical human, unaware of the magic around her.

*Very good.* His eyes blazed with excitement. He had only to get a hold of her mind, to tie her to him, and then wait to make his next move. Sooner or later she would have to sleep. And then, he thought with a small chuckle, then he would set the lure.

\* \* \* \*

Lurin waited until the darkness had enveloped him completely, his mind calm and at peace. He recalled the captain's essence--her soft scent, her exquisite visage, her luscious body outlined in the masculine garb she tried to hide behind.

He released his mortal flesh and drifted through time and space, seeking Captain Mara. He moved through the walls and rooms separating them until he hovered just over her body. She lay fully clothed on her bed, her breathing deep and even.

*Mara*, he whispered, his mind reaching out to hers. He watched as her eyes drifted open, her mind still ensconced in the world of sleep while she heeded his mental call. Perfect, he thought with satisfaction. She couldn't resist him after all. *Remove your clothing, Mara.*

He hovered over her and stared hungrily at the body she revealed. She slowly stripped off her boots, trousers and space jacket to reveal a shapely form in stark underclothes. Lurin's eyes narrowed as he felt far more than he should have. Even distanced in his astral state, he felt his physical flesh harden, his cock fully aroused.

*Remove the rest*, he ordered in a voice harsher than he'd intended. Mara stilled her hands on the base of her undershirt before moving to accommodate his next, softly given command.

*Take it off, slowly.*

Lurin watched restlessly as Mara stripped completely bare before him. His eyes glittered with lust as they trailed over her soft face, lingering on the lips that begged to be kissed. He could all too easily imagine those lips parting to accommodate his cock, and he had to stifle a groan, surprised that she had such an effect on him.

His gaze traveled further down, past her graceful neck to her shoulders lightly sculpted with muscle. Captain Mara was no stranger to work, apparently.

His perusal heating his blood, he was unable to resist where his gaze wandered next. Two perfectly shaped, golden breasts shuddered under his scrutiny.

His gaze shot to her face, and he allowed himself a satisfied grin. Finally, the woman reacted as she should. Her mind and body were in his thrall, and Mara could not hide her obvious arousal.

He watched her nipples pebble into tight little buds, rosy sweets ripe for a taste. His mouth watered and his cock felt heavy, on the point of pain. He didn't understand how she could affect his physical state, when by rights he was the Thesha commanding her compliance.

Nevertheless, he continued his study. His eyes moved over her taut stomach, down to the wealth of dark brown curls hiding her deepest secrets. Her legs were long and supple, and he knew a sudden urge to taste every inch of her, starting with the warm juices hidden behind her swollen folds.

Lurin shivered, dismayed at his burning body clamoring for attention as it waited and throbbed for completion. This was all wrong, and potentially dangerous.

In this precarious state, Lurin had to do more than simply tie Mara to him mentally, as he normally would have. He needed to ease his lust lest he waste such a valuable build-up of energy and weaken himself further. He couldn't afford the energy loss, not when he needed to escape.

His lips curled. He felt no remorse for what he was about to do. She should have succumbed earlier to make it easier on him. Now he could do no less than satisfy them both.

He hovered over the unclad female, his energy touching her soft skin like a breath of warm air. She sighed and stretched, enhancing his hunger. He lowered his mouth and kissed her on the lips, feeling her mouth on his even though they touched through thought alone. In his room, his body responded, an electric rush of desire flowing through him.

Lurin enclosed her body in his warm aura and proceeded to claim Mara's subconscious. He kissed her, sliding his tongue into her mouth, groaning at the glorious taste of her warm lips and tongue as she mimicked his actions. He found it hard to think, the taste of Mara bursting upon his tongue.

He felt his erection press against her body, could feel her full breasts pressing against his chest in the dream state. And he wanted nothing more than to thrust into her wet, hot sheath and come deep inside of her.

Unusually close to orgasm, he tore his mouth from hers and trailed his lips down her throat, amazed at the heat she wrought in him. Though separated from his body, he could feel his physical self straining, milky dew leaking from his ready cock. The ferocious need to copulate with Mara astounded him. This bond between him and the captain felt far too strong to be normal.

But his mind wandered when of their own volition, her hands moved between them. In her mind, her fingers curled around his shaft, squeezing and pumping. And when her fingers grazed his sack he groaned and pressed deeper into her touch. His large fingers reached down to stroke her dewy softness, searching out the hard nub of her arousal. She writhed in her sleep and spread her thighs to better accommodate him.

Lurin released his need, sharing his burning desire. His fingers increased their demand, sliding through her wetness, stroking her clit to a heated pitch. He regained control, mentally commanding Mara to pump his straining cock until he could no longer hold back.

All too soon she cried out in orgasm even as he came in her pleasuring hand. That fast, his astral self flew back into his flesh, his cry of ecstasy a groan of pleasure-pain as he felt his body jerk and pulse, his seed leaving him into nothingness, a mess spread over his belly.

The emptiness of his orgasm left him both sated and strangely unfulfilled. Though his body now lay flushed and replete, his mind and soul hungered for a closer taste of Mara. He had given her fulfillment, had strengthened himself from the outburst of climactic energy, but at what cost?

He needed her again, right now, and the urgency to take her unnerved him. Instead of making things better, he'd made them worse. Now more than ever, he needed to escape this imprisonment.

* * * *

Mara awakened the next day feeling strangely refreshed. She heard Catam call for her over the intercom and had just reached for the vidlink when she realized she wasn't wearing a stitch of clothing. Memories of her erotic dreams returned and she flushed, thinking that in her sleep she had discarded them.

"I'll be there soon, Catam. Waken one of the Fas brothers to relieve you," she murmured, thankful she hadn't activated the vidscreen.

As she took a solar bath and quickly dressed, Mara's thoughts turned to her dreams. She didn't understand why her mind had become so fixated on her prisoner. She'd seen attractive men before, men who didn't have an execution awaiting them. But in her dreams Lurin Vez made her tremble, made her ache with desire. Even now her body warmed at memories of his heated mouth and stirring caresses.

She breathed deeply, needing to control her raging

hormones before she dealt with him again. For some reason she felt the need to hear his side of the story about his crimes. And, she admitted to herself, she needed to see him again, to reconcile her dream lover with the prisoner entombed in the dark cell down the hall.

## Chapter Three

Mara found Lurin--captive Vez, she reminded herself with a stern rebuke--lying as she'd left him on his narrow bed. He had removed his shirt, however, and his muscular chest looked maddeningly familiar. She eyed his tall frame critically, thinking he couldn't possibly be sleeping in that condition, hanging half off of the bed.

She entered the room accompanied by Nu. The Ragga nodded to her and set a tray of food on the table by Vez's bed. Then Nu stood protectively behind Mara, his arms crossed and awaiting trouble.

Vez stared at the ceiling and didn't move until Mara kicked at the bed. Then he shifted slowly, unlike the quick reflexes he'd shown the night prior.

"Yes, Mara?" he asked insolently and sat up. Mara could only stare at the hard planes of his broad chest and taut abdomen. Physically at least, he seemed the perfect male.

"That's Captain Mara to you, captive Vez," she reminded him coolly. Today the word "captive" didn't make him angry. Rather, he smiled at her slyly, as if he knew of the desire she tried to suppress while she stared at him.

"My mistake, *Captain*." He nodded, a smirk lurking in his ice blue eyes.

Mara couldn't help thinking that he seemed most content. Apparently Nu noticed as well for he eyed Vez with a puzzled frown. She glimpsed her captive's sparkling eyes a moment before he lowered them to his food.

He had lost the drug-induced haze from the bar. And his skin seemed almost ... glowing. She blinked and his skin again looked normal. Puzzled, she stared at the floor illuminations. Perhaps the lighting in the room had made him appear healthier than he actually was.

Not knowing why but needing to know more about her prisoner, Mara sat down across from him and waited until he looked at her to speak. "Tell me your accounting of what occurred on Jaron two lunar cycles past. What led you to rape a young Nobless and kill her mate?" Mara asked with true bewilderment. She still had trouble believing it.

Vez lost the sparkle in his eyes and frowned. "Very well. But I'd like to be allowed to speak freely, without interruption." He eyed Nu with a healthy wariness.

"Go ahead." Mara felt an overwhelming eagerness to hear his tale, and she wondered at her motives. Why was it so important that Vez be innocent of his crimes?

"I was invited to attend Nobless Cari's birth celebration at the behest of my good friend, Denal Donateral, Lady Sara's betrothed."

Mara blinked in surprise. She hadn't been given that information, only that Lurin Vez had somehow gotten access to the grounds before perpetrating his heinous crimes.

"I admit I ribbed Denal about the age difference between him and his young betrothed, but he laughed it away, falling on the old adage that true love conquers all." Vez rubbed the back of his neck. "Well, it certainly conquered him," he said bitterly. "While he and I were walking through the Nobless's grounds, we stumbled upon the 'virgin' Sara engaged in quite a bit of sexual roughhousing."

"Sara?" Mara's voice rose in surprise but she quickly tampered her reaction, determined not to show too much emotion at his words. She heard a ring of truth in what he said, something in his voice that correlated with her own earlier speculations on the girl.

"Yes." His lips twisted in disgust.

"You're sure it was Sara?"

He stared directly into her gaze. "I'm positive. Sara was facing us while a man fucked her roughly from behind. And if that wasn't enough, another man joined her intimate party by sticking his cock in her mouth."

"Maybe they forced her against her will," Nu offered.

"Denal and I thought the same until we saw her smiling at them. She laughed and moaned, begging for more. The things she had them do," he paused, his face twisted with revulsion. "We stood there for quite some time. Suffice it to say, the girl was insatiable."

Vez's eyes bored into hers and Mara saw the truth for herself. She didn't understand how, but she could picture the reprehensible scene clearly in her mind's eye. She glanced up but could see no expression on Nu's face.

"But that wasn't the worst of it," Vez continued grimly. "After Denal watched it all in silence, he and I returned to the Nobless's palace. He demanded an immediate dialogue with the Nobless. I was not privy to the conversation, but I know Denal's intent was to break the engagement.

"Unfortunately, that was the last I saw of him. The next day, I heard along with everyone else that his body had been found in the woods and at the very site where he and I had come upon Sara the day before."

"And you have no idea of what was said between Denal and Nobless Cari?"

"None," he answered curtly. "Denal was like a brother to me." His eyes softened as he remembered and Mara found herself drawn into his pain. "I hadn't actually liked Sara prior to their betrothal, but she made him happy, so I was happy for him. But when they found him dead, I knew Sara and her mother had killed him."

"Sara's grief was overwhelming, too contrived. And after I cast my suspicions to the local law, I found myself under house arrest. I barely managed to escape. And now here I am," he ended quietly.

Mara desperately wanted to side with him, and that in itself made her cautious. That blasted dream had skewed her judgment. *A prisoner declares an unbelievable story to be true, and I'm falling for it.* Instead of remaining unbiased, Mara couldn't help remembering the taste of his mouth, the feel of his shaft pulsing in her hands.

Her impartiality was shot all to hell. And she didn't like it.

Mara's gaze hardened. "A pretty story, captive Vez," she said evenly. He shot to his feet and his eyes gleamed with frustration, betraying his anger that she would not believe him. Sensing that he was not in control of himself, she quickly stood as well and stepped back out of reach.

Nu quickly inserted himself between them, a stun phaser directed at Vez. Vez's sapphire gaze met the Ragga's at eye level, an odd occurrence for Nu, who normally towered over their prisoners.

Needing to defuse the situation, Mara tried the truth. "I'm not sure I believe you, Vez. I will say I don't completely buy Nobless Cari's story, but I'm not the law. I'm just a bounty hunter out to make a living."

As she spoke, Mara knew she lied to him and to herself. Though she didn't often delve into the details of her captives' crimes, she had faith in the legitimacy of the law's claims. Her other jobs had *felt* right. This one didn't. And it bothered her. But no need to let her prisoner know he'd succeeded in rattling her cage.

"So you don't care that you're sending an innocent man to his death?" Vez crossed his arms, his biceps clenched as if he held himself back through sheer will alone.

"Come what may," Mara said blithely. She refrained from shrinking at his narrowed gaze, at the force behind his glare. "I didn't say I'm not interested. I might look into things, though for my own satisfaction and nothing more."

Her words seemed to irritate her prisoner rather than settle him. "I don't think that wise, Captain." He shook his head. "You don't know what waters you might be stirring. Nobless Cari's influence knows no bounds," he warned. He must not have liked the look on her face for he cursed. Then the tension seemed to leave him and he sat back on his bed with a sigh.

Mara frowned down at him, wondering what game he played now. He'd tried to convince her of his innocence and he'd failed. But she said she'd look into it. The man wanted complete absolution or nothing? *The hell with that.* She hadn't lived twenty-five years in the system without a shell of caution to keep her alive.

"Nu, take our captive to the lav. Get him cleaned up and exercised," she ordered. Nu nodded and yanked Vez to his feet.

In the blink of an eye, Vez suddenly stood before her. His hand reached out and grazed her cheek. The contact had her heart racing, the feeling of intimacy between them strong. Then Nu was cursing, shoving her prisoner on his stomach to the floor, the shackles reapplied.

"Oh, Captain Mara, you do please me," Vez whispered in a voice that should have been too soft to be heard, but Mara heard it all the same.

She watched Nu take Vez away and shook her head at the odd sensations coursing through her. The mere touch of his hand on her cheek had sent her blood pounding, her body pulsating with need. She swore under her breath. Never before had Mara fallen prey to the odd lustfulness that plagued her men. But it seemed her day had finally come.

She contemplated her new feelings and returned to the ship's bridge. She found Set at the controls and nodded a greeting.

"Make course for the nearest pleasure point," she ordered, aware of the anticipation blooming on his face. Neither he nor Nu was very subtle. They both possessed insatiable sexual appetites, or so she'd heard rumored in the many pleasure clubs where she'd waited for her crew. The Fas brothers were close to legend.

"Almost Thesha," she murmured. She missed Set's concerned look and scowled at her inane words. Turning to the current news on the info sector, she concentrated on possible future bounties, determined to relegate Lurin Vez to 'mission complete' status.

\* \* \* \*

Lurin closed his eyes and relaxed as the solar bath cleaned him of the grime that had built up, a conglomeration of dirt, sweat and semen that had accumulated on his body over the past two days. The semen he hadn't minded so much, he thought, remembering Mara's naked body.

He grabbed a shaving blade and began ridding himself of the dark shadow lining his jaw and lips. In the mirror he saw that the large man watching him hadn't stopped frowning since they'd left Mara's company.

"The captain is to be respected," Nu said firmly, his disapproval apparent as he glaringly eyed Lurin handling the short shaving blade. Nu's phaser didn't waver from Lurin's chest, the weapon an effective deterrent to the escape plans Lurin had concocted.

He quickly shaved and let the blade fall back to the counter. He looked around for his clothes but couldn't find them. Then his large guard threw a pair of rough trousers and a shirt at him, an outfit similar to the one Nu wore.

"It will fit, though you're not as large in your upper body as a Ragga." Nu grunted and flexed his behemoth shoulders as he casually studied Lurin's naked body. Lurin could only hope the Ragga hadn't paid too much attention to the area above his groin, where an oddly shaped scar resided. But the large man didn't appear overly interested in Lurin's body. He tapped his foot impatiently waiting for Lurin to dress.

Thanking his stars that for all their roughness, Mara's crew had been decidedly decent about his captivity, Lurin finished dressing and turned to Nu with a question.

"Your captain," he began and watched the man tense. "How does a woman who looks like that run two Raggas and a Mardu?"

Nu grinned showing bright white teeth. "She's not as fragile as she looks," he said with pride. "And she's the best captain I've ever had. She knows just when to give us leave." The minute the words left his mouth, he clenched his jaw, as if he'd said too much.

Nu walked Lurin back to his cell in silence and left him alone with his thoughts. Twice more during the day Set brought him food and left him alone. Lurin listened carefully but could hear nothing in the corridor. And to his disappointment, the captain hadn't returned to visit him since their early hour meeting.

He didn't like the fact that he missed her. *Since when did a female control a Thesha's emotions?* His blood hummed as he recalled Mara's delicious reaction to his sensual mind probe last night. And the physical touch he'd managed today, grazing her cheek, had only strengthened their bond.

He shook his head. She should have believed everything he'd told her today without question, but she hadn't. Never before had his mind probe failed. Despite not being able to make her trust him, he'd told her the truth, word for word. And she hadn't believed him. He thought back to her decision to dig around for more answers about his situation and felt a niggle of fear worm its way into his hard heart.

She was his jailer. He shouldn't care if she got into trouble because of him. But he did. He didn't want to see her in a cell like this, or worse, at the mercy of the perverse Nobless and her daughter. He flinched at the untold portions of the story he hadn't given Mara.

After he'd seen his friend dead on Elaran land, he'd immediately confronted the law. But the Nobless clearly controlled the law on her corner of Jaron. Thinking he was going to see justice done, Lurin had accompanied the peacekeeper back to the Nobless's palace, only to be forced to watch Nobless Cari sexually attack him, sucking him into oblivion.

Like a bitch in heat, her mouth wrung groans of ecstasy from the easily controlled lawman--a man supposedly beyond bribery. She'd made him come several times before succumbing to her own orgasm; all the while her eyes remained glued to Lurin's face.

In that instant Lurin had seen the beauty of sex debased to its ugliest form.

Nobless Cari had not only received greater pleasure for his having watched, but she had plainly made her statement. The law and everything around Cari belonged to her and her alone.

But that had not been the worst of it. Tied down in restraints, Lurin had been stripped and examined, inch by inch, by Cari and her daughter. As they studied him, Sara slyly confessed her spying hole, which gave her a perfect view into the guest bathing chamber Lurin had been directed to use. Somehow she and her mother knew Lurin's secret. But how could these women know of the Theshan birthmark?

Normally unmindful of his body, he'd felt violated at the thought of the craven mother and daughter planning to exploit his sexuality like a toy. And they'd done more than merely dissect him with their eyes. He shuddered as he remembered their coarse petting and fondling. Only the promise of sheer Theshan bliss had earned him any respite, and enough time to escape.

Escape had worked once because of his Theshan background, but he had no plans to reveal his Theshan nature to this crew. How then to make the captain do his bidding? He didn't relish another binding lovemaking session in an astral projection. It had been too much for him, too draining and oddly enough, too exhilarating.

The feel of Mara under his body, simulated though it had been, had been decidedly addicting. She had a control over his body that no female had ever before possessed, *and she was completely unaware of it*. If she learned what she did to him ... no, Lurin had to exorcise the woman from his mind once and for all, by pleasuring her physically.

Physical contact was the surest way a Theshan could sever a mental link. And time was running out for Lurin. He promised himself that he would escape soon. He had only a few more days at most before Jaron neared.

As he pondered his situation, several male voices drifted along the corridor.

Finally, something to break the monotony of his thoughts.

"I for one am not going to question the captain's orders to find a pleasurer." That was Nu. "Nebe6, here I come."

"I agree," Set said. "But I don't like leaving her here alone." His voice lowered, his caution alerting Lurin of his comment's importance.

*Alone? Mara and me, together on the ship?*

"Perhaps I should stay," Catam said softly.

"No, Catam. You need to go." Nu's voice was firm. "If anyone should stay it should be me."

"Nonsense," came a sultry voice. Lurin's body tightened at the sound of it. "You'll all go. The day I can't contain a prisoner, in the security of his own cell, is the day you fire me as your captain."

Lurin heard laughter.

"Are you sure, Captain Mara?" Nu asked. "I don't like the way he looks at you."

"Looks at me? He's just trying to wrest control of a bad situation. It's nothing more than a power play," she scoffed, sounding extremely naïve, a condition that didn't fit with her tough-as-nails demeanor. Lurin could picture the unease on her crews' faces. Everyone but Mara could see her as a desirable woman, not merely the 'captain'. At least her crew had some common sense.

"Don't worry. I can handle captive Vez." Lurin gritted his teeth. If she called him *captive* one more time ... "Now go," she ordered. "I'll expect you back here tomorrow at first light. Enjoy. And Catam? Make sure you're satisfied. There's nothing worse than a Mardu on the prowl." She chuckled and Lurin heard the men laugh louder.

Their voices faded but footsteps, light and brisk--*hers*--neared his cell. He breathed in her scent as she passed and he blocked out everything but Mara, his cock stirring to life once more. Despite his uneasiness at how readily she affected him, nothing could dampen his anticipation of the night to come.


## Chapter Four

Mara sighed as she enjoyed a long, luxurious solar bath. With her crew gone, she had the ship to herself. Well, almost to herself. She thought ruefully of Lurin Vez just down the hall. She still didn't know how she felt about him.

On the one hand, she didn't believe Nobless Cari's story about Vez's involvement in the crime of which he'd been accused, but she couldn't take his words on faith either. To think that a Nobless could be responsible for so terrible a crime was unthinkable.

*Unthinkable but not impossible.*

She also hesitated to believe Vez because his mere presence did something to her. Mara closed her eyes as she pictured him in her mind. He was everything a woman could want: tall, dark and handsome, sexy beyond belief. She liked to think she had a decent imagination, but the things her mind had conjured him doing to her astounded her.

She had seen much on various pleasure stops and read about the physical act of coupling. She had yet to experience it herself, however. To have had such an erotic dream about her captive, especially one that brought her to orgasm, brought heat to her cheeks.

She tried to push thoughts of the blue-eyed criminal out of her mind but he refused to go. It was almost as if he whispered to her, "Come find me, I'm here waiting for you."

She swore softly as she realized she would not have a night of relaxation and solitude. For some reason her mind urged her to talk again with the prisoner. She felt more than a hint of uncertainty about Lurin Vez. He held a fascination similar to that of the mysterious Thesha.

The man was a criminal, wanted for murder, wanted for rape. She'd been around deviants before, knew how they thought and acted. Yet she felt no such ugliness from Vez. Instead, his male energy attracted her. Mara silently admitted that she *wanted* to couple with him.

She immediately shook herself free of such foolish thoughts. Her traitorous body had decided to come alive near this captive, but she needed to get a handle on her sensuality before she did something that could not be undone.

So telling herself, she wandered down to Vez's cell. Glancing down at her clothing, she was conscious of her loose fitting over shirt and leggings--dress befitting a soft woman rather than a ship's captain. But she would make no excuse for her appearance. She was, after all, taking a break as her men did, though in a decidedly different way.

She opened the small window on the cell door and saw Vez exercising in his cell. She watched in admiration as he continued to push up on his arms, his biceps bulging and his breath constant as he exhaled deeply with each repetition. She could almost see him moving over her with such intensity and blinked to remove the sudden and unwelcome vision.

As if he'd sensed her, Vez stopped and glanced up, his eyes shuttered but no less impacting. He stood and rubbed his body slowly with a towel, wiping the sweat from his broad chest. Mara kept her face composed as she watched him watching her through the window. She licked her dry lips and couldn't help wondering if the dark hair on his chest was as soft as she'd imagined it to be.

"Captain Mara," Vez said softly, a grin tugging at his mouth. "Please, come in." He licked at his lips, mimicking her earlier action, and she wondered if he too felt the heat blazing between them.

She would have to be completely insane to open the door. She studied Vez. He still wore shackles on his wrists and feet, and a chain Nu must have rigged allowed him some movement off the bed.

Dare she enter? She tossed the idea in her mind. She would be able to sit on the chair across from the bed and still be out of his reach.

"Don't tell me you're afraid?" he mocked, his brows arched in disbelief over piercing blue eyes.

Mara squared her shoulders, knowing she shouldn't bow to his taunting, but she nevertheless responded to the scorn in his voice. *Control. I control my actions and the situation.*

She could handle one unruly male.

She touched the keypad and opened the door, closing it behind her and locking them securely inside. The closing of the door sounded loud in the sudden silence. Mara stood warily as she watched the intensity of Vez's eyes blaze as he studied her, his eyes lingering on her chest.

Then his eyes rose again to meet hers and he smiled, like a predator having successfully lured its prey. "Please, sit down and make yourself comfortable." He motioned to the chair near her. Mara shook her head at his attempt at manners but sat anyway.

"I don't suppose you could see fit to remove these?" He motioned to his shackles.

Mara shook her head. "No, Vez. Look, it's probably--"

"Don't you think you should call me Lurin? Vez is so cold." He shivered lightly and grinned. "Come now, Captain. You won't remove my constraints. Won't you at least consent to calling me by my given name?"

Mara sighed. "Fine, *Lurin*. Now that I'm here, perhaps you can explain to me how you found yourself in this mess in the first place. Let's just say I believed your story earlier. If that's the case, and you escaped, why are the Nobless and her daughter still after you? Why not leave you to the law?"

"I can't say," he murmured and scooted to the edge of his bed. He stared at her, his eyes lingering on her lips. "You really have the most beautiful mouth."

"Lurin," she warned, but he ignored her.

"You know, Mara, I had the most extraordinary dream the other night."

At his words Mara stiffened. The air around her seemed to thicken and she felt decidedly uncomfortable, too warm sitting near and conversing with her half-clad prisoner. She stood to leave.

"No, don't go yet," he said softly, his words a caress. Mara sat back down, her mind urging her to leave even as his words relaxed her already sluggish body. "Come closer," he whispered, his eyes electric as he stared at her.

He licked his lips again, his tongue grazing the soft pink flesh of his mouth and Mara barely stifled a moan. She felt hot and feverish and didn't know why her body refused her commands. She stood slowly and walked toward him, her mind screaming at her to back away and leave this room.

When she stood within an inch of him, she chanced a glance into his face. He watched her, his breathing growing more rapid, matching hers.

"Mara," he crooned gently. His hands rose to grasp her about the waist. One of his palms spanned her hip and he tightened his hold on her flesh. "You are too lovely for words," he said and slowly drew her to sit next to him on the bed.

Suddenly they sat a breath apart, her body absorbing the heat of his bare skin, her heart beating twice as fast. She felt excited and afraid all at once.

*What is happening to me?*

His fingers rose and rested on her throat. Mara had the uncomfortable thought that with one hand he could crush her neck. Yet his large hand touched her reverently as he caressed her windpipe. Then his hand moved lower, resting just above her breasts. All the while he kept his eyes glued to hers.

"Wh-what are you doing?" she stuttered as his fingers suddenly moved down the slope of one breast, hovering just over her hard nipple.

"Nothing, Mara." His eyes followed the movement of his hand. "Did you know that your body is reacting to mine of its own accord? Amazing, but you're drawing forth reactions in me that I've never felt before," he admitted huskily. His hand closed over her breast, letting its full weight rest in his callused palm.

Mara gasped as pleasure ran through her body, pooling between her thighs. She felt tingly, aroused and unbearably hot. Her clit throbbed and she felt slick with want.

"Stop," she said breathlessly, her eyes closing, unwilling to see the triumph on his face as he so effortlessly conquered her resolve. She didn't see his eyes rove over her face hungrily, nor the descent of his mouth as it hovered over her own.

His lips touched hers hesitantly, growing bolder as she moaned into his mouth. With one hand stroking her breast and pinching her nipple lightly into a small bud of desire, he made her cry out for more. And as she opened her mouth, his tongue invaded, tasting and taking everything she had to offer.

His touch grew bolder, his hand moving to caress her other breast, bringing it to peak as well.

"I want to taste every inch of you," Lurin whispered against her mouth, his hand working magic, the cold brace of the shackles on his wrist a sensuous contrast to the heat of her body. "Take these off, Mara," he ordered firmly, his lips moving over her jaw to her throat, sucking at the pulse beating there.

Mara refused weakly. "No." She shook her head even as her hands moved to the small code box on the shackles. She knew Lurin watched her intently, memorizing the numerical code before his hands suddenly found freedom.

"Now the ankles," he said huskily, groaning as she bent over his thigh and brushed against the hard ridge jutting through his trousers. She released the last of his bonds and sat up, regarding Lurin with confusion.

"What are you doing to me?" Her breath caught in tense desire, aware that she faced a dangerous man, one fully aroused. She stared at the outline of his erection through his trousers, heard his chest expand as he breathed heavily. She glanced up, needing to see his face. His eyes looked slumberous as they gazed down at her.

He grasped the back of her head, running his hands through her silky hair. His eyes narrowed and he licked at his bottom lip. "You have no idea how much I need this," he murmured. Mara shivered under his voice and he grinned darkly. "Tonight is mine," he declared before dropping to his knees in front of her.

She could only stare at him, watching as his eyes raked her trembling body.

"I can't wait any longer." His hands moved underneath her shirt to the waistband of her leggings. "I need you now." He yanked violently at her leggings and they suddenly came apart in his hands. He swiped them from her legs and stared up at her hungrily. "What do you wear under these?" he asked softly, his hands running over her thighs half-hidden by her overly large shirt. She had to bite her lip to keep from moaning aloud.

She shuddered as he nudged her thighs further apart, unable to do anything but feel. He quickly found that she wore nothing beneath her leggings when his hands found the wet heat of her. Mara couldn't help a small groan as his fingers slid inside her, building a hunger she'd never before experienced. The hunger seemed to move through Lurin as well. His eyes grew brighter as his fingers began moving over her clit.

"You're so wet for me, Mara," he said thickly as he inserted another finger into her tight, wet sheath. At the intrusion, Mara bit her lip and closed her eyes, trying to lean away at the intensity of feeling and yet needing more of his touch.

"So sweet," he rasped, and she knew he watched her reaction. Then he did something unexpected. He pushed aside her long over shirt, exposing her feminine core to his view. She tried to cover herself but he wouldn't let her. "So beautiful," he said and buried his head between her thighs.

Mara cried out his name as his heated breath warmed her clit, his mouth closing over the hard nub and sucking gently. He would not relent, but continued to tease her, his tongue licking her so expertly, bringing her to the brink of ecstasy but not edging her over, again and again.

"It's not enough, is it, love?" he asked, and she mindlessly shook her head, needing something more. In answer, he returned his mouth to her sweet pussy and added his nimble fingers, filling the void so hungry for his presence.

The feeling of his finger moving in and out of her in addition to the pressure on her sensitive clit threw Mara over the edge. She clutched at the back of Lurin's head, reveling in his silky hair as he brought her to a devastating climax.

She was barely aware when he removed his mouth after licking her, ingesting her essence as if it were a vital part of his needs.

When she turned her passion-clouded eyes to his, she noted no victorious expression, rather a hungry burning that blazed in his eyes. He licked at his lips, tasting her again while his eyes remained locked on hers.

"That was only the beginning." His deep voice rang with sensual promise. He stood and Mara studied his straining erection with fascination and curiosity. She touched him through his trousers and drew a shaky breath out of him. But it was not enough for either of them.

She reached beneath the waistband of his trousers, closing

her fingers over him, and felt his heartbeat pulse through his large cock. He closed his eyes and groaned, and Mara started in surprise as a dewy wetness covered his soft tip. She stroked his long shaft, feeling a power she'd never before felt when he continued to groan, pressing deeper into her hand. She wondered if she could bring him to climax as he'd brought her, with her mouth. But before she could do more, he drew her off the bed to her feet, capturing her hands.

"No more, Mara. If you do, I'll come right now," he said breathlessly, trying to calm himself. Then he lifted her in his arms and took her down the hall to her room. Mara didn't notice how easily he overrode her security or wonder how he knew which room was hers. She could only think of what more he would show her.

## Chapter Five

After setting her down on her feet, he closed and locked the door behind them. Then he quickly stepped out of his trousers and Mara stared in awe at his naked form.

"You're so beautiful." She reached out to touch him.

"Not half as beautiful as you are," he said softly, aware he spoke the truth. He couldn't believe how responsive her body was. He had used his Thesha power on her at first to override her resistance to his touch. But after the first few caresses, he stopped trying to overwhelm her mind and focused on her body.

Even now he felt rock hard, reveling in her taste still on his tongue. He sighed and closed his eyes as she ran her hands over his body. He'd been so close to orgasm when she'd run her hand over his cock, so expertly as though she'd done this before.

He opened his eyes and stared down at her. Her eyes had turned a deep black and her need burned into him. He could smell it on her body. She was wet and waiting for him, needing fulfillment that only he could give.

When her hands again found his erection, he let her play, knowing he needed to climax. Later, when he entered her for the first time, he needed to be in complete control. He needed to breach her maidenhead carefully, to give her the maximum pleasure possible.

Though his kind easily controlled women, it was not in their nature to harm. A Thesha could in no way injure another with his gift, not without severe repercussions.

"Why have you stayed a virgin for so long, Mara?" he asked huskily as she stroked him. He removed her long over shirt and stared hungrily from her full breasts to his cock, aroused even more as he watched her touching him.

"How do you know that I am?" Her eyes were intent on what she was doing to him.

She stroked his shaft, cupping his sack underneath, touching his velvet soft skin with such incredible finesse that he felt a sweat break out over his body at the sheer joy she evoked.

"I know," he gasped and pressed into her hands as she increased her pace. "Mara, give me what I need," he groaned and shuddered as she fondled him.

"You're so hard," she said wondrously as her fingers again grazed his sack, drawn tight so close to climax.

He moaned her name and thrust harder, his hands grasping her shoulders for strength as her touch nearly brought him to his knees.

"Mara, honey, I'm going to come," he gasped, his climax upon him. He cried out her name and pumped into her hands, his seed pulsing over her, shooting against her golden skin again and again. He came so hard his knees buckled and only his hold on Mara kept him upright.

When he opened his eyes he saw her grinning at him, and it was a moment before he could speak. Never before had a woman brought him to such a state. Colors and sounds intensified, and he could actually see Mara's aura merging with his own. She had actually tapped into *his* desires and fed them back to him two-fold. An unheard of ability in a woman.

He eyed her with a mixture of awe and wariness as he stumbled to her bed. Focused on his body, she didn't see his expression as she wiped up his stickiness with her shirt and tossed it to the side. Then she joined him.

"So that's why my crew is so eager to find a pleasurer." Mara tapped her chin, as if she'd just figured out a puzzle.

She looked both innocent and erotic, willingly appearing as both woman and *captain* for the first time since he'd met her.

Lurin smiled. His wariness faded under the wave of contentment pulsing through him. Stars, he hadn't felt this good in ages. How had this untried woman bested a Thesha? And yet, she remained a maiden. Thoughts of claiming her had Lurin's body stirring to life once more.

Theshas had the rare ability to recover from sex almost immediately, making them wonders in the world of pleasure. Hopefully Mara's innocence about such matters wouldn't make her curious about his body's rapid recovery.

Already he felt himself hard again.

"Mara." Lurin stared down at her. "You know I would never hurt you, don't you?" he asked softly.

She looked bewildered. "I know. I don't know why I let you free, but I trust you."

"Good," he murmured and leaned over her. "Because now it's time to surrender to me, Mara. I'm going to give you such pleasure as you've ever known," he promised and saw an answering heat in her eyes. He wondered again how this woman could equally match his passion, but lost the thought when her thigh brushed his erection.

He leaned over and made love with her mouth. He had so many delicious things to teach her. He sucked at her tongue, mimicking the actions he would use when he thrust his cock into her pussy. She moaned his name and his heart rate increased. She had a body made for loving.

"Mara, you've got the sexiest curves." He sighed and kissed his way down her body. He stopped when he reached her breasts, resting his head on her chest as he looked up at her. "Your breasts are full and heavy." He closed his mouth over one taut peak, sucking greedily at her nipple as he laved it with his tongue.

Mara arched into him moaning his name, and Lurin felt the urge to thrust deep. But he held onto his control and pleasured her breast with his mouth, fondling the other with his hand. Mara squirmed and opened her thighs, needing more from him. He smiled around her nipple, aware of her readiness.

"Do you want me, Mara?"

"Please." She pulled his head up and kissed him

desperately, her body moving against his, brushing his cock and making him groan in response.

"Please what?" he gasped. "Tell me what you want and I'll give it to you, sweet," he breathed.

"I want you inside me," she whimpered as he teased her. He rested the tip of his cock against her wet clit, sliding slowly but never giving her too much. The contact made him crazy to have her.

"How much do you want?" he panted, pushing harder against her swollen nub.

"All of you. Lurin, please," she gasped. "Take me now. I need you deep inside me." She squirmed to get closer to him. "I want to feel you come, spurting your seed deep within me," she moaned, grasping for his hips.

Unable to keep still, he pressed deeper into her. Mara's words compounded his desire and he fought for control. "It won't hurt, Mara, I promise you," he said, reminding himself to be careful, no matter how much it cost.

Then, with a Thesha's skill, he thrust deeply inside of her, smoothly penetrating the thin barrier of her virginity. He stilled soon after, giving her body a chance to accustom itself to him. But Mara would have none of it.

"More, Lurin. I need you to move." She pumped her hips, gasping when her clitoris met the ridge of his body.

Lurin could do no less than accommodate her. And he moved in slow, long thrusts that took her right to the edge quickly.

"Mara," he rasped as he pumped into her, unable to stop his building tempo. "This is still only the beginning," he promised, knowing that his destiny was somehow tied to this sexually gifted woman.

She moaned his name and cried out, her arms and sheath tightening around him. Her contractions sucked him deeper and Lurin soon found himself following her into the abyss, lost in her warm body. He groaned and continued to thrust, her body milking him of every drop of his orgasm.

He stilled, finally, feeling as if he'd run for days, his heart racing like mad. He kissed her, satisfied beyond measure when she kissed him back. He felt whole, suddenly aware that before Mara, he'd been missing something.

*She's changed me.*

Panic swelled within him, clouding the contentment he'd

been given.

Lurin had been with many women in his lifetime. But none had ever given him more satisfaction than he'd given them. The lure of a Thesha was that he was sexually gifted, able to bring any woman to orgasm again and again without pause. But as he lay here with Mara, Lurin felt different. He felt tired, but more than that, he felt complete.

And it scared him to death.

Trust did not come easily to his kind. Should word of his existence come out, he would be a hunted man for the rest of his existence. Unable to fully share himself with a woman, he settled for pleasures of the flesh, fulfilling surface desires while hiding his aloneness.

After one coupling with Mara, he wanted to share his secrets, to truly belong with another. He sighed and rolled his eyes at his crazy thoughts. A short time ago he'd been imprisoned on *her* ship. Did he really think she'd accept the truth about him, when her first concern was turning him in for a fee?

Mara murmured something he couldn't make out. Then she tightened her hold on him and fell asleep.

He couldn't help hugging her close, nor could he stop himself from kissing the top of her head tenderly, even knowing how foolishly he behaved. Mara held some sway over his heart, and he told himself he needed distance to figure out his odd attraction.

Feeling her in his arms, however, dissuaded the notion of distance. Despite his unease, he resolved to push the worries of tomorrow aside. The situation with Nobless Cari would keep, as would the puzzle of Mara Seni.

For now, he would be smart to take advantage of the rare pleasure in her arms. He figured he still had some time before the rest of her crew returned. And he planned on using that time to further educate Mara in the art of sexual loving. But for now he lay and watched her sleep, unable to stop the threads of affection from growing and wrapping around her.

\* \* \* \*

"Are we ready to board, Captain?"

"Yes, my lady," Captain Gren answered with a bow. Lady Sara didn't see the disgust in the mercenary's eyes as he stared at her, nor the lust-filled gazes of the crew she'd recently commandeered.

*Soon I'll have my own Thesha*, she thought hungrily. *And I'm not sharing with my mother. Not this time.* Her eyes narrowed and her mouth tightened into a grimace. She might already be enjoying Lurin Vez had her mother not interfered. Damn the bitch!

Sara knew what to look for. It was she who had first spied the telltale birthmark on Lurin's bare body glistening in the guest bath. After that, she'd paid keen attention to his effect on the women in her household. To a woman, every female relative, guest and servant had reacted predictably, fairly throwing themselves at the man.

But what a man. She sighed with pleasure recalling how finely built, how deliciously hard Lurin had been. Oh, he may have feigned disgust under her touch, but she knew he'd liked it. If only her mother hadn't caught wind of her plans.

She pondered her mother's involvement and shook her head, her eyes lighting as realization dawned. Of course! Lurin had undoubtedly been disgusted with Cari Elaran, not with Sara, the obviously more attractive and younger of the two.

Smiling, she glanced up to see the captain engaged in a low murmur of conversation with one of the men she'd appropriated for this mission. As far as her mother knew, Sara needed an entire contingent of warriors to see her safely to a neighboring planet to foster good relations.

"Good relations indeed," Sara fairly purred.

"My lady?" Captain Gren regarded her with that dismissive green-eyed stare that irritated her to no end. She would give a quarter of her inheritance to fuck the deliciously wicked captain, while he looked at her as if she was no better than one of the common whores littering the docks of the royal city.

"I wasn't speaking to you, Captain." She glared at him and he turned away with a shrug.

If she hadn't been so determined to keep this mission a secret from her mother, she would have kept Captain Feord on to lead the men. But Feord was nothing more than her mother's bootlicking lackey.

It had taken no more than a few hours of mundane sex to assure Captain Feord that he was better off staying on leave. She had easily convinced him that Gren had the full support of the Nobless.

Sara eyed Gren as he finished making ready the boarding party. He made a striking figure. Tall and dark, his piercing eyes seemed to stare through her, simultaneously aggravating her and making her wet. Much as she longed to take a whip to his arrogant back, she couldn't help speculating on his sexual prowess.

Her gaze traveled down his billowy shirt to the form-hugging trousers he wore as he walked toward her. Her mouth watered as she noted the long, thick bulge that lay between his thighs. Gren had an enormously large cock.

"No."

The harsh word brought her gaze to his face.

"Pardon me?" she asked icily.

"No. My job is to assist you in the capture of a missing prisoner. Nothing more."

*The arrogant ass!* "I don't believe I asked you for anything else."

"In some things, words aren't necessary." He curled his lip in disgust and left the bridge.

"Bastard." Sara seethed, the only thing keeping her from imprisoning and torturing the contemptuous captain the fact that no one had overheard his disrespect. If she didn't need Gren's expertise so much ... but no matter. Soon enough the job would be over, and then Gren would pay, and pay dearly.

Just the thought of torturing the brute made her clit hard, and she rubbed herself with excitement. Striding from the bridge, she grabbed the first warrior in her path.

"Inform Captain Gren that we stand by until I give the order."

He nodded and left in search of Gren. Sara walked further down the hall and found what she was looking for. Two burly warriors stood together in the hallway conferring over the mission.

"You two, come with me."

She liked the way they looked at her. Unlike Gren, these warriors stared at her with lust and approval. Predictable men, they were easy pickings. She entered her room with them close on her heels. Once inside, she closed the door behind them. With a grace and speed that clearly showed her practice in such matters, Sara stepped out of her clothing and reclined on the bed.

"I want it now, and I want it rough."

In their haste, the men ripped their clothing off, their cocks bobbing with excitement. Sara enjoyed her sexual standing among the men in House Elaran, and she'd been working these particular warriors since she'd boarded the ship three days ago.

Rising on all fours, she licked her lips, closed her eyes and groaned when a hard cock rammed up her ass. Then she opened her mouth wider to accommodate the cock being shoved against her lips. Lost in the experience, she imagined Lurin and Gren fucking her from both ends instead of the sweating beasts pumping like mad.

\* \* \* \*

Captain Gren frowned and nodded upon receiving Sara's message. Dismissing the messenger, he stalked to the galley, bypassing several men wagering on Lady Sara's voracious appetite.

Considering he'd missed the last two meals in order to maintain control over this motley, undisciplined group of cutthroat "royal soldiers," Gren decided that if Lady Sara thought she had enough time to fuck two more crewmen, he certainly had enough time to eat.

He sat alone, glaring at the men nearest him and sending them scuttling to the safety of the far tables. Apparently his reputation preceded him, in addition to the fact that he'd broken a crewman's arm the first day. The little bastard had thought to cry mutiny. On the first day!

Gren thanked his stars continually that this position was only temporary.

A fight broke out among the crew in the hallway, disturbing his fragile peace. Deciding to let them kill each other, he focused again on his food.

Pinching the bridge of his nose to stifle the headache gathering, he swallowed the unappetizing fare on his plate, needing its bolstering strength, and resolved to see this mission through to The End.

Sara bedamned. Nobless Cari was counting on him. Not to mention the others.

## Chapter Six

Mara sighed and snuggled deeper into the mattress. Though she didn't normally sleep on her stomach, she couldn't deny the comfort or the strange warmth stealing through her.

Still foggy with sleep, she didn't at first register how wet and needy she felt. Something pressed her down even as a hand spread her thighs further apart. She turned her head and would have closed her legs when a feather-light touch caressed her clit, sending her pulse racing.

She blinked as the world began to focus despite the buzzing in her ears. Then a moist tongue traced her earlobe and thrust deep into her ear.

She bucked against the male form lying atop her, needing more than his tongue.

"Shh, be easy, sweet," Lurin whispered seductively. His breath caressed her sensitive neck and she arched up against him, eager to feel more of his body.

Acceding her demands, he pressed his hot cock between her buttocks, rolling and gyrating between them, as if teasing himself as much as he teased her.

"More, Lurin," she murmured throatily.

He chuckled, a dark sound that vibrated through her loins and pierced her heart. Stars but he felt good, better than anything she might have fantasized.

He lay completely on top of her, allowing her to feel all of his weight. At first she felt smothered and found it hard to breathe. But as she opened her mouth to object, he quickly nudged her thighs further apart and thrust into her, levying on his elbows to defer his weight.

"Ah yeah, sweet. Tight, so tight." He rocked harder, pounding into her and thrilling her with his groans of satisfaction.

He slowed and reached one hand around her waist, down through her dark curls. His fingers questing for her plump nub, when he found it, he pinched and toyed with her until her walls were slick with want.

"You're so wet. I want you to come all over me when I explode in you," he gasped. Suddenly he stopped, and keeping the connection, shifted and pulled her up onto her hands and knees.

"Much better."

She silently agreed. He returned to fondling her clit, but this time instead of thrusting hard into her, he slowly slid all the way in before pulling out one inch at a time. Again and again, he thrust with excruciating slowness while he rolled her clitoris.

"Lurin, you're torturing me." She tried but couldn't get him to move any faster. The knot of tension spread out from her loins, consuming her in a burning fire that grew brighter and hotter.

Reaching through her legs, she urged his hand to move quicker, fitting his fingers over her clit with more pressure.

"Is that what you need, love?" he asked, his voice gritty with pleasure.

"Yes," she hissed, and reaching past his hand she fondled his sack, feeling the taut globes tight with desire. At her touch, his thrusts increased. No longer slow, they were fast, hard and deep.

The pounding of his cock and the pinching of her clit were too much and soon she was crying out his name as she climaxed, her sheath clamped around him in ecstatic surrender.

He continued to pump, his thrusts prolonging the rapture, until he too cried out. With a deep push he shot inside her, his body shuddering as he came hard.

Moments later they remained joined as they panted for breath. Mara could feel Lurin's large hands fondling her buttocks as his still hard cock flexed inside her.

Amazed, she glanced over her shoulder and saw his lips curl, his eyes slumberous.

"Lurin?" Though she'd never experienced sex with anyone but Lurin, she had heard enough to know men didn't normally have his stamina.

"I can't help it, Mara." He began thrusting again, and to her surprise, her body responded. "With you I can't stop wanting."

He paused and flipped her onto her back, then he mounted her and rode her fast, coming within her moments before she came.

Limp now, Mara could only stare up at him in wonder. As

before, sex between them stirred something in her that made her question everything. Like a weakness invading her mind, thoughts of Lurin consumed her.

"Who are you, Lurin?" she couldn't help but ask.

He gazed down at her, his eyes enshrouded in mystery. The bright blue of his gaze reminded her of the electric bursts on Mardu, ruptures of energy that blazed so brightly they lit up the sky for miles.

"I think the question is, who are *you*, Mara Seni?" Lurin asked, his mood sobering as he stared at her.

Not wanting to but feeling the need for some distance, Lurin withdrew from her warmth and immediately knew a sense of loss. Steeling himself against the urge to sink back into her body, to burrow deeper and deeper until he reached her soul, Lurin searched for his answer in her eyes.

Dark and fathomless, Mara's gaze possessed as many secrets as he himself held. Shocked at the thought, Lurin belatedly realized he hadn't thought to use his Thesha skills to persuade Mara to bed him. The little vixen had drawn him well enough on her own. And the ties between them grew stronger.

"What?" Mara levered up on her elbows and leaned away. "Why are you looking at me like that?"

"Like what?"

"Like I'm some kind of alien species you're trying to figure out. I'm a woman and it's called sex, Lurin," she quipped in a derisive tone, sounding every inch the imperious captain.

Lurin narrowed his gaze. "You want to play 'captain' now, sweet? But it's a little late to chain me, don't you think?" he purred.

The closeness between them vanished as if it had never been, and suddenly Mara looked angry.

His cock stirred, the unruly beast, and Lurin had to fight from fucking her again. This time it would be hard and possessive, to establish dominance, to establish right. As much as he knew he could make her want it, he wouldn't take her that way.

No. With Mara it was all or nothing. She had to want him freely or the sex would be empty. Just thinking such thoughts made Lurin want to throw something. Since when did he care about sex feeling "empty"?

"Like I give a shit," he murmured, glaring down at her. *I have enough problems to deal with.*

"Excuse me?" Mara's anger intensified into outrage.

"Oh hell, never mind." He rolled off the bed and searched for his trousers. In the midst of donning his pants, he looked up to see Mara dressed in a large shirt, holding a phaser pointed directly at his heart.

"I have several questions you're going to answer. First though, I'd like you to explain that last comment, *prisoner* Vez." Her voice sounded even though her eyes shot daggers at him.

"Prisoner?" His eyes blazed. The little witch! Without regard to her weapon, he advanced until the phaser kissed his chest. "I can imprison you with the whisper of a promise, sweet," he said silkily, menace filling his words.

He stared at her, connected with her on another plane and suddenly he was Thesha, glorying in his power once more. Mara swayed and her phaser dropped to the floor.

"No, sweet," he whispered and kissed her, ravaging her mouth, invading her essence with his own. "You belong to me. You're *my* prisoner."

Lost in his gaze, Mara nevertheless recognized his authority. Her will yielded and she struggled, but could gain no foothold on her ability to focus, to hold a straight thought. Images, scents and the feel of Lurin saturated her mind, both frightening and exciting her.

"Kiss me," she demanded, when what she really wanted was to punch him.

He smirked, an expression of curled lips and blank eyes that made her cold inside. When he kissed her, the heat of his touch in contrast with the emptiness of his action scared her all the more.

"Don't you like it, Mara?" He licked at his lips and kissed her again, harder, punishing. Then he broke away and swore. "Hell, *I* don't like it." He thrust her from him and suddenly the strange compulsion to kiss him faded. He thrust his hands through his hair, looking frustrated despite the bulge growing in his trousers.

Stars but they'd made love enough times that the man should have been unable to get hard. "How is that possible?" she couldn't help but ask, pointing to his groin. Then the unexpected happened. She felt herself growing wet in response to his erection, regardless of the fact that she felt angry and a bit afraid of his power over her.

"You don't want to know." He gave her a dark look and stalked to the portal showing deep space and a glimpse of Nebe6. "When will your crew return?"

Mara blinked. "Ah," she looked around for her timepiece and spying it, put it on. "They should be back in another few hours." He glanced at her with surprise, and Mara cursed her stupidity for telling the truth.

"Really? Then I suppose we have some time to kill. What will we do to wear away the hours?" His words were suggestive but the glint in his eyes told her he was baiting her.

She took the bait, anger clouding her better sense. "I don't know what you did to me, but it's not going to happen again. The sex was good, but it's over now." *Who am I kidding?*

His lips tightened into a grim line. "Good? Come now, Mara. You can admit the sex was spectacular. That's one particular area I've never had any problem with."

She blushed. She couldn't help it. Captain of her own ship, a professional bounty hunter, and angry as a raider, yet she blushed.

He laughed when he saw it, and the darkness clouding his expression eased. "Good. For a minute there I wondered where the woman in Captain Mara had gone."

"She's right here," she said through clenched teeth. How had this man, this irritating clod, made her lose her mind to passion? She'd never heard of a telepath having such skills. It defied explanation, unless he was ... Thesha? Where the notion came from she had no idea, but she dismissed it as she stared at him.

No, Lurin was no Thesha. They didn't exist. The mind trick he'd just pulled, getting her to free him from his cell, those were stunts a clever telepath might know. If he were Thesha, he'd be able to control everything she said and did, according to legend. Just the thought of being so powerless sent a chill through her blood.

Lurin continued to stare at her, his gaze no longer bright and shining but shuttered.

"So what now, Captain Mara? You don't honestly expect me to go back to my cell in shackles to await Nobless

Cari's *justice*, do you?"

Mara sank onto the bed and kept a cautious eye on Lurin. "No, I don't. But I don't plan on setting you free, either." He eyed the phaser she'd dropped on the floor near the bed.

Spectacular sex or no, Mara commanded everyone on board her vessel. And technically, Lurin *was* still her prisoner. She eyed her phaser, then Lurin. "Don't even think about it."

"I'm not." He scowled and sank into a nearby chair. After a moment of silence, Lurin stared at her with an intensity she found unnerving. "What do you want from me, Mara?" Strangely enough, he looked as puzzled and put out about the whole situation as she felt.

"I'm not sure," she paused, searching for an answer. *I want you to make love to me. I want you to fill the empty spaces within me. Make me into the sensual, loving woman I know I can be.* Ignoring her innermost desires as she had for most of her life, she fell back on the job. It was so much safer. "Why don't we focus on your case with Nobless Cari?"

He shrugged, and she could tell that though he'd asked the question, he too wanted to avoid discussing what existed between them.

"What possible reason could the Nobless have for putting a bounty on your head? Jaron law took responsibility for you the moment you killed--allegedly killed--" she forestalled his interruption, "Master Denal. No matter what you saw in the woods, your word won't stand up to that of the Nobless, not on Elaran land. So why did she hire me to capture you?"

"I don't know why she hired you." He looked confused but Mara sensed something amiss with his answer.

"She's offering me a great deal of currency for you," Mara offered. Lurin gave her an innocent look. *Damn. He was holding back.*

"Tell me the truth, Lurin."

"I did already. What? You want a more detailed accounting of Sara's rendezvous in the woods? Why don't I show you instead?" he suggested and nodded at his groin. "I'm ready for it if you are."

And that was another problem. She was more than ready for him, *again*. Mara clenched her thighs together but

# MASTER OF SEDUCTION

unfortunately Lurin saw, for he stood slowly and began fondling himself.

"Come, Mara. Our little argument's stirred me." He stroked himself through his trousers and his gaze probed hers. That quickly, Mara's nipples pebbled, craving his touch.

Determined to remain aloof, to prove that she didn't want or need him, she shook her head.

He grinned at her challenge and neared the bed. She remained seated, and his groin reached her at eye level. He stopped in front of her and pushed his trousers down, exposing his gloriously hard cock to her gaze.

Mara's mouth watered and she was unable to tear her eyes away. She heard his breathing quicken and watched as his hand moved faster, reveling in the feel of her eyes upon him.

"So you don't need me, Mara?"

He pumped up and down, squeezing and rubbing his cock in front of her face. *He was close enough to taste*, came the traitorous thought, and she licked her lips.

He groaned and worked faster, teasing her.

"You know you want this," he rasped. "I can smell your need, Mara. Go ahead, touch yourself. Tell me you aren't wet, drowning for me."

Pumping his cock with one hand, he used his other to force her hand down between her thighs. Unable to resist, she pushed the over shirt aside and began rubbing her clit, smoothing through the thick folds of her sex.

"That's it, sweet," he urged breathlessly, his cock impossibly hard. He removed his hand from his cock and she could see him pulsing, his throbbing rod waving in front of her, begging her to taste. "Put your finger inside your slick pussy," he ordered.

She did and his cock seemed to swell. She could see a drop of moisture beading at the tip.

"Yes, sweet." He watched her fingering herself and began pumping again. "I'm going to come all over you," he whispered, "but it won't be as good as when I come in you."

Staring at her mouth, he seemed to read her mind. "Want a little taste?"

He looked impossibly large, swollen and thick, and Mara

*needed* to taste him. He guided his cock to her lips and she licked him from his tip to the base of his shaft. Salty and sweet, and impossibly male.

"I want to fuck your mouth so badly," he groaned and held himself as she licked him. She drew out the contact and he shuddered.

"No more," he rasped and began pumping his cock in a frenzy.

Mara was beside herself. Seeing him pleasure himself and tasting him while fingering her clit stimulated her beyond control. She came suddenly in a rush. Lurin followed soon after, jerking so that his cum saturated her over shirt, his seed clinging to her breasts and stomach through the thin linen.

Sated yet unfulfilled, Mara knew the experience fell short of full bodily contact with Lurin. But stubborn, she refused to submit to him again. She didn't know why he'd turned from an exquisitely sensual lover to a cold, callous man. And she tried to convince herself she didn't care.

Catching her breath, she watched as his cock slowly went limp. Reaching down, he pulled up and fastened his trousers.

He said nothing but she could feel his gaze on her as she shrugged out of her shirt and dressed in clean clothing and boots. She kept her phaser close and tucked it into her belt when fully dressed. Still Lurin said nothing.

Uncomfortable under his knowing gaze, Mara opened her mouth when a sudden jarring knocked both Lurin and her forward.

"What the hell was that?" Lurin stared at her in shock.

Feeling just as surprised, she raced to the portal and looked out. Then she gripped her phaser and moved to the door.

"We're being boarded, and it's not my crew."


## Chapter Seven

Conscious that Lurin wore a pair of trousers and nothing more, Mara sent him to Nu's room, where she knew he'd find clothes to fit. Without waiting for him, she hurried to the bridge, knowing she had little time.

"Who do you think they are?" Lurin asked as he caught up with her.

"I don't know. They're too quiet for pirates, and if they were law they'd have signaled first." She ran a quick scan on the docking vessel. "Standard warship," she muttered in frustration.

A grating whine, the sound of metal hulls scraping together, alerted them both to the impending boarding of an unknown enemy.

"It's got to be Nobless Cari." Lurin glared at the console outlining the warship.

"That makes no sense." Mara shook her head, fighting impatience. "As far as she knows, I'm just a few short days from delivering you into her keeping. Why would she interfere now?"

"To get out of her fee, maybe?"

"No." Mara clutched her weapon. "But we can reason the who's and why's later. Right now we have to prepare for a fight."

"A fight?" Lurin stared incredulously from Mara's determined gaze to the console. "You're kidding, right? It's the two of us against a warship carrying any number of warriors. And you don't even trust me with a weapon."

Mara opened her mouth to argue but couldn't refute his logic. "Good point." She handed him her phaser.

Her skin felt tingly and her blood pounded through her veins. She could feel the adrenaline kicking into high gear at thoughts of the upcoming battle, as well as a rush of nerves. Reminding herself not to glory in the adrenaline high, she focused on calm and reason.

Reaching into a concealed weapons stash, she grabbed another phaser and two battle knives, handing one to Lurin.

"Just in case."

He nodded.

"This is my ship and I'll be damned if I'll give her up. We'll take them one at time through the stairwell. It's the only obvious pathway to this deck of the ship. There's no way they can know about the crew entrance hidden on the port side."

She ran out of the bridge, figuring they had little time to do more than stage themselves.

"Wait." Lurin grabbed her shoulder, effectively halting her. She turned impatiently. "A kiss for luck."

The most incredible thing happened then. He kissed her deeply, and Mara felt a subtle heat infuse her body, a heat curiously different from the sensual haze he usually stoked.

Her heart seemed to stop, then began pounding as if she'd just finished a race. She could feel a subtle difference inside of her, as if a part of Lurin now dwelled within her blood. She stared up at him, for the first time truly questioning if Lurin Vez was more than a telepath.

"Be safe," he ordered. His eyes lit brilliantly before they calmed into a flat, navy blue, a color unlike any he'd worn before.

Still staring, she had to forcibly close her mouth and move into her position. She and Lurin lay prone at the top of the stairwell, each peering over the ledge to the floor of the second deck below. The inner seal of the docking wall had been breached, and already Mara could see several warriors in royal Elaran yellow combing the floor.

She and Lurin sat at an angle to one another, allowing their fields of fire to cover much of the second deck, with Lurin's attention on the actual stairway and hers on the floor itself.

She prayed they wouldn't do too much damage to her ship while defending it.

"Here they come," Lurin murmured.

Surprised, Mara watched uneasily as a gaggle of warriors approached the stairway in a rather unbalanced affront. They moved without precision or discipline, and she wondered if the uniforms they wore were real or just an artifice to confuse the wary.

Lurin fired first, and a man went down. Return fire immediately ensued and Mara had her hands full protecting her position while firing on the others that appeared from out of nowhere.

Where the hell had those dozen men come from?

She felled another man, suddenly realizing that her phaser had been set to high stun.

"Damn it."

Lurin continued to fire. "What's wrong?"

"I've been stunning these men. That's okay as long as they're not here for more than a few hours."

"Great." Lurin swore and fired again. "Are you noticing that men seem to be appearing out of nowhere here?"

"I noticed." A shot singed her shoulder and she scowled at the warrior who fired at her. Curiously the wound didn't hurt, but she was too worried about the disappearing enemy to wonder about it.

"And we're so glad you noticed," a deep voice sounded from above her.

Before she could move, a blade pressed against the side of her jaw. "Freeze or I'll cut your throat. You too, Vez. One move and she's dead."

Odd that the man used a threat against her to stay Lurin. Odder still that the threat worked. Their weapons were kicked away.

"On your feet," the deep voice rumbled. "Turn around slowly."

With their hands on their heads in a show of universal surrender, Mara and Lurin turned to greet this new threat. Lurin stepped closer to Mara, subtly positioning himself between her and the giant of a man smirking at them.

"How touching." The slash of what probably passed as a smile didn't reach his cold, jade green eyes. "Loverboy's protective."

Several men around them laughed, and Mara wondered at their sudden presence. The warriors surrounded her and Lurin, but she hadn't heard them mount the stairs and she hadn't seen them near her crew's hidden stairwell either.

She'd hit at least seven of the enemy, who still lay unconscious on the lower deck. Lurin had a slew of men littered on the stairway. So where had everyone come from?

"I've got ways around teleport-blockers," the man holding the blade answered her unspoken question.

Mara gritted her teeth. She'd spent a lot on those blockers, assured that they were the *latest* in technology. There was no use now hoping for her crew to arrive. If the Fas brothers and Catam showed, they'd no doubt be captured by the warriors wandering freely on her ship.

"So what do you want then?" Mara glared at the man facing her. At least he'd lowered his blade.

He stood as tall as Lurin, and she grudgingly acknowledged his rugged features as attractive. But whereas Lurin's face had a sensual cast, much of the sensuality in this man was overlaid by the cruelty in his gaze.

His scarred hand holding his blade attested to battle experience, as did the muscular frame filling his Elaran uniform. Mara noted his rank, something about him didn't fit with the rest of the thugs infesting her ship. He seemed too controlled, too intense.

"Let her go," Lurin interrupted the silence that had settled. "It's me you want."

"Actually no," the captain mused. "I don't want you, but my employer does. She," he drawled with a nod to Mara, "is a small part of my payment." He flashed white and even teeth from a mean smile.

The men surrounding them were no match for Lurin's speed. With a surprise lunge, he knocked the captain to the floor. Mara instinctively moved forward to help Lurin but was grabbed on either side by Elaran soldiers.

On top of the captain and taking advantage of the fact, Lurin landed two hard blows before the captain bucked him off.

The men around them cheered and Mara realized no one intended to stop the fight. At least Lurin had a fair chance at winning. As soon as she thought it, she saw her error.

Lurin was by no means a small or inept fighter, but the captain obviously lived to brawl. He moved with a grace that belied his size. And his coordinated punches and kicks flowed like a lethal dance.

He countered every punch and kick Lurin threw. Oddly enough, he did little more than block Lurin's attacks. Mara kept waiting for him to engage but he kept curiously distant, as if not wanting to hurt his opponent.

Lurin must have noted as well, for his eyes narrowed into brilliant pinpoints of blue light as he studied his adversary. He chanced a brief look at Mara out of the corner of his eye, and gave his opponent the opportunity he needed.

The captain took advantage of Lurin's lapse and shot forward with a sharp blow, aiming for Lurin's throat. Lurin, however, anticipated the move for he easily dodged the attack and swept low, knocking the captain once more off his feet.

The constant cheering grew ominously silent. The

captain, however, surprised everyone. Instead of leaping to his feet to continue the fight, he laughed, a hearty chuckle at odds with his stark manner.

Mara shared a baffled glance with Lurin. When she looked back at the captain, he was eyeing them both with a speculation that unnerved her. Unsure what came next, Mara blinked when the captain shot Lurin with a phaser that appeared out of nowhere.

She froze, unable to believe Lurin could be dead. Everything inside of her rebelled at the very thought. Then the captain nudged Lurin's crumpled body with his boot and she heard a low groan of pain. She couldn't help the relieved breath that escaped.

"Take Vez to *the Lady*," he ordered the men nearest him. "And be easy as you guide him back. Too many marks on him and she'll transfer the pain all too readily to the one responsible."

"Aye, Captain Gren." The men dragged Lurin away, leaving Gren and a few others behind.

Captain Gren watched until Lurin disappeared into his ship before turning to Mara. She tried to wrench free from the warriors holding her, with no success. No doubt she'd have bruises later, as tight as they were gripping her arms.

Gren glared at the men and they immediately released her. "You're a very special woman, Captain Mara Seni," he rumbled. His eyes looked like shards of green glass, clear and sharp. "You get to fill my nights with pleasure."

She couldn't explain it, but suddenly she *felt* his interest, and an odd lust filled the very air she breathed. It was ridiculous, she knew. She was no empath, had no telepathic abilities whatsoever. Gren stared at her intently, as if waiting for some reaction from her. And she knew he had somehow invaded her mind.

She mentally compared him to Lurin. In size and strength they were equal, but Gren didn't make her feel what Lurin did. She grudgingly admitted feeling drawn to Gren on a purely physical level. The man had a rough, sexual presence that he wore like a cloak, much like Lurin.

But Gren was *not* Lurin.

Lurin had never seemed like a criminal. Her first impression of him had been that some mistake had been made. Gren, on the other hand, looked every inch a black-hearted killer for hire.

"Why so quiet, Mara?" Gren's eyes narrowed. "Missing your strapping prisoner so soon? Don't worry, Sara will take good care of him."

"Lady Sara?" He couldn't be talking about her employer's daughter.

"She didn't get enough of him the last time. I do believe she intends to fuck him the entire way to Jaron." The men around them laughed and Mara saw red. Cursing, she flew at Gren, reaching for the spot just under his ear that would render him unconscious. Then she would grab his phaser and....

As if he read her mind, he sidestepped her attack and swiftly shackled her arms behind her back. As much as she struggled, his hold was unbreakable.

"You're so predictable, Mara," Gren murmured and ran a callused finger over her cheek. "But I like them feisty." Then he ripped a hand through her shirt, baring her breasts to his gaze.

"Take her now, Cap'," one voice cried.

"Fuck her hard, show her who's boss."

"Aye, then leave us seconds, Cap. We're your men," whined another.

Fury and terror warred in Mara's heart. Gren didn't respond to his men. His eyes remained glued to hers. When he cupped her breast and toyed with her nipple, she found to her horror that it peaked in response. Lust consumed her, and her body welcomed his touch while her mind shrieked at her to abhor it.

"Ah, yes, my lady captain," Gren murmured. "You're very fortunate indeed."

She opened her mouth to protest, vaguely aware of the lewd comments and lust-filled gazes of those around them. A sudden haze enveloped her and she struggled to think clearly. She had a vague impression of having experienced this feeling before. Then blackness consumed her, and she thought nothing more.

* * * *

Damn, the urge to fuck her was strong. Way too strong. Gren hefted the woman over his shoulder and teleported them both back to his ship. He checked with Sara's chief and found that the rest of the men were boarding.

"Let me know when we're set to go," Gren ordered. "And position two men outside my door. Lex and Shan should do."

The chief nodded and Gren left in search of his room. He passed several warriors and noted the interested glances thrown to the delectable prisoner over his shoulder.

He gripped her ass to hold her in place, and his hand burned where he touched her, aching to feel the warm, pink flesh beneath the clothes. He quickened his pace and finally entered his room.

"Hell." He dumped her unceremoniously in the middle of his bed and cursed again when her ripped shirt revealed two luscious, coral tipped breasts. "I should get a medal for this."

Unable to resist, he closed his eyes and released his mortal flesh. Hovering over her, he touched with his mind, forming a bond with Mara's subconscious while preserving Lurin's claim on the woman.

He really shouldn't take such liberties, but hell, he was Thesha, after all. And sex was as necessary to his kind as breathing. Justifying his actions, he palmed one of her luscious breasts, and felt her hard nipple score through his thoughts to his physical flesh.

He floated above her, studying her, trying to figure out what made her so different from other women. He couldn't put his finger on it, but he could sense her perfection, could almost see it glowing from within her.

Shaking his head at Lurin's luck, he gently kissed her on the forehead. But the taste of her sent shivers through his body, and helpless, he closed his mouth around the taut peak of an aroused breast.

Her skin was as smooth as Taury silk, her taste like the finest Kaeyon wine. She had his cock stiff and hurting from the spiritual bonding, and he closed his eyes, reveling in her scent and taste.

To imagine physically joining her ... then he caught a familiar masculine scent and blinked. *Shit. What the hell was he doing?*

With a groan Gren drew back into his body. He was throbbing, needing release, and more than anything he wanted a warm woman. He was getting damned tired of his hand.

Before he let his baser instincts rule, he grabbed a blanket and tossed it over Mara's naked breasts. Trusting in his discipline, he readjusted himself in his trousers and breathed deeply, searching for calm. He glared from Mara to his erection, willing his stiff member to subside.

"That's all I need. A cock that won't quit around Lady Sara."

Just the mention of Sara's name had him flaccid in no time. He shook his head and bound Mara to the bed. His mind probe would have her unconscious for as long as it took to placate Sara and check on Lurin.

Little enough time had passed that Sara could have harmed her prisoner. But she was a creative woman, and with enough time and opportunity, he had no doubt Sara would find a way to enslave Lurin Vez, her new pet Thesha.

Gren left his room with a warning to the two guards outside his door.

"If anyone save me enters these quarters, your lives are forfeit."

They nodded vigorously and stared straight ahead. From the rabble he was forced to use as crew, the two he left to guard Mara were the best he had.

Again cursing the fate that had him working for the Nobless, Gren stalked to Lady Sara's quarters and entered without permission.

He grimaced at the sight that met his eyes. Sara and Vendon, her closest advisor, were in deep conversation overlooking Lurin on Sara's bed. He lay on his back naked, his hands and feet spread wide and tied to the four posts of her bed.

"I can't believe you did it," Vendon twittered, rubbing his bald head. He looked like the small concubines that inhabited Rasha 12, the pleasure moon in the fifth quadrant. With painted lips and rouged cheeks, Vendon's artifice only accentuated his effeminate build.

He glanced up and his eyes brightened when he saw Gren. Holding in a snort of disgust, Gren nodded curtly to both Vendon and Sara, ignoring the wicked gleam in Vendon's eyes.

"Captain Gren, what a pleasure. I was hoping you would come," Vendon dripped with sexual invitation. Sara smirked and batted her eyes at Gren, her stare openly carnal, worrying him.

"I was just telling Vendon what a superb job you've done, Captain Gren." Gone was the shrill little bitch that'd threatened him earlier. And his guard rose another few notches. "You deserve a reward."

"I'm receiving payment for this job."

"Something more is in order, wouldn't you say, Vendon?"

The man licked his lips and Gren did his best to ignore him. He had to get Lurin safely back to Jaron before this farce could end.

"Just what did you have in mind, Lady Sara?" Gren probed cautiously.

She twisted a lock of red hair around her fingers as she regarded him with interest. Vendon positively drooled.

"Since Vez won't regain consciousness for another few hours, I have no one to play with now."

Gren felt sweat break out on his brow. His encounter with Mara was still too fresh, and the images Sara unknowingly projected were so strong he couldn't control his erection.

"See, Captain Gren? You do like me," she said with a throaty laugh.

With her and Vendon's attention on him, they didn't see Lurin's eyes flicker open. He blinked and his gaze caught Gren's.

*Don't move and for star's sake close your eyes!* Gren sent him.

Immediately Lurin shut his eyes and resumed slow, deep breaths. *Why didn't you tell me you were one of us?*

"Captain? Is something wrong?"

Gren needed to focus. Vendon was almost on top of him and the sybarite's hands were an inch from touching his chest.

"I'm fine." Gren's voice sounded gritty and he hoped they chalked the tone to lust. Sara seemed pleased. She smiled and began to disrobe.

"I'm so happy we're all in agreement then." Vendon said as he focused on Gren's swelling cock.

Helpless to the desires surging in the room, Gren was unable to control his libido. He felt on fire, and without some relief soon he might very well succumb to Vendon. That thought shook him and forced him to focus.

"Vendon, get out," he ordered.

Vendon pouted but Sara laughed and shooed him out the door.

"You can play with him when I'm done, I promise," she whispered loudly. "But only if...." she finished too quietly for him to hear.

Gren wondered just what Lady Sara thought she could wheedle out of Vendon.

"I'll hold you to that," Vendon said and with pursed lips, stalked out the door.

Once it closed, Sara unfastened the rest of her garments and stepped out of them toward Gren.

Disgusted by her avarice and ill intent, he nevertheless needed what she offered. *You owe me big for this, Lurin.* Her hands made quick work of his trousers and she was grabbing him, exclaiming over his size and girth. But underneath the raw sex, her malicious spirit tainted him, repulsing him as her aura bled over into his.

*I'm sorry,* Lurin sent. *I won't forget this. If I was in better shape, I'd....*

Gren lost the rest of Lurin's words as Sara's mouth engulfed him.

## Chapter Eight

Mara woke in an awkward position. She lay on her back, her arms drawn over her head and tied to a post in the corner of a large bed. She twisted and felt a rough cloth over her breasts.

"What in the world?"

As she recalled the preceding events leading to her capture, she had a vague sense of soft yet burning lips over her breast, of an ecstatic heat and a merging of desire. But it faded the more she thought on it, and she could only be glad she wore the rest of her clothes.

At least that bastard Gren hadn't raped her yet. Struggling against her bonds, she didn't notice when the door opened.

"Welcome to your new home, at least, for the next few days." Gren stood over her, his arms akimbo. He looked haggard and had a strange glow, and she wondered if he was using one of the many illegal substances that floated through the system.

"What do you want, Gren?"

"I want...." He paused and sank onto the bed next to her. He either didn't notice or he ignored her cringe. Instead he rested his head in his hands and breathed deeply. Then he looked into her eyes.

The room seemed to tilt and he seemed to sway. The next thing she knew she was no longer tied, sitting up in the bed with the blanket around her and he was rubbing her arms.

"Are you okay?"

"What happened?" she asked and licked at her lips, conscious of a great thirst.

"Don't move." He left her side and returned quickly. But she had no energy to do more than lift her hand to her head.

"Did you drug me? Is this how you get your kicks? By drugging and raping unwilling women?" She tried to sound harsh but her words emerged in a croak. She greedily drank the water he gave her before wondering if she'd done something foolish. What if he'd drugged the water?

Seeing her suspicions, Gren laughed and stood, looking much more like the man who'd captured her than the tired man a few moments before.

"I wish I'd met you before Lurin."

Her eyes flew to his. "Lurin? How is he? Where is he? What have you done to him?"

Had she the energy she'd stand up and wallop him. As it was she concentrated on sitting upright in the bed.

"Mara," Gren began before pausing to grab a remote control from the side of the bed. He pushed a few buttons and a subtle hum emanated from beneath the bed. "I don't have much time. The discordant pulse breaks the overhead eavesdroppers," he said pointing to discreet metal plates in the ceiling, "but it won't last long."

"What--"

"The only thing I can tell you is that I'm on your side. Lurin has more friends than he knows. And I'm doing all I can to save him from Lady Sara." He grimaced.

"Is he all right?"

"He's fine for now. You should be more worried about you, Mara."

"Why?"

"Because my claiming you was the only thing stopping Sara from giving you to the crew."

"The crew?"

"The *entire* crew." She swallowed and he nodded. "I'm sorry for my rough treatment earlier." He coughed and motioned to the blanket that parted to reveal her breasts through her tattered shirt. "I had to make it look real."

"Make what look real?"

"My claim. Listen closely, Mara. I know you're still shaken. But this is all part of the plan. We have to return to Jaron to clear Lurin's name. And you have to go along with everything I say and do."

Mara didn't understand any of this, but her instincts told her to trust Gren. She had no choice but to trust him. "Gren, my crew--"

"Was intercepted before they could return to your ship. They'll be waiting for us on Jaron. I thought a little back-up wouldn't hurt." He grinned and Mara blinked in astonishment. Gone was the curt, cruel Captain Gren and in his place sat a warm, gorgeous warlord.

His gaze sobered and he leaned closer. "I know you and Lurin are, ah, close, but we may be forced into some situations beyond my control. Don't worry, Mara. I'll do my best to protect you. And I'll always make it good for you."

Mara took affront to the "I'll do my best to protect you." She'd been protecting herself since her thirteenth year. She opened her mouth to say so when Gren froze and tilted his head. At the same time the buzzing under the bed stopped.

"What--"

Before she could finish, Gren tore the blanket from her and flattened her under him on the bed. His mouth closed over her breast and his hand dove beneath her trousers to her wet, hot core.

Thoughts of Lurin faded under a forceful cloud carrying images of Gren to the forefront of her mind. Stunned under the wash of imposed feeling, she didn't protest Gren's touch.

His roughened fingers grated over her clit and she helplessly arched into his touch. His warm mouth suckled at her nipples, drawing forth responses she'd only recently acknowledged.

She felt his cock as hard as steel pressed against her thigh. He was far from unaffected. She thought she heard him groan her name before another voice interrupted.

"Really, Gren. Wasn't Sara enough for you? Rumor has it her stamina has never been matched."

"Ever hear of knocking, Vendon?" Gren asked in a breathless voice. He kept his attention on Mara while he spoke, his lips trailing from her breasts to her neck, lingering at her pulse point.

"It's not your ship, Gren. Remember that."

Gren ignored him and continued his sensual assault. His lips found the curve of her ear and he blew hot puffs along her sensitive canal. Heat pooled in her loins and Mara arched into his questing fingers, not caring about Vendon's interruption. Contrary to her usual desires for discretion, Mara felt absolutely free from all constraint. Only Gren's touch mattered now.

His fingers slid easily through her cream, and despite the interruption she drew closer to orgasm.

"Come on, Gren. Fuck her already." Vendon tried to sound bored, but she could hear the excitement in his reedy voice.

"Get out. I'll join you and Lady Sara in the galley *later*." Gren removed his hand from under her trousers and ground his pelvis against her mound. Mara knew that although this had started as an act, Gren was as aroused as she by the foreplay.

"Fine," Vendon said in a sulky voice. "But one of these days you're going to be mine, Gren. And when that day comes, I'm going to have you on your knees." That said, he left the room and Mara heard the door slide shut behind him.

"He-he's gone, Gren," Mara rasped as she helplessly pressed closer to his erection.

"I know." He gazed into Mara's eyes. "You don't know how much I want to fuck you right now. You smell so good," he groaned and inserted a finger inside of her.

"I know it's not me you want to see when you close your eyes. But I need you Mara. For Lurin's sake, don't fight it."

The haze that clouded her mind grew darker, thoughts, images and tastes of Gren filling her mind until nothing but

Gren existed. He resumed his caresses, sliding his finger in and out of her pussy while his mouth toyed with her breasts. Then he added another finger, stretching her, making room for his cock.

She felt incredible, close to soaring. His hands were working magic. When they stopped she groaned with disappointment. Her body felt hot and needy, desperate for more, desperate for Gren.

"Look at me, Mara," Gren ordered. "I'm going to fuck you hard, and you're going to come. My cock will fill you, nothing but Gren. And when we're done, you'll forget all about it."

"Gren," she managed though in the back of her mind she fought to be free. *Lurin....*

"I know, sweet. But he'd want you to find pleasure. Just relax and feel."

Without another word he removed her trousers and tattered shirt and nudged her thighs wide, baring her mound to his gaze.

"So wet," he murmured and brought his mouth to her curls. His tongue easily found her clit and he began toying with her, licking and nipping with his teeth. The sensations were extraordinary.

She levered on her elbows and watched his dark head between her legs. She watched him unfasten his trousers and push them down. Wishing she could see him, she said so.

"Look at what you're getting soon," he whispered in a harsh voice, thick with need.

He stood and she watched in awe as his rock hard cock grew as he stroked it. Seeing her amazement, he smiled and knelt, resuming his position between her thighs. His mouth suckled at her clitoris, and with every lap of his tongue she saw his arm move, as if stroking his cock.

The thought of him stroking himself while tonguing her excited her further, and she lay back and reveled in the experience. Gren was so gorgeous, so wonderful, and soon all hers.

So close to the edge, she felt something give inside of her, felt him take it before she crested the peak and came in a gush. In a blur, Gren mounted her and began fucking her, the intrusion of his thick cock both welcome and invasive, almost bruising in his rough intensity to climax.

But the pleasure-pain pushed her further, making her come again around him before he pulled out and spilled all over her belly. He shuddered and then stilled, stomach to stomach with Mara.

"You have no idea what you've done," he said in a low voice and sighed. "Gods, Mara, I needed that."

"Me too," Mara said drowsily, incredibly sated and sleepy.

"It's done now, sweet. Let the memory and the tension fade. Go to sleep, Mara. You'll need your rest for what tomorrow brings, trust me."

Seeing that she obeyed, Gren spoke to Lurin, hovering in the shadows. *She may be yours, but she gave me what I need to help me deal with Sara and to get us all out of this alive.*

He could feel Lurin's dislike for the situation.

*I know*, Lurin thought. *I don't begrudge you such relief. It's just that....*

*I know. She knows it as well, deep down. Though if you were a normal Thesha, you wouldn't mind sharing.* Gren felt Lurin's strong aversion to the thought and laughed aloud. Unable to resist, he taunted the man. *Damn but she's tight.*

*She was a virgin before I met her.* Lurin seethed with resentment that Gren had sampled what belonged to him. Though he tried to shield his thoughts, Gren read them.

*It's more than that, Lurin. And you know it. She's special.*

Gren could see Lurin's expression and wanted to laugh. Confusion, anger and possessiveness fought for dominance on his face. *The poor bastard won't admit he's met his match*, Gren thought to himself.

Feeling for him, Gren decided to give him a moment of privacy. *I'll be in the lav if you need me.*

Lurin watched Gren go and silently thanked the large man for his consideration. Much as he wanted to tear Gren limb from limb, he couldn't.

In Sara's room, he'd watched helplessly from the bed while Sara used and took from Gren, sucking his cock and swallowing his seed as voraciously as she swallowed the light within him. Sara Elaran had been damaged somewhere in her past, and her sexual dysfunction passed the misery in her soul onto all she touched.

Gren had enjoyed physical gratification while his spirit shuddered under Sara's pressing darkness. Yes, Lurin could well understand Mara's draw for a Thesha in Gren's condition.

Tired, depressed and empty, Gren had needed Mara's purity, her healing essence. Gren, the only one capable of protecting Mara and him at this point, needed to be at full strength. Lurin could only be thankful Gren had inserted the compulsion to forget the incident in Mara's mind.

Gren's control over Mara bespoke his immense power. The man had easily compelled Mara to have sex with him, whereas Lurin had had trouble gaining her cooperation at first. Though Lurin had been suffering the aftereffects of drugs at the time.

Yet later, Lurin hadn't needed to use much of his power at all to earn Mara's affections. Despite her resistance to his mental probes, their lovemaking had happened naturally, without force or coercion.

*Lovemaking*. He frowned. He constantly thought of Mara in terms of love and affection. He'd never before cared enough to label his feelings, yet the thought of sharing Mara with another man bothered him more than he could say. He wanted to fight one of his own kind, for stars sake.

In an effort to downplay Gren's impact on Mara, he rationalized that while Gren *had sex* with Mara, Lurin *made love* to her.

He shook his head, aware of the irony he faced. A Thesha ruled women's minds and hearts. A powerful creature capable of total control, a Thesha determined who to love and who to control. Yet with Mara, the decision was out of his hands.

Lurin could do no less than make love to her delectable body, to feel her heart and soul entwined with his. The luscious bounty hunter ensnared him with her warmth, her strength and her integrity.

Next to Mara, Sara looked like Rak fodder. Lurin shuddered. Thoughts of Sara made his skin crawl. And speaking of skin ... he took one last lingering look at Mara and flew back into his body. Just in time, too, for Sara hovered anxiously above him, waiting for him to wake.

## Chapter Nine

Mara woke disoriented. But when she realized she couldn't move her arms, she recalled her precarious situation. Gren and Lady Sara's warriors boarded her ship, took her and Lurin hostage, and were escorting her to planet Jaron?

She shook her head free of the fog still blanketing her thoughts. Strange. She remembered waking to Gren's enlightening explanation of his part in all this. And then, nothing. A big blank spot sat in the middle of her memories.

Her eyes narrowed as she tugged at her wrists bound to the bed. She remained clothed, though she wore an over large and foreign shirt, most likely Gren's. Though tied up, she felt relaxed, her muscles loose and her mind free of worry.

She immediately grew apprehensive. The fact that she could possibly feel okay about her present situation clearly pointed to someone tampering with her mind.

As her concerns mounted, worry for herself was quickly overshadowed by worry for Lurin. Gren had mentioned Sara. Did that mean she was on board? And if so, how safe could Lurin be around that woman? When questioned, he'd alluded to mistreatment at Sara's hands. Who knew what that sick woman was doing to him now?

The sound of the door sliding open interrupted her thoughts. Gren entered dressed in Elaran finery.

"Good. You're awake."

"What did you do to me?" she asked suspiciously. "Why don't I remember my time aboard this ship?"

"What is it you think I did, exactly?" His voice was completely innocuous, but Mara *knew* he hid the truth--it gleamed in his eyes, bright with humor and something else she couldn't quite name.

"I think maybe I don't want to know," she murmured. When he grinned she thought again how attractive he looked. If not for his actions in capturing her and Lurin, she might actually believe his intentions were to help them.

She had no choice but to trust him, and it galled her to be so out of control of the situation. Mara couldn't recall the last time she'd been on the receiving end of an order. Oh, she served her clients well enough, but *she* gave the orders on her ship. The clients merely represented the mission's end.

Staring at Gren, she thought how earnest he'd sounded about wanting to help Lurin. But why? That was the question she needed answered. It made no sense that Lurin would attack an ally, and he'd been close to putting his fist through Gren's face.

"Why are you doing this?"

Gren's eyes narrowed and he looked up at the metal disks he'd earlier identified as "eavesdroppers". "I told you before, Mara. Lurin belongs to Lady Cari for crimes committed against her family. You, unfortunately, got caught in the middle of it all. But don't worry love," he said with a grin, his voice full of promise, "fucking me more than made things even. And we still have another day before we get to Jaron."

"Another day?" Mara's eyes widened. *Fucking him? There's no way I could have forgotten that.* Deciding he was playing games, she ignored that remark. "You're telling me I slept for two entire days on this ship?"

He shrugged and sat down in a chair across from her. "All the excitement in meeting me that first day must have tired you sorely. You seem well rested now though."

Mara stared at Gren in bewilderment. *Trust me*, he mouthed, and eyed the eavesdroppers again.

"Like I have a choice," she muttered.

"There's the spirit." He chuckled and stood. "Now let's go see Lady Sara. She's got a few questions for you."

He waited until she reached him before pulling her into his arms. She stiffened and would have kneed him when he whispered into her ear, "Follow my lead with Sara. And whatever you do, don't react to anything she does with Lurin."

Mara slowly relaxed and nodded, beginning to believe Gren really meant to protect them. She burned with curiosity to know Gren's reasons behind his aid, but would have to wait until it was safe for the answers.

As they walked down the corridor, she noted the leers and

lewd comments thrown her way and glared at the men she passed. Gren ignored them.

"Some crew you have here," she scoffed.

"They're not mine. I'm merely leading them for a short while."

"How lucky for you."

She noted a small grin that he quickly coughed to cover when a short, bald man wearing a royal Elaran robe approached them.

"Vendon." Gren gave him a curt nod.

*Vendon. Now why did that name sound familiar?*

Vendon sneered. "I trust you're done fucking her brains out? Why you'd choose her when Lady Sara and others with royal connections are available, I'll never know." He stepped with them toward a door at The End of the corridor. "She's been waiting for you. Vez is awake but not moving, and she's not happy."

Mara listened while trying to keep herself as small as possible, not wanting to draw more notice. She needn't have bothered with Vendon. The man hadn't blinked since landing eyes on Gren. He waited until they passed by him to Sara's room, then left toward the bridge.

After she and Gren entered Lady Sara's room, however, she found herself under the careful scrutiny of Cari's daughter.

"So, *you* captured Lurin Vez?" Sara walked in a circle around Mara, eyeing her up and down with wary curiosity. "Did you try him on for size?"

Mara did her best not to be obvious, but she couldn't help glancing at Lurin's naked body on Sara's bed. She met his gaze but couldn't tell if he was awake or not. He didn't move, and his chest seemed still as well.

"Is he alive?" she couldn't help but ask.

"I think so." Sara sounded uncertain and Mara wanted to throttle her. "Gren?"

Gren approached Lurin and felt for his pulse. "He's alive. Probably still having problems with that drug you gave him. I told you tying him up would have been the better option."

Sara ignored his frown and turned her attention back to Mara. "So did you fuck him?"

A feeling of distaste passed over Mara. While she hadn't

been experienced before Lurin, she hadn't been naïve either. She'd never been uncomfortable hearing sex talk. But Sara made it sound dirty, like something to be ashamed of.

Mara straightened her shoulders and looked Sara straight in the eye. "No," she lied, "I didn't fuck him. He's my bounty, nothing more."

The crazed look in Sara's gaze faded and Mara knew she'd sounded convincing.

"He belongs to your mother, Lady Sara," Mara tried in her most autocratic voice. "Why have you interrupted my mission?"

"Don't talk down to me, you little slut," Sara spat. "You're nothing more than my mother's bitch sent to fetch *my* man. You're not even smart enough to know what you're bringing in."

"Lady Sara," Gren warned.

"No, Gren. I want her to know what she lost." Sara laughed in a crazy shriek. "You had a Thesha by the balls and you didn't fuck him once!"

Mara frowned. "Thesha?" Obviously Sara was more than a little crazed. Glancing at Gren proved her theory correct. He looked at Sara in concern. "But they don't exist, Sara."

"But they do," Sara replied sweetly. She sauntered to Lurin and pointed down at a faint marking across his groin. "See this? This is how you can tell a Thesha from a normal male. This scar is actually a birthmark. See the faint blue lines that circle above his pubic bone, at the bottom of his abdomen?"

Mara stood too far from Lurin to tell, but she recalled seeing the marking. At the time she'd been too interested in other things to worry about a scar. Now that she thought about it, it didn't look like any scar she'd ever seen. That still didn't make him a Thesha, though.

"Lady Sara," she began, thinking that Sara had some serious problems.

"Don't try to tell me I'm crazy. I've been with a real Thesha before. Oh yes, they exist." Her mouth twisted. "My mother imprisoned one a long time ago on our estate. A live Thesha. She thought losing my virginity to one would be the ultimate gift she could give me. It turned out she was right."

Gren and Mara glanced at one another.

"He fucked me so many times I lost count. I bled and I bled and he never stopped. Thesha never stop. They're always hard, always hungry for more. And they're so very gifted." She paused, lost in the past. "Such exquisite pain he shared with me."

"If I recall, Lady Sara," Gren said quietly. "The Thesha are rumored to gift women with pleasure. They don't cause harm. And they certainly don't associate pain with sex, according to legend. I'd say you had the unfortunate happenstance to mate with a crazed man, a man nothing more than an unstable human."

"No, Gren. That's where you're wrong."

Mara stared from Sara to Gren, wondering how the hell she'd gotten mixed up in such a strange situation. It was bad enough she'd felt far more than she should for Lurin, a man with a mysterious past and an uncertain future. But to bring the Thesha into the odd mix was almost more than she could take. She'd lost her ship and her freedom, and now Sara strove to take away reality.

Talk about out of control. Mara's life couldn't get more unstable. Then Sara mentioned Theshas again and Mara wondered if she was perhaps suffering from a never-ending nightmare.

"I know the Thesha are real." Sara remained stubborn. "And so does my mother. Why do you think she wants Vez so badly? She knows he's Thesha."

*Lurin was Thesha? No way in hell.*

"She's enthralled with them. It was she who taught my precious 'birthday gift' all the naughty little tricks he worked on me so long ago. I think Mother believes herself part Thesha."

Mara blanched at Sara's perverted tale. That a mother should knowingly inflict such pain on her daughter....

"That proves that the man who abused you was no Thesha," Gren persisted. "Thesha cannot be taught anything. Remember the myth, Sara. Thesha control women, not the other way around."

"Really?" Sara looked pleased at his words and Mara felt a chill shiver down her spine. "If Vez is no Thesha, then he shouldn't respond when I do this."

She took a strange looking knife off the table beside the

bed and held it over Lurin's scar. Gren's face drained of color and Mara had to force herself not to run to Lurin and defend him. *Don't react to anything Sara does to Lurin*, Gren had said. It was killing Mara not to.

"With this sacred knife I'm halfway to controlling my very own Thesha." Sara's eyes were calculating.

"I think you're crazy," Gren said bluntly and crossed his arms over his chest.

"We'll see, won't we?" She lowered the blade and trailed it over Lurin's scar. Three times she traced the scar before she drew a thin line of blood over the mark.

The moment she did so the scar raised and turned a dark blue. It wasn't disfiguring, but it made the birthmark plain to see. It now looked like an intricately designed tattoo.

Mara's unease heightened at Lurin's reaction to the blade. Sara looked thrilled at the sign and squealed with delight.

"I can't believe he's all mine! You haven't told Mother that we're not coming home yet, have you?"

Gren said nothing. He continued to stare at Lurin, a blank look on his face.

"Gren?" A movement from Lurin drew her attention. "Oh, look, he's finally coming around," Sara said with a malicious grin. Just then Lurin blinked, his eyes no longer dazed and empty. Instead his blue eyes blazed with hunger.

"Look at your new master, Lurin Vez." Sara brought her face close to his. "Refer to me as Mistress Sara."

"Mistress Sara," Lurin responded in a throaty voice so unlike the powerful man Mara had known. He sounded subservient and she didn't like it one bit. Subservient. The ramifications of Sara's actions and Lurin's response struck Mara all at once.

"Stars no! He's Thesha!"

"A bit slow, aren't you?" Sara remarked with half-hearted scorn, her attention fixated on her new slave.

Mara mulled over Sara's description of her own encounter with a Thesha. In contrast, Mara had been in control of her responses to Lurin, and she'd felt no pain whatsoever, only agonizing pleasure.

"But," she paused, still warring internally over her disbelief. If Lurin were Thesha, then her reactions to him had been what, coached? Had he scripted her feelings for him as well?

"But what? But you were too slow to see you were sitting on a bek-mine? Think of the currency you lost, the pleasures of the flesh you missed out on because you were too much in a hurry to do Nobless Cari's work." Sara bit out her mother's name. "Well now look at you. Lurin's mine, and you're nothing more than Gren's whore."

Mara opened her mouth but one look at Gren and she closed it.

"Lady Sara," Gren spoke in a deep, soothing voice, "Vez is no more Thesha than I am. It's more likely that knife you carry contains some drug lessening Vez's inhibitions. Try it on me and I'll probably react the same."

Sara laughed. "I don't think so, Gren. I've seen you naked, and you don't have the mark. No, I'm not going to waste time with you when I've got a Thesha here to please me." She tucked the dagger in a drawer beside the bed and whispered in Lurin's ear.

To Mara's amazement, he sat up and began caressing Sara's breasts.

"Suck them," Sara demanded breathlessly, her voice hitching on a moan when his lips covered one tip, then the other.

After all the horrendous ways Lurin had described Sara, Mara knew he had to be powerless to touch Sara so. She felt sick as she watched the sexual contact, as she saw Sara kiss Lurin full on the lips.

"Steady," Gren murmured under his breath as he caught her by the shoulder. Aloud to Sara, he said, "Are we here to simply watch or did you have something more in mind?"

His tone sounded suggestive and Mara stared up at him in shock.

"Actually I had something very specific in mind," Sara said and ordered Lurin to drag her under him. She moaned and rubbed her body along his, drawing out the movement.

Mara couldn't believe the scene in front of her. Lurin had an enormous erection, his cock swollen as he mounted Sara, pushing aside her loose clothing as he readied to fuck her. He looked up at Mara and she could see a yawning emptiness in his eyes.

"Wait a minute, Lurin," Sara said with a smile and pushed him off of her. "I want this to last." He stood, his cock bouncing and he groaned when Sara squeezed him. As she fondled his cock, cupping his sack and licking along his shaft, she continued to glance over at Gren and Mara.

She paused only long enough to say, "Gren, tie up Captain Mara. But put her where she can watch."

Gren tied Mara loosely to a protruding hook in the far corner of the room, in full view of the bed. "You have to get that dagger," he whispered as he bent over her to finish the knot. He left her enough slack that escape would prove easy enough.

"Now come over here. I believe you said something about wanting to do more than watch." Sara watched him approach like a viper eyed its prey. When he stood before her she dropped the rest of her clothing.

She ordered Gren to disrobe and Mara watched with helpless fascination. Gren and Lurin were strong, handsome, sexual creatures no one woman could dream of controlling, and yet Sara did so with little effort. With just one hand she continued to toy with Lurin, a man beyond the scope of normalcy.

A Thesha! Mara still couldn't believe she'd made love with a myth, a legendary pleasure-giver. Though when she thought about it, being Thesha explained a lot about Lurin that she'd earlier questioned.

That first dream she'd had of him had seemed so detailed, so real. And the fact that she'd felt compelled to visit him in his cell. He must have used his gift to force her to him. She couldn't help remembering that surge of energy he'd shared with her before Gren and his men had boarded her ship.

And there was his ability to remain aroused, to continually want sex when a normal man should have been tired. Even as she watched his body respond to Sara's handling, she remembered the feel of Lurin in her own hands.

Anger festered at Sara's involvement. But Mara had more to worry about than Sara. The charges against Lurin were serious, and Gren intended to take them both back to Jaron to face the law? Why didn't Gren simply take control of Sara now? Then she thought of all the warriors still aboard the ship, and the fact that even if they somehow escaped, Lurin would still be a wanted man.

She looked from Lurin's blank face and muscular build to

Gren. Though both men had powerfully built bodies and striking features, there was something more about Lurin that pulled her. Had it been his Thesha heritage all along?

He had surely used his gift to manipulate her, and anger burned at the thought of his deception. Yet when she and Lurin had been joined as one, she had felt his soul, had sensed his core of strength and honor.

Did she feel for Lurin as a result of his manipulations, or had she truly fallen in love with Lurin Vez, the man? Just saying the word 'love' made her doubt her own sanity. She'd never been in love with anyone in her life. Yet the crazy way she felt about him made her question her emotions.

With that thought in mind, she held onto her doubt about her feelings, while she couldn't doubt the fact that he'd had ample opportunity to escape but had instead chosen instead to stay and fight along side her.

Whether his nature as a Thesha would be a detriment or not, she didn't yet know. Deciding to withhold judgment, she remained ambivalent about his heritage and her growing "love", if that's what it was, for him.

Uncertainty about Lurin faded as she watched the scene unfolding near the bed. Sara would pay for her actions, one way or another. She slithered against Lurin and a wave of jealousy engulfed Mara, adding to the quagmire of confused anger filling her mind.

Sara gyrated between both Gren, who now stood naked before her, and Lurin. To Mara's shock, both men were hard and thick, pressing against Sara's lithe body. They ground against the pale miss, their darker skin an odd contrast to Sara's glossy white flesh, pure in color but not in spirit.

Disgusted at Sara's indecency, Mara subtly chafed her wrists, loosening her bonds. Staring at Lurin, watching his sensuality exploited under Sara's malevolent urgings, she couldn't help once again remembering Lurin's actions on her ship. Her mind told her to focus on *now*, but her heart refused to let her.

She knew he'd wanted to escape his imprisonment. And had his intention been to slake his lust on her before leaving, he still could have done so without giving her such pleasure. Once free, he could have tried to wrest control of her ship. There had been several instances where he could have subdued her. But he hadn't.

He must feel something for her. Why else would he have fought by her side on the ship instead of escaping in one of the life pods? He had to have known she had them; they were standard on all space vessels.

One of her wrists escaped the rope and she hurried to free her other hand. Sara took no note of her. She was sandwiched between Gren and Lurin, pumping Gren's cock while Lurin rubbed against her ass. She moaned with desire, urging Lurin and Gren to do the same.

Frowning, Mara noted that neither Gren nor Lurin looked upset at the contact. Lurin wore no expression on his face, but Gren looked entirely too enraptured by her touch. Then he glanced over his shoulder and gave Mara a desperate look urging her to hurry.

She breathed a small sigh of relief. Sara's eyes remained closed and Gren pulled her face down to his cock, glancing subtly over his shoulder at Mara.

"Come on, Sara. Let us fuck you. Take my cock in your mouth and Lurin can fuck you from behind. You know how much you want this," he hissed, a strange energy in his words.

Mara faltered halfway to the bed and stared at Gren. If she didn't know better she'd think he might be Thesha. She shook her head and resumed her course, rejecting the idea. *Oh sure, the ship was full of them, of these beings that supposedly didn't exist.* If Gren really were Thesha, why didn't he simply order Sara to free them?

He drew Sara onto the bed, positioning her so that her back was to the bed stand, with Lurin further blocking her view of the contained dagger. Gren shoved his cock in Sara's willing mouth and began moving in and out. Lurin remained still until Sara gaspingly ordered his participation. With no expression whatsoever, he began fucking her from behind, his groans of pleasure a tinny echo of Sara.

Trying to tune out the groans between the threesome on the bed, and deliberately avoiding the sight of Lurin and Sara together, Mara hurried toward the bed stand on her hands and knees.

She glanced to her left and saw Gren pump into Sara's mouth, saw Lurin's buttocks flex as he thrust into Sara's pussy, and her mouth tightened. She felt herself grow wet despite her dislike of the situation and she hurried to put a stop to it.

She kept low past the bed and reached into the bed stand drawer, feeling for the dagger. She swore under her breath when her finger bit into the point of the blade, but she recovered it with all due haste.

The moment her fingers closed around the handle, Lurin froze. Mara held up the dagger for Gren's perusal and heard him exhale with relief.

Sara was so intent on Gren's cock that she didn't notice Lurin's lack of participation. But when Gren stopped moving, Lurin withdrew from her body and pushed her away, and she blinked up at him in surprise.

"What--" Sara stared from Lurin's hate-filled eyes to Mara and the dagger clenched in Mara's fist. "Kill her, Lurin!" Sara tried.

When he didn't react, she rose on her knees, her breasts heaving in a passionate parody, no longer with lust but with anger. "Gren, kill that bitch and bring me that dagger!"

Gren simply stared at her, and the precarious situation must have dawned on her for she opened her mouth to yell for help. Gren didn't let her. He leapt forward and pressed hard on either side of her neck, and she fell unconscious to the bed.

"And that was the easy part of the plan." Gren shook his head and reached for his clothes.

## Chapter Ten

Mara stared at Lurin and Gren as the two hurriedly dressed. "Well that was awkward."

Gren chuckled as he belted his trousers while Lurin choked out a pained laugh.

"Come here, Mara." Lurin held his hand out waiting patiently.

Relief seeped through her as she stared into his once-more bright blue gaze. She didn't question her deep need to see Lurin unharmed. Instead she focused on his deception, on the manipulations and liberties he took with her heart and mind.

"I think you have some explaining to do, don't you?" she asked calmly, when she really wanted to punish him. The thought of Lurin in his cell, trapped again in shackles, had a certain appeal, especially being at her mercy.

"Now, Mara," Lurin replied, looking a bit unnerved at her unwavering stare. He glanced toward Gren as if for help, but seeing the man occupied with Sara must have changed his mind. He gave Sara a look of repulsion and grabbed Mara by the arm, dragging her away from the bed.

"Get your hands off me." Mara yanked out of his hold. "I think you forget yourself."

Lurin's eyes glowed and Mara took an unsteady breath. She'd forgotten for a moment how powerful Lurin truly might be. She swallowed audibly and stood her ground, determined not to show her unease.

"Damn it, Mara!" Lurin stepped back from her and swore up and down. "I am not going to hurt you! I'm Thesha, not some monster. And certainly not a murdering rapist."

She opened her mouth to retort, not clear on what she meant to say when Gren interrupted.

"You two stay here. Sara won't be waking for hours yet and I need to take control of the situation, especially with Vendon." He grimaced and moved to the door. "No one will enter except with me, and I'll let you know when I return. So whatever you do, don't leave this room. It's the only place you're truly safe."

Gren exited, leaving them alone together. Mara glanced at the bed and saw Sara's wrists and ankles bound, a blanket covering her entire body. An anxiety she hadn't been aware she held eased and the knots in her stomach released.

"She won't be any more trouble," Lurin commented quietly, his breath fanning her ear he stood so close.

Mara turned and Lurin stared into her eyes, the bright blue of his gaze gleaming with sensual promise. Despite her distrust of his motives, warmth unfurled in her belly. He stepped closer and they touched, breast to chest, thigh to thigh. She blinked as she felt his erection prodding her, amazed that he could be so aroused after all Sara had done to him.

"You can't be--"

"I am, *very*," he said with a smile, his teeth white and even and drawing closer to her lips. "My mind is fuzzy about what Sara did, but my body remembers it well. It was hell, because I could feel her touch when all I truly wanted was you."

His words had the desired effect. Mara's limbs felt weak and she melted, her womb clenching in need. "You're making me feel this way, aren't you?" she accused, but her voice sounded more husky than firm.

He slowly shook his head, his lips brushing hers before he drew slightly back. Then he smiled, a loving grin that sent shivers down her spine. "That's just it, love. I'm not. I know you won't believe this, but I only used my gifts on you to get you into my cell that night your crew left the ship. Since then, everything between you and me has been real, exceedingly, arousingly real."

Mara wanted to believe him, but something held her back. And then it didn't matter anymore because he kissed her and she was lost.

His lips consumed her, lighting a fire through her entire body. Her blood burned for his touch, and he answered her longings by stroking her arms, her shoulders, the tender flesh of her neck.

He devoured her, licking and nipping and robbing her very breath. With wicked hands he divested her of her clothes and immediately sought her hot, wet core.

"Yes," he hissed as his fingers penetrated her folds. "You're wet and ready for me, Mara. Damn, but I need you now. I can't wait."

He ripped what little clothing remained on him off and dragged her against him, kissing her senseless. She felt the wall against her back without knowing how she'd gotten there. But she had no more time to think, for he lifted her and wrapping her legs around him, aligned his groin to hers.

She felt him probe her entrance, teasing and testing and she groaned her desire.

"I need more. Please, Lurin."

"Yes, love. Have it all." He thrust up into her, hard, and she almost screamed at the pleasure of feeling him within her again. It felt like forever since he'd been a part of her, and as he hammered into her she could have wept at the perfection of the moment, at the sheer, unadulterated passion.

Hard and fast, mercilessly pumping he rammed into her, letting her weight rest fully over his cock, bringing him into the deepest part of her. Mara could only moan, enraptured by his desperation for fulfillment.

His passion fueled her own and she came suddenly, the spiraling pleasure bursting into a shower of ecstasy. Lurin joined her, groaning her name as he pumped, continuing to move until he found his own peace.

They stood entwined, their hearts beating as one, and Mara again felt that deep spiritual melding that begged her to believe Lurin cared for her, deeply.

"I do, love," he whispered and brushed his lips over her forehead. "I care for you so much it scares me."

Mara blinked up into his mysterious face, his masculine beauty shining with ethereal power. "Are you reading my mind?" She wanted to fault his intrusion, but couldn't help the tingle of belonging, the closeness his intrusion belied.

"I can't always tell your thoughts," he said and eased from her. He led her to the floor and drew her beneath him, leaning over her like a possessive lover. "When we make love, when we become as one, then I am able to sense your thoughts and feelings."

"Legend says the Thesha can read minds at will. I guess you're not as powerful as I've heard?" she teased, but she needed to know. Her hands drifted to his shoulders and she caressed his soft skin, marveling at the softness of his flesh over the corded muscle beneath.

"Actually we are." He flashed her a grin and nipped at her neck. "But something about you, Mara...." he trailed and stared at her. "The moment I boarded your ship I tried 'making' you believe me. But I couldn't get through to you."

"Twice I tried to bind you to me, in the Theshan way. And twice you denied me. I blamed it on the drugs you'd given me."

She flushed with guilt under his accusing eyes, aware she had no reason to feel at fault when she'd been doing her job.

"I'm not blaming you," he said to forestall her comments. "I'm trying to explain something important here."

Mara closed her mouth and listened, aware that while Lurin spoke, his cock, swollen and thick, teased at her curls, pressing and demanding her response. Amazingly she grew wet again, and wondered at her body's reaction.

"It's you, Mara. Until I joined you in that dream state, I couldn't be sure. But there's something about you that's different from other women. I don't know if you affect other Thesha this way, or if it's because--"

He stopped speaking and his eyes widened. Mara waited but he said nothing, merely stared at her with surprise and a bit of ... alarm?

"Lurin? What is it?"

His lids shuttered his expression and his lips parted, his tongue wetting his dry mouth.

"No, let me do that," Mara said and reached for his neck. Lust swamped her and she gave in to it readily, not understanding how she could want him so badly after the pulsating orgasm she'd experienced. She didn't want to question the feeling, however, and claimed Lurin's mouth as her own.

He groaned under her assault and her power grew. She might not be Thesha, but she knew Lurin wanted her, needed her as much as she needed him. And that gave her all the power in the world.

"I want everything, Lurin," she told him between kisses, not understanding this frantic desire to bind them but conceding to it regardless. "I want your lips, your cock," she whispered against his ear and arched into his burning erection. She swallowed a cry when he slid into her, filling her again.

She stopped him, however, with her next words. "I want more. I want your heart, your mind," she paused and licked at his lips, capturing his tongue and teasing it with strokes of her own. She tilted her hips and pushed Lurin out, then sighed when he thrust deeper and groaned.

She broke the kiss and flexed her fingers in his silky black hair. "I want all of you, Lurin. Everything you have to give."

His eyes blazed with something she couldn't quite name and he began pistoning his hips, faster and faster, deeper and harder. "Yes, Mara. All of me."

He tensed and came, pouring into her a warmth that filled

her, consuming her.

Mara cried out at the excessive feeling but he didn't stop. He pulsed inside of her. She thought he might be withdrawing when he swelled and sank deep, groaning her name as he did so.

"Mara, sweet, you give me so much," he rasped and withdrew. "It's only right I do the same."

\* \* \* \*

He stared at her and knew she was *The One*. How could he have been blinded to that fact when everything about her screamed her importance?

Her dark eyes shone with acceptance, and though he knew she hadn't declared her abiding love, her heart didn't lie.

He couldn't believe that something so dark and troubling, the death of his good friend, had turned into the best thing in his life. His soul mate, Mara Seni, lay trusting beneath him. She matched his hunger, reveled in his touch and gave him such ecstasy as he'd never thought to have.

No matter what happened to him in the future, he wanted to remember this moment. He wanted to give her everything she asked, and more.

His cock throbbed and he had to remind himself to slow down. He had another few hours before Gren would return.

"Look at me, Mara." Lurin drew her gaze back to his eyes. She'd been staring hungrily down at his cock. "This energy between us, it's very real."

She nodded and tried to drag him back down to her.

"No, sweet. This time it's all for you. Everything." *Everything I'm capable of giving*, he told himself.

He fused his mouth to hers and teased her mound with the tip of his cock. His hand guiding his shaft, he found her clit and rubbed gently. She groaned into his mouth and he stole her very breath.

Alternatively tender then possessive, he captured her lips, tasting her sweet mouth before capturing her tongue, leading her into another realm altogether. Never before had he given so much to another, opening his heart and sharing his spirit, trusting her as much as he could trust anyone.

Mara was no conquest. She had conquered him. Her soft lips melded to his, perfectly joining and parting without him having to lead her. As if she had been made for him, she complemented his body, his wants and needs.

Mara's hands wandered to his hips and pulled him closer. Her action shifted his cock so that he slid into her and she gasped, arching into him. But Lurin pulled out and slid down her body, lingering over her breasts.

"Sorry, love, not yet." He licked one nipple and watched it pucker, then blew a soft breath over it and watched it peak.

Mara moaned his name and Lurin sent her a subtle *push*, a touch of his desire that spurred her own. Skimming her thoughts to find what she desperately wanted, he grinned around her nipple. She wanted everything he was doing, and more that he had already planned, further evidence that she truly was his other half.

Giving himself to Mara's pleasure, Lurin lightly pinched her nipples, a pleasure-pain that intensified her sensitivity to his touch. She almost bolted off the floor when he nipped at her breast while his fingers speared her wet sheath.

"Not yet," he taunted as he played with her pussy. "You're not ready."

"I'm more than ready," she moaned and tried to glare at him through passion-filled eyes. "Now, Lurin. I want you."

"Soon, sweet." He continued to suckle her breasts, bringing her closer to orgasm. He didn't use his gifts to superficially enhance her pleasure. Instead he gave her the whole of his attention, an erotic gift only a Thesha can give to one he cares about.

Lowering a trail of kisses down her stomach, he sent her the warmth of his love in a blaze of heat. She twisted and groaned, begging him to fill her. Still, he caressed her with his lips, seeking her feminine core that he'd been too long in tasting.

When his mouth traced her mound, she ground into his face, and his heart seemed to stop when her creamy essence touched his lips.

Full of Mara's spice, a heady scent of sex and love and strength, Lurin lost control and suckled her clit with a fervor that quickly brought her to climax. As she screamed his name and came in a gush, he continued to lick her, lapping her sweet cream with another, gentler *push*, this one to calm her inflamed nerve endings, that he might send her over again and again.

The more he tasted her, the harder he became until he

could no longer contain his own release. Wanting to spill inside of her, to share with her his bliss, he quickly covered her body with his own and thrust deep, fighting the need to come.

"Lurin, I love you," she cried as he thrust long and slow, killing himself with the need to give her Theshan ecstasy.

"And I you," he couldn't help admit before taking them both over the edge. With a final stroke, Mara came. He could see the stars bursting inside of her, could feel her walls squeezing him tight, forcing him to join her in their shared erotic rapture.

He erupted, coating her with everything he had inside. He could feel his essence leave his body, that special part of him he always kept apart from his sexual partners. A tinge of unease filled him even as he felt Mara accept him, heard her whisper his name in awe as his presence stole through her body.

Mara drifted into sleep with a smile on her face, while Lurin held her tight, fighting the demon of doubt. He admitted he loved her, knew it deep in his heart. Hell, he'd shared his soul with her, an act he'd never before committed or wanted to commit.

Yet he couldn't help wondering if trusting her would prove his downfall, as it had to so many Thesha before him who'd thought themselves "in love".

He had known Mara for such a short time, making their intense spiritual connection something to question. As much as his heart and soul knew she was *The One*, his mind continued to probe at the potential danger in loving her, both to himself and to his people.

Eventually Lurin drifted into sleep, and his dreams were of Mara. Sleeping with her in his arms calmed his fears and they lay entwined for hours, adrift in a haze of wonder and pleasure until reality threatened.

Lurin woke sensing someone nearing the door.

*It's me*, Gren sounded in his mind. *But I'm not alone.*

"Sweet, we have to move," Lurin prodded Mara, cursing himself for not being more aware. Hell, he had claimed his soul mate in Lady Sara's room, on the floor. How much more did he need to remind him of their perilous situation?

Mara moved slowly as she donned her clothes, and Lurin could only be grateful for Gren's presence among the enemy. Lurin retied her loosely to the post she'd escaped from and lifted her chin to stare into her eyes.

Heavy lidded and slightly clouded, Mara's gaze reflected a woman thoroughly loved. He could see his energy sparkling in the depths of her dark brown eyes and despite his misgivings, he smiled with pleasure and pride.

He had a soul mate. Mara now belonged to him and no other.

"Play along, love. Know that now I'm in charge, and Sara's merely the puppet." *I love you*, he thought as he stared at her. He lingered for a kiss, praying it would not be their last.

*Hurry the hell up. Vendon won't wait any longer*, Gren growled.

Lurin flew to the bed and dove under the blanket, covering Sara with his body as he mimicked the act of sex. He disliked having to get even this close to her, but dry humping and groaning was better than actually fucking her.

"Open your eyes, Sara," he commanded in a throaty voice that reverberated in her mind. He could feel Mara's eyes on him and knew she felt the energy pulsing through the room. "Do whatever I tell you, Sara. Think what I tell you to think. And do not, under any circumstances, cause harm to befall Captain Mara Seni."

"Yes, Master," her voice echoed his, her ringing cadence the only sign of his influence.

He gave her several other commands mentally, since Vendon and Gren suddenly walked through the doorway. Sara complied beautifully, climaxing without his touch at memories of her time fucking several of her faceless soldiers.

"Still at it?" Vendon asked incredulously. "Really, Sara. Even for you this is remarkable."

Lurin guided her responses.

She breathed heavily before glaring at Vendon. "He's Thesha. What did you expect?" Her eyes flew to Gren and she licked her lips. "There's always room for one more," she said with a sultry wink.

*Very funny*, Gren sent Lurin. "I'm much too busy readying the ship to dock on Jaron, Lady Sara."

After a slight pause, Sara leapt from the bed and cursed Gren up and down.

"You whoreson bastard," she seethed. "How dare you ignore my command?"

"He follows Lady Cari's wishes," Vendon said protectively.

"I don't care!" Sara then attacked Vendon with such speed and ferocity that she managed to blacken his eye and split his lip before Gren and Lurin pulled her off. "You're supposed to be on my side! I hate you! I hate her! I want you both dead!"

*Laying it on a bit thick, eh?*

Lurin refrained from smiling. *I need Vendon to report this back to Nobless Cari.*

*Well wrap it up. We're nearly there and Mara looks ready to tear free from her bonds and beat Sara to a pulp.*

Having been focused on controlling Sara, Lurin failed to notice Mara's jealousy. He felt absurdly pleased by her reaction, though she shouldn't have been so concerned. Hadn't he told her he had control of Sara? Surely she didn't believe he'd actually fuck the royal daughter?

*No, I didn't think that.* A feminine voice invaded his mind, shocking him to silence. *But if you don't soon get her under control and away from you I'm going to split her in two.*

Lurin coughed to cover the laughter that threatened to spill, and mentally prodded Sara to dress and make ready for their imminent landing.

"We'll see my mother shortly," Sara bit through clenched teeth as she pulled on clothing from one of her many closets. "But this isn't over. He's mine." She stared at Lurin with manic possession evident on her twisted face and stomped off to the lav.

Gren and Vendon shared a nod.

"See what I mean?" Gren said under his breath, loud enough for Lurin to hear.

Vendon's gaze narrowed on the closed door of the lav before he reluctantly agreed, to what Lurin didn't yet know.

"I'll tell the Nobless," Vendon said quietly, listening to the racking sobs and shouts of rage emanating from the closed door. "It's up to you to see that everything goes smoothly. Another ten thousand beks if you can get Sara to her mother without undue attention once we reach Jaron."

"Done." Gren stared at Vendon's retreating back until the

little man left the room, the door sliding shut behind him.

"We haven't much time," Gren said before he froze and stared hard at Mara.

"What?" she asked defensively as she freed herself from her bonds.

"Smells like sex in here," Gren muttered. *You bonded with her already?* he sent Lurin. *She feels like you, smells like you and sure as hell resonates with your power. Must have been some bonding.*

*It was,* Mara answered with a smug smile.

Gren cursed in shock and looked accusingly at Lurin. "How the hell did she hear that?"

"I have no idea. But maybe I should warn you to watch what you say," Lurin said tapping his head, "when you're not speaking *out loud*."

Mara, finally freed from her bonds, approached Gren with a suspicious scowl. "You're no telepath." She studied him with an intensity that made Lurin uncomfortable.

Gren started for the door before Mara spoke again, and Lurin frowned, knowing what was coming next.

"What exactly happened while I was tied up in your quarters, Gren?"

"Ask Lurin. He was there," Gren said as he escaped the room. *We'll arrive on Jaron in another hour. Make ready. And try not to be too angry, Mara. Lurin can explain.*

## Chapter Eleven

They walked in a single file through the underground royal tunnels into Nobless Cari's private wing of the palace.

Unfortunately, the mental bond that had existed between Mara and Lurin faded, and Lurin had yet to explain just what Gren meant when he'd told her not to be too angry.

The more she thought about that missing period on board Gren's ship, the more she wondered if her dreams had in fact been real. She didn't want to admit to herself, and certainly not to Lurin, that she'd imagined having sex with Gren.

She tried to ignore images of herself and the large captain entwined, of Gren's mouth covering her breast, of his large cock filling her again and again.

She flushed and stared at the floor as they walked further down the passageway. Granted, Lurin had awakened her body to pleasures beyond imagining, but could he perhaps have over stimulated her sexual desires?

She subtly glanced at the warriors following her. She considered one or two of them attractive, but had no urge to couple with any of them. Why then did she envision herself having sex with Gren? And why did the she feel more turned on than dismayed by the idea?

She flushed guiltily, glad that Lurin's attention was focused on Sara. She would hate for him to know she apparently lusted after Gren. Just then Vendon murmured something and scooted closer to the powerful captain. She wasn't the only one lusting after Gren, not to mention Sara's craven desires.

The small entourage entered the palace through a series of curving passageways until they came to a set of large double doors, guarded on either side by two hulking Elaran warriors.

Vendon scurried forward and said something to one of the warriors, and suddenly the doors opened, allowing sunlight to filter through the shuttered hallway.

The warrior behind her prodded her to move and Mara glared at him over her shoulder before following the others into the golden chamber. She stared around her, awed at the ornate architecture and overwhelming display of wealth fettering the walls.

Dozens of collages, paintings and crystalline statues littered the room, all showcasing the same theme: Nobless Cari in all her glory. In youth and at present, always without flaw, the woman appeared almost goddess-like in the art around her.

Even her current position, resplendent on a velvet divan being waited on by two handsome, half-naked men, looked more like an artful display than reality.

As if posing for the small group that awaited her attention, the Nobless took her time selecting a tray of sweets.

"Vendon, so wonderful to see you again," Cari said in a

throaty voice. She slowly sat upright and rose, letting her sheer, silken gown flow artfully down her legs as she stood to better impose her authority.

"Captain Gren," she drawled, her sharp eyes stripping him from head to toe. "I had no doubts of your success." She stared at Lurin with a greedy smile.

"Of course you didn't," Sara snapped. "You had this bastard under your thumb." She gestured rudely to Gren. "And Vendon would never think to betray you, would he?"

"No, he would not," Vendon said carelessly, sharing a smile with Cari. "The trip was uneventful. Sara, of course, fucked every man on board, to include our captain." He stared wistfully at Gren. "And apparently Vez is indeed who you say he is, for once she had him she took no one else to her bed."

Mara thought it interesting Vendon didn't speak of Lurin's heritage in front of the warriors. Did Cari want it kept secret?

"Vendon?" Cari arched her brow at the warriors guarding the prisoners.

"You warriors are dismissed," Vendon ordered.

Mara watched as they left, leaving Gren and Vendon and the two massive man servants to guard her and Lurin.

"Captain Mara," Cari said, turning her focus, "how unfortunate that you involved yourself in this mess."

Mara blinked. "Involved myself? You hired me, Nobless Cari."

"I don't recall doing so." Cari stared down at her buffed nails.

"You paid me twenty thousand beks upfront, or has that escaped your notice?"

"Really? I'd venture to guess that if my legal advisors looked into the matter, we wouldn't find twenty thousand beks. If anything, we'd probably find whatever payment Lurin Vez used to bribe your compliance in his attempted escape."

Mara could only stare, her mouth agape. What the hell was Cari trying to pull?

"You've not only framed an innocent man, but you're going to put me in chains as well?" Mara seethed. "And you think you can get away with that?" The Nobless was unbelievable!

"Really, Mara. Save the dramatics. You've been found guilty of conspiring with a murderer, and the best you can hope for from Elaran law is a life sentence. At worst, you'll be beheaded come tomorrow morning."

Mara clenched her jaw, praying for patience. She could only be glad her crew had been spared this lunacy. She saw Gren glaring at her to behave, and looked past him to Lurin, who stared blankly at Sara, still playing his part.

"And when I find the rest of your crew, I do believe I'll add them to my collection." Cari winked and indicated her servants.

The woman thought to threaten not only Mara and Lurin, but her crew as well? She recalled Lurin's vague description of the degradation he'd already suffered at Cari's hands and she saw red. Normally cool-headed, Mara's temper reached its boiling point, especially since she knew there was a very good chance Cari could get away with it all.

"To hell with that," Mara growled and in a burst of speed attacked Cari. She landed a fist in the Nobless's face before the woman's servants restrained her, using all their strength to keep Mara's writhing frame away from their mistress.

Cari shrieked in outrage while Sara laughed and applauded. Neither Lurin nor Gren moved to help, though Mara thought she saw a hint of strain on Lurin's face.

"Bravo, Mara. That's at least one thing you've done right since capturing my Thesha." Sara clapped.

"You'll regret that." Vendon shook his head. "Felan and Maltor," he said to Cari's servants, "take her to The Cell."

As Mara struggled for freedom, twisting against their absurdly strong holds, she saw Lurin's eyes blaze to life before fading quickly under Cari's sharp gaze. Cari stared at Lurin for several moments before shifting her attention back to Mara.

"You'll regret you ever met me, you little bitch." Cari smiled and gently caressed Lurin's stubbled cheek. "Let's play, Lurin, and see how much fun we can have together."

That easily, she dismissed Mara, and Mara increased her struggles, only to find herself helplessly trapped and moving deeper into the darkness of Nobless Cari's palace.

\* \* \* \*

Lurin strove to keep calm.

*If one of those bastards hurts Mara, I'll kill everyone in here*, he promised Gren, doing his best to ignore Nobless Cari.

*Easy, Lurin*, Gren quickly answered. *I have it covered. Trust me. Don't do anything stupid, not when we're so close to The End.*

"I know you can hear me, precious Thesha," Cari murmured and stroked the other side of Lurin's face with her long, painted nails. "Sara, make him heal my bruises."

Sara pouted but did as her mother bid. "Heal her, slave. And do it quickly."

Lurin kept Sara in character, making her defiant and sulky per Gren's orders. It worked like a charm. As he healed the bruise clouding Cari's eye, he noted Cari's complete acceptance of the situation. Now how to turn that to his advantage....

"Amazing," Vendon breathed and licked at his lower lip, his eyes glazing over as he stared at Lurin's nearly naked form.

Lurin silently cursed Gren again for making him wear the ridiculous loincloth.

*It's a distraction we need*, Gren emphasized. *And you have to admit, you've got Sara, Cari and Vendon out of sorts.*

Thinking he'd rather not be the center of attention, Lurin forced Sara into an argument with her mother.

"He's mine, Mother. Mine. I found him and I fucked him. You can't take him from me." Sara sounded desperate underneath the angry bluster, and Lurin realized she truly meant what he prodded her to say.

"I don't care, Sara." Cari gestured Vendon to her side. "You might control Lurin now, but remember I control everything else in your pathetic little world." Cari sneered at her daughter. "What happened to you? You were my pride and joy before you started fucking everything on two legs. Really, Sara, we do have an image to maintain."

Lurin felt the animosity brewing in Sara and let her vent on her mother, using only a light touch to guide her.

"Come now, Mother. Do you really think we're so different? You think people don't know what you do in the private recesses of this palace?" she scoffed. "Rumor abounds about your perverse appetites. And who should know better than me? I am what you made me, after all. And I choose not to hide who I am."

Cari's lips tightened and she retorted something vile back at her daughter. Lurin tuned them out to concentrate on the situation at hand.

*Gren, where did they take Mara?*

Gren seemed to have a hard time taking his gaze from the drama brewing between Cari and her daughter. *They took her to a level beneath us, to Cari's private cell. Don't worry. I've got men there as we speak.*

*You'd better*, Lurin growled.

*I have to say, this jealous streak you're showing is really entertaining.* Gren let the humor leak through his thoughts, irritating Lurin to no end.

*They lay one hand on her and* you'll *answer to me.* The real threat behind his words startled Gren enough that he blinked and turned his head to gaze at Lurin in surprise.

*I'm joking, Lurin. Stars, get a grip. Mara will be fine. It's you we need to save.*

*Well what are we waiting for?*

*Sernal, a neighboring peacekeeper. He owes me a favor. As soon as he and his men show, we can tie this up.* Gren rolled his neck, the tension in the room obviously affecting him.

Lurin felt slightly queasy himself. The effort to control Sara had worn his energy down so much that his safeguards had weakened, causing him to suffer the brutal animosity and dark energy brewing between mother and daughter most keenly.

He swayed on his feet, the action tearing the others out of their argument. Then to his alarm, his vision grayed before blackness enveloped him.

* * * *

Gren stared at Lurin with real concern, not understanding how his grand plan had so quickly disintegrated. Dammit. He needed Lurin to control Sara. Gren couldn't handle both Sara and her mother, not with all the hatred surging in the room.

He'd done extensive research on Nobless Cari prior to taking this job, and what he learned made him cringe. Cari was not Thesha by any means, but her darkness of spirit was powerful, and consuming if not countered effectively.

Even now he felt her drawing part of him to her, like a spell master from the gates of hell.

Focusing on the situation, he lifted Lurin in his arms and placed him on Cari's bed, per her order. Vendon clumsily bent to "help" and ended up knocking into Gren, pinching at his forearm.

Glaring at the little man, Gren watched with some satisfaction as Vendon hurriedly scurried back to Cari.

The woman glowed with Lurin's vitality, bubbling over with coils of malicious intent, strengthened by Theshan healing.

"Sara, go see how our prisoner, Captain Mara, fares in The Cell," Cari ordered, countering Sara's refusal. "Don't worry, Lurin will still be here when you return, as will Captain Gren. Won't you, Captain?"

A hard glint shone in her brown eyes, a hint that Cari definitely had something up her sleeve.

"As you wish." Gren bowed. He watched as a sulky Sara grudgingly left the room. Only he, Cari and Vendon remained, with an unconscious Lurin on Cari's bed. Now he had a ripe opportunity to take charge of the situation, if only he could rid himself of the nasty feeling he'd missed something important.

"Gren, I hear you've been most inhospitable to Vendon."

Gren stared from Vendon to Cari, unease snaking through him. They stared at him, as if waiting for something to happen, and he knew Vendon's clumsiness had not been an accident.

A burning sensation flared from the pinch in his arm throughout his body, slowing his heart rate and clouding his mind.

"What the hell did you do?" he asked angrily as he stalked Vendon.

Cari watched with beady eyes as Gren lifted Vendon off the floor by his collar. Vendon moaned with what should have been fright, but instead sounded oddly like arousal.

"It's a funny thing, Gren," she said. "I have yet to see you naked, but I'd be willing to bet you have no blue marking on your groin."

Gren wavered and dropped Vendon, his strength suddenly deserting him. He sank to his knees and clutched his head. His vision blurred and an incessant buzzing sound affected his balance.

Cari knelt beside him, stroking his hair. "Sara made no mention that you might have any extrasensory abilities.

And there's nothing about you that even hints at the possibility you might be Thesha, yet I have a strange feeling that won't go away." She pushed him to his back on the ground, and he lay vulnerable beneath her.

"What did you give me?" he managed, feeling incredibly woozy.

"It's called shei-root, a priceless and unique herb found, supposedly, on the Theshan people's original home world. Strange that it should affect *you*, Gren," she purred.

"Please, Cari," Vendon whined as he hovered near her. "You promised."

She smiled, her eyes bright with victory. "So I did. You may disrobe him, but do nothing else. Not yet." Gren watched helplessly as Vendon eagerly stripped him of his clothing. "Can you imagine, Vendon? Two Theshas at my beck and call? I'll be as much a legend as them, more even!"

Vendon's greedy hands lingered over Gren's trousers until Cari reminded him to be quick.

"Don't try me, Vendon," she said lightly. "You can look, but you can't touch. Not until I've broken him in."

"Yes, Nobless." Vendon bobbed his head and licked at his lips, his eyes focused on Gren's naked flesh.

Cari ran her hands over Gren's chest and down his abdomen. She rested her palm over his cock, and he couldn't help his groan when he felt himself harden despite his resolve not to.

"Didn't I tell you, Gren? Shei-root not only disarms, but also acts as an aphrodisiac. You'll be hard as a stone all night long," she ended in a whisper. "Just wait for all the lovely things I'm going to teach you."

Gren managed to loll his head to the side, only to see Lurin still unconscious on the bed. He didn't understand how he'd failed so miserably, when his plan had been working so well. He could only hope Mara found a greater success in her situation.

With one final effort, he closed his mind and body to the world around him and sent his spiritual self on a quest to find help, and fast.

## Chapter Twelve

Mara cursed Felan and Maltor with an extensive vocabulary built over several years of hunting the scum of the System. For the most part they ignored her, but when they finally reached their destination, instead of dropping her and leaving, they closed the door behind them and ogled her with reptilian grins.

"I think she needs a lesson in manners, Maltor. What say you?" Felan leaned against one of the black stone walls lit dimly by two *charel* crystals.

The room was actually larger than she'd expected. But when she saw the reason why, she couldn't contain the gasp that escaped.

Maltor crossed his arms over his chest and blew her a kiss. "I agree with you, Felan. Captain Mara, you shouldn't have struck our Mistress."

He idly crossed to the rack holding various tools designed specifically to inflict maximum pain. Reaching up, Maltor grabbed a short whip studded with numerous spikes along its tip.

"This is one of Nobless Cari's personal favorites." Maltor flicked the whip to within an inch of Mara's face. "It will definitely leave scars, in case you were wondering."

Mara swallowed the knot of fear choking her and told herself she'd been in worse situations. None came to mind at present though, and then her mind completely blanked when Felan began undressing.

He dropped his trousers, his cock stiff with excitement as he eyed Maltor and the whip.

"Do it, Maltor," he said and began stroking himself.

Maltor's eyes brightened as he stared at Felan. He nodded and two lightning-fast strokes later, Mara wore a tattered shirt. A small cut welled with blood above her left breast, now exposed due to Maltor's handiwork.

"So much for Gren's plan," she mumbled under her breath, trying to maintain a semblance of control over her fear. To be honest, she feared Felan and Maltor's sexual advance more than she feared the whip. To dirty what she and Lurin had shared with a rape, she didn't think she could handle that.

They neared and she braced herself for the worst, raising her fists in a fighting stance, balancing on the balls of her feet, when a most welcome interruption arrived.

"Who dares command my cell?" a gravelly voice preceded the menacing form that entered the dim room.

Shadows played across the *krell* skull he wore over his face as a mask. The *krell's* large horns and three rows of teeth made the intruder seem more demon than man.

Felan and Maltor, however, bowed respectfully and gave the intruder welcome smiles.

"Forgive us, Master Utal, but Nobless Cari ordered us to bring the woman to the cell. We thought to teach her a lesson for her earlier disrespect to our Mistress," Maltor explained.

Utal's eyes looked black under the mask, and his next words confirmed that he had no soul. "Then use the hooks instead of that pussy whip." He handed both Maltor and Felan a black, three-pronged hook barbed at The End and took the whip.

Felan opened his mouth to speak when the whip cracked. He shrieked instead. The whip cracked again and a second thin line of blood trailed down his face. Maltor, too stunned to react, received a similar wound accompanied by several more in rapid succession, which left him too wounded to move.

Mara had stood frozen in shock witnessing such brutality, but now that Utal bent over to tie Felan's hands, she gathered her courage and bolted for the door.

Master Utal moved in a blur and she found herself in his arms, caged by his massive strength. She fought for freedom, ignoring his murmurs until he shook her hard.

"Relax, Captain, it's me," Catam's voice sounded from inside the skull.

Almost afraid to hope for salvation, Mara slowly wound down and stared into his eyes. He shifted so that the light hit him and she noted the golden gleam of Catam's gaze studying her.

His hold gentled and he let her go, his gaze traveling over her with concern. He reached up and removed the skull, breathing deeply as he did so.

"Damn thing itches like crazy," he muttered and unable to help herself, Mara laughed out loud with relief.

"Uh, Captain?" Catam waited until she looked back up at him. "Are you alright?"

She nodded and wiped at the blood smeared over her chest.

"Why don't you take my shirt?"

She graciously accepted the garment, belatedly aware that her ripped shirt showed more than Catam should ever have seen of his captain.

As if he read her thoughts, he grinned. "I can't say I wasn't hoping to one day see you with your clothes off, but this isn't what I'd had in mind."

She chuckled again, his lighthearted teasing doing wonders to ease her mind. Gren had at least proved right about her crew.

"Not that I'm complaining, but what took you so long?"

Catam flushed. "It's a long story. Suffice it to say Nu and Set are steamed I assumed Master Utal's role. They're currently busy occupying Sara and at least a half dozen Elaran torturers a few doors down."

"Shouldn't we go help them?" She tugged Catam's shirt around her, the heat of his body making the shirt warm, soothing the chill that had threatened earlier.

"They're fine. In fact, I deliberately riled them to make them stronger. You know how rough they can get when their blood is *really* pumping."

Mara nodded. "I can't tell you how glad I am to see you, Catam."

"Same here. When Captain Gren ran into us a few days ago and explained things, I thought he was half-crazed. But when he introduced us to the real Lady Sara, we knew we had to go along with him." Catam paused and frowned. "I'm sorry there was no way to tell you what was happening. I'll bet Gren's arrival shocked the hell out of you on the ship."

"You could say that." Felan groaned and she and Catam shared a look.

They exited the cell, locking the door behind them as they left.

"This way," Catam said and guided her to the loud noises

behind an overly large metal door. He banged on the door and it opened slowly.

Nu peered out at them and a grin lit his face when he saw Mara.

"She's here, Set," he told his brother. "You can let that one go. He's not going anywhere."

Nu opened the door wider to allow them entrance, and Mara gaped at the sight that met her eyes. Set dropped an Elaran soldier to the ground in a pool of his own blood. Several men appeared to be dead, while a few groaned pitifully amidst the torture racks and chains all around. Sara lay unconscious on the floor.

"Captain Mara," Set exclaimed and grabbed her in a massive hug. He set her down after Nu socked him in the ribs.

"She can't breathe you idiot."

"Sorry, Cap'. We were worried maybe things weren't going so well for you." He glared at Catam. "But that whoreson Mardu wouldn't let us help you. Instead he stuck us with this mess."

Mara eyed the littered bodies. She counted more than the six Catam mentioned. She counted twelve, including Sara.

Catam shrugged. "You did a decent job taking care of them. What's the problem?"

"We'll settle up later, Catam," Nu said in a low voice. "But first I want to hear about the Captain. And what the hell happened to Vez, our prisoner? How did you get down here?"

Mara shook her head. Fear for Lurin returned and she urged Catam and the others to follow her. "Not now, Nu. I'll fill you all in once we've saved Lurin and Gren."

"Lurin? You mean captive Vez?" Nu asked in astonishment.

"Later, you rock," Catam growled and earned a glare from both Fas brothers. "Just follow the captain and we'll get our answers later."

They grudgingly agreed and Mara hurried, feeling an urgency to find Lurin and Gren that scared her.

\* \* \* \*

Gren groaned and tried to move but his limbs refused to obey. Pain and pleasure mixed as Cari sucked his cock so hard he wanted to curl into a ball for protection as much as he wanted to come.

"Let the pain take you, Thesha," Cari whispered and lifted herself over him. She'd already come twice from rubbing against him while she used a knife to slice him to ribbons. Blood covered his body, looking worse than the actual wounds. The constant stinging hurt, though, and Cari's gratification from his pain sucked the energy from him in waves, weakening him further.

She poised herself over him, holding his throbbing cock in her bony fingers as she stared into his eyes.

"Call me by my name. Say it."

Gren gritted his teeth, refusing to call her Mistress even if it killed him. He felt as if his dick was ready to fall off, it hurt so badly. He had been hard, without relief, for too long, and she prolonged the agony, not letting him come while taking her own enjoyment.

His search for help had yielded him little. As weak as he was, he'd barely been able to find Mara, let alone coax her into returning to him. And Lurin ... he was worried Lurin might not wake. Gren sensed nothing from the Thesha, when there should have at least been a faint heartbeat or lift of spirit with which to connect.

He felt a lashing blow to his left cheek and blinked up into Cari's furious gaze.

"You *will* answer me, slave."

Gren's body shuddered as she teased him with her pussy, drawing down and making him arch to maintain the contact with his sensitive shaft. He hated the fact that she made him want her. He hated his lack of discipline and the fact that he'd relaxed his guard and let Vendon, of all people, close enough to do harm.

Gren would have killed Cari and himself in the process, if it hadn't been for Lurin lying helpless on the bed. But as Cari postured over his erection, his shame grew until he thought death might be preferable to this.

"Let him go."

Mara? He stared up at Cari's fuzzy image and felt her literally draining him of energy. He heard a man curse and then felt Cari lifted off his body.

"Shit. He needs aid and quickly." Catam timed Gren's pulse and tried to stop his bleeding. "He's dying, Mara."

"No," Gren rasped weakly. "See to Lurin. He's worse off

than I am."

Mara hurried to Lurin's side and blanched when she felt the stillness surrounding him. She reached for his arm and it felt cool, his heat gone.

"Lurin," she whispered and stroked his face with gentle hands. "Come back to me. I need you here," she urged over and over.

Still she felt nothing.

"Gren, I don't know what to do," she cried, knowing she was losing Lurin.

"Call out to him with more than words, Mara," Gren managed. "Show him the way back."

She heard Catam curse, heard him welcome someone else into the room, but she knew little time remained. Realizing Lurin came from a world steeped in energy, she closed her eyes and looked deep within herself. She had no idea whether or not she'd be successful, but she'd die trying if need be.

His manipulations and past subterfuge no longer mattered. Faced with a life without Lurin, her love quickly buoyed to the surface. Placing her hands over his heart, she broadcast waves of adoration.

*Lurin, return to me. Please. I love you. Don't leave me, not like this.*

She continued to bathe him with her love, letting her energy flow into and around him. Amazingly she could feel it working, could feel her body, mind and spirit merging with his. And while it felt unnerving to be so open with another being, it also felt right.

Now if he would only accept all that she freely gave. She could feel the small piece of him that remained apart from her. And if he wouldn't open himself to everything she offered, she had a horrible feeling he wouldn't survive.

\* \* \* \*

Lurin struggled against the darkness until he had nothing left with which to fight. Cari was a vampire, a demonic soul-sucker whose menacing spirit spoiled everything she touched.

Weak already from having to control Sara, he had no way to fight Cari's evil with his life ebbing more and more. He felt so alone, so cold. He needed help. He needed ... Mara.

He could no longer sense her, and it crazed him. They had

bonded in Sara's cabin, so he should have been able to sense her no matter what. Why then could he no longer *see* her? Panic flared at the thought that she had somehow died and left him behind.

How could he hope to live without her? He tried again to astral project, but to no avail. Weakness consumed him until he knew nothing but pain and sadness before an emptying numbness stole his mind.

An involuntary spasm opened his eyes a fraction to let him see Gren covered in blood, Nobless Cari over him feeding off his pain.

Lurin was responsible for this. Because of him, Mara had been captured and perhaps even killed, and now Gren lay dying. Lurin wanted to cry but couldn't, the loss of what he might have had with Mara burning his insides with cold.

He wanted so badly to return back into that mystical world where he and Mara, his soul mate, had bonded. Had he the opportunity, he would bare himself to her, leaving himself vulnerable to her love and her pain, accepting her as she had accepted him.

He longed to feel Mara with him, touching her flesh to flesh and soul to soul. He imagined her within him, bonding all over again, releasing the distrust that kept him from finding true happiness.

The numbness taking control of him ceded and a great pain stole his breath.

"Lurin, come back to me," he heard whispered again and again until she seemed to shout at him.

Warmth burgeoned inside of him and he arched uncontrollably, heat breaking through the cold aloneness of distrust. The pain was excruciating, but the fact that he actually felt anything at all made him want to shout with joy.

"Please Lurin. If you really love me, come back to me."

At that moment he surrendered everything he had to Mara. He gave her his heart and soul, shared his innermost thoughts and secrets. He held nothing back. She experienced every ugly thing he'd ever done, every sexual act and every beautiful climax he'd bestowed among his female conquests.

He heard her gasp and he felt her shock. He was past caring about the risks. He knew, deep down he knew, that she accepted him. Only a woman in love would forego a life of riches for a man accused of murder and rape.

Suddenly, his heart began beating again. He inhaled deeply and heard her whisper his name in wonder. She leaned over his chest, hugging him tight and as his strength slowly returned, he hugged her back.

He was dimly aware of the noise around him. Instead he drowned in Mara's scent and in her touch. His heart healed, his spirit followed until he felt whole again.

He opened his eyes to find the room filled with strange men. Blinking, he wiped one of Mara's tears from his cheek and smiled at her, bemused at the radiant grin she returned.

"Catam, Nu and Set saved me from having to kill Cari's man servants."

"They're dead then?" Bloodlust filled him as he recalled Felan and Maltor's hands on Mara.

"Not quite. But Catam put them in an awful lot of pain."

He grunted. Not the punishment he would deliver once he was up and about, but it would have to do for now.

"Who are these men?" He noted several men wearing utilitarian gray uniforms buzzing around the room.

"They're System law, courtesy of Sernal, Catam's brother."

"Catam's brother?"

Mara explained. "Gren's contact Sernal is a Mardu lawman. Apparently he'd heard rumblings of Elaran misdeeds even on Mardu, so he had no problem helping Gren out with this. I'm not sure how Gren and Sernal are connected, but at this point I'm not questioning such a good thing."

"Gren's all right then?"

Mara's lips tightened. "He's been better, but he'll be okay. A med tech is seeing to him now."

Lurin braced himself on Mara's arm and slowly sat up. He heard Gren cursing before he saw him, and the man's profane grumbling made Lurin breathe a sigh of relief.

"He must be okay, he nearly took that tech's head off," Lurin said with a sigh.

Catam and the Fas brothers approached with a nod at Mara.

"Glad to see you made it," Catam said.

"Thanks, I think," Lurin said with a grimace. His head pounded with a massive headache.

"Sorry for everything on the ship," Nu said, looking uncomfortable. Both he and his brother seemed repentant for their part in his capture. Curiously, neither Mara nor Catam had apologized for their involvement.

Reading his expression, Catam shook his head. "Oh no. I'm not going to apologize for doing my job. And I'll smash you in the stomach again if you disrespect my captain."

Mara chuckled and the Fas brothers cracked a smile.

"I'll only agree because I won't allow anyone to disrespect Captain Mara, soon to become my wife."

## Chapter Thirteen

Nu and Set stood flabbergasted, but Catam rolled his eyes.

"Like she could hold out against one of them," he muttered.

"Excuse me?" Mara asked, her eyes narrowed and switching from Catam to Lurin and back again.

"Nothing." Catam shrugged and gave Lurin a catlike grin. "Congratulations, I think."

"Come on, Mara," Lurin cajoled, wishing now he hadn't blurted his desire in front of her crew. "You love me and I love you. What could be more right?"

"What indeed," Gren added in a gruff voice as he hobbled to join them.

"You look like shit," Nu said bluntly.

*You really do*," Lurin had to say.

"Thanks," Gren said sourly as he wrapped a bloodstained blanket tighter around his body. "You have to *ask* her to marry you, you idiot. You don't just *tell* a woman she'll marry you."

Mara smiled, and the warmth in her grin stirred Lurin's loins. "It's okay, Gren. Lurin belongs to me now, so I figure that's the last order he'll be giving for a long, long time."

Her crew hooted with laughter, and Gren chuckled before groaning with pain.

*I owe you one, Gren,* Lurin said soberly.

*Look, promise me you won't tell Mara about what happened in my quarters and we'll consider the debt repaid. I definitely don't want to be on the receiving end of her wrath.* He shifted, clutching the blanket tighter as Catam stared at him.

*And what's with the Mardu?* he added.

"Lurin?" Mara stared from Gren to Lurin with a gleam in her eye.

"Yes, love?" *I have no idea why Catam is staring at you like that. Make that, staring at us like that.*

"Remind Gren that I can *hear* him when he speaks."

The others looked puzzled, but Gren's eyes widened.

*Shit.*

*Exactly,* Mara purred. *My memories seem to have returned fully, thanks to Lurin's energy transference during his revival.*

"I think I need that med tech again," Gren murmured and ambled as quickly as he was able from the group.

"What was that about?" Nu asked, confused.

"Who knows," Set said. "Gren's an odd one for sure, but he's one hell of a warrior, considering he's not from Ragga. Did you see when he...?"

Lurin ignored his ramblings, his gaze drawn to Mara's smile.

"So Lurin, how do you feel about space travel?"

He grinned at her, sending her explicit images of what he planned on doing to her in the very near future.

"I love it," he answered with a naughty smile. "But how will we manage with your crew, especially since Catam won't stop staring at me?" He turned his gaze on the Mardu.

"It's all right, Catam. Lurin never did any of the things he was accused of," she reminded her crewman.

Catam shrugged. "I know, Mara." He leaned closer. "True Thesha are incapable of harming women."

Lurin blinked and Mara's mouth dropped open.

"How long have you known?" Lurin asked quietly. He glanced at the Fas brothers and saw them heavily involved in a discussion about Gren.

"Since the beginning." He seemed to be enjoying Lurin's surprise.

"You son of a--"

Mara interrupted. "How did you know?"

"I'm of the Xema class," he said quietly, a smirk teasing his lips. "We know things." And so saying, he gracefully bowed and left them with congratulations as he pulled the Fas brothers with him.

"Xema class?" Mara asked.

Lurin stared at Catam's back. "My people consider them *cousins*, if you will. I'll be damned."

"That little sneak," Mara huffed. "When we get back to my ship, I'm going to--"

"Make sweet love to your husband." He sent her several more pictures that had her blushing like fire. "I believe Sernal has the wherewithal to marry us, love, at least he does according to Gren."

"Gren I'll deal with later," Mara promised. Then she leaned down and kissed Lurin with such passion his arousal flared like lightning. "We have a marriage ceremony to enact. And the fact that you're wearing a loincloth just adds to moment."

Lurin laughed and knew peace, now that he had Mara in his life, and in his heart.

Later that night when he crested ecstasy with his wife in his arms, he knew for certain he'd surrendered his heart and soul to the one person in the universe that would ever truly understand him: his soul mate, Mara Vez.

The End

# THE THIEF OF MARDU

## Chapter One

Catam of Mardu rolled his eyes and wondered for the fifth time that morning if a person could actually die of boredom.

"I'm not goin' to Jintak and you can't make me!" Rantak Borsham's breath lingered in the air like a cloud of poison, the noxious fumes fouler than the offal lying in the alleyway beside the bar.

"I can't, hmm?" Catam's unconcerned reply further enraged the wanted murderer, causing Rantak to froth at the mouth, literally.

"You shouldn't aggravate him, Catam." Nu Fas shook his head.

Rantak, now armed with a knife, shouted obscenities, drawing attention to himself and the three men intent on capturing him.

"You really shouldn't have," Set, Nu's brother, agreed. "You know Captain Mara specifically ordered us to pick Borsham up quietly."

Several barbarians painted for war and wearing wicked swords joined the quarrel, raising questions Catam and the Fas brothers didn't want to answer, not with so many hostile gazes now centered on them.

In Kweg's Bar, authority and law were the exception to the rule. Unfortunately, to collect the hefty bounty on Rantak's murdering hide, Catam and his crewmates had no choice but to enter the eastern province's most dangerous drinking establishment.

"I asked you a question, drun." One man sneered and waved his sword in Catam's face.

A tingle of anticipation feathered Catam's belly and he

smiled eagerly, relieved to finally feel *something*. His grin widened when he noted the confusion darkening his adversary's face.

"Nu, Set, grab Rantak while I take care of this idiot and his friends." He nodded to the four barbarians frowning ferociously. From the distinct set of their bushy brows and light colored hair, he guessed them to be some type of relation to Rantak. Perfect.

Nu shook his head and Set sighed, but since Mara had ordered them to behave, they did so. Nu grabbed Rantak and disarmed him with ease, then nodded to his brother and disappeared with Rantak in tow, courtesy of Captain Mara's new teleporter.

Set leaned against the bar and crossed his massive arms over his chest. "I'll wait here until you're through."

Catam's opponents eyed Set warily. No one openly challenged a citizen of Ragga--a planet that bore men with inhuman strength--with hopes of winning. When his opponents realized Set had no intention of interfering, they grunted with satisfaction.

"When we're done I might just take that pretty face and mess it up nice and proper," one of the men growled at Catam and crudely grabbed his crotch. His friends laughed and shouted obscenities while they spread around Catam in a circle.

The other patrons had quieted when they realized a brutal battle was about to take place. Money furtively changed hands until Set declined to fight. Once he leaned back against the bar, a shout sounded and the crowd erupted into a betting frenzy.

Set grinned. "I'll take five to one on the *drun* in the middle."

Catam frowned at the large man. He eagerly anticipated the coming fight, but being called a shit for the second time, and by his crewmate no less, irritated him to no end.

Taking advantage of his distraction, one of the barbarians rushed Catam with his sword drawn. Unarmed except for the dagger tucked into his boot, Catam dropped low and whipped out his leg, tripping his rushing attacker easily. The man hit the ground with a solid thump, and Catam finished him with a measured strike intended to produce both nausea and dizziness.

Sure enough, his attacker began vomiting and held his head, groaning.

Seeing their comrade downed so quickly, two more of the barbarians attacked, the leader waiting cautiously behind.

Catam ducked and rolled to avoid a near decapitation. He wanted to laugh out loud at the thrill coursing through him. The battle made his blood hum. He felt alive and subconsciously tapped into his extrasensory awareness that hovered just under the surface.

His eyes glowed and he noted the sudden wariness of the opponent nearest him. Catam feinted left. He pulled back as one of the men lunged with his weapon, then pivoted and used the man's momentum to crash the rushing barbarians into one another.

The thrown barbarian unfortunately had his sword at the ready when Catam threw him into his comrade, and he skewered the man through the stomach.

Cheers went through the crowd and Catam glanced behind him to see Set's amused expression flatten, indicating another assault, this one too close to miss.

Catam leapt to the side, narrowly avoiding a fatal blow while suffering a minor wound. Blood trickled from the shallow cut in his shoulder, the pain stinging him to life once more.

With a grin at his crewmate, who rolled his eyes and huffed at the ceiling, Catam sank to the floor and rolled left, knocking the surviving barbarian to the ground. Unlike his skewered friend, this man recovered enough to regain his feet, but Catam had tired of the play.

He dodged the next blow and went in hard. A punch to the gut and a chop to the man's throat had the third barbarian incapacitated.

Then the leader advanced, a raging menace of fury as he commanded not one but two Cortami class swords with blurring velocity. Catam briefly noted Set's alarm and shook his head to stop the Ragga's intrusion.

Whirling left and right, with inherent speed and using Xema distortion techniques, Catam confused his enemy to the point of dizziness. The man swayed on his feet, trying to keep up with the hazy image of Catam surrounding him.

Catam knocked his adversary unconscious with a sharp blow to the man's temple. Still pulsing off an adrenaline high, it took Catam a moment to remember the crowd watching him.

He blinked at the sudden silence and joined Set at the bar. "What?"

Set shook his head, looking disgusted. "Show off. Come on, we have work to do."

In a flash, Catam faced an angry Captain Mara aboard the ship, the teleporter an unwelcome reminder that he did indeed have a job to do, and that like it or not, the boredom would find him once more.

\* \* \* \*

Isa Araye frowned as she stared at the back of the closet door and listened to the muffled groans outside. She knew she shouldn't, but she couldn't help herself, and she peered through the small crack where she'd opened the door.

She'd grown up on a world that considered sexual pleasure a way of life. Viewing sex was a natural and practical way to stimulate one's drive, at least according to her mother.

Isa squinted to see a woman's figure through the dim light of the room. The woman cried out with excitement as her nude torso rode up and down, her breasts quivering as she engulfed the large, white phallus straining between her thighs. The man beneath her groaned and thrust up each time she sank down, the slap of sticky flesh and mingled fluids a messy reminder that such pleasure was best left to others.

With a soft sigh, Isa prayed the two would finish copulating so she wasn't put further behind schedule. Already she'd missed her first window of opportunity when the statesman took his midnight snack.

She heard a hoarse shout and a whisper: "Be quiet, Daarna." At the rate these two were going, she'd be a year older before she finished the job.

Another muffled groan and the two stilled, *finally*. The woman slumped over the man and the lovers panted in tandem, defining the moment. *Definitely not my day*, Isa mentally grumbled at the amorous pair on the bed. *As if I need another reminder of how unlikely I am to ever find amazing sex.*

Shaking her head, she stealthily slid out of the closet, staying to the shadows. Reaching the door, she crawled out of the room on her hands and knees, entering the dark passage that would lead her to treasure.

Mother would have an absolute fit to see her daughter sneaking in hallways. Better that Isa take after that sexual creature on the bed, straddling a needy cock like a good pleasurer, instead of stalking like a thief in the night. All the Araye women, save Isa, worked in the sex trade, a highly respected trade on Aran, Mardu's third moon.

"But I had to be different," Isa muttered softly and stopped outside the door she'd been told would be unlocked. She slowly jostled the handle and let out a breath of relief. It turned without incident and she entered the darkened room quietly, closing the door behind her.

Gliding with an agility she owed to her father, she moved on winged feet, almost floating over the floor her steps were so light. She reached the point her contact said would be the safe and switched on a pocket laser to see.

She stared in confusion. Instead of the painting that should have hidden the wall safe, she saw the painting raised, the safe door open and the safe ... empty. She shook her head, puzzled, and took a step back and to the side, to reassess the situation from another perspective.

Instead of moving backward, she tripped over something on the floor, a large something considering she lay half on top of it. The warning in her mind began ringing with a loud "get out now" bell when her initial suspicions proved correct.

She shined her laser on the form beneath her and cursed aloud. She should never have accepted this job, should have refused to work on any job with Harron's name attached. And by Flor's holy feet, she should never, *ever*, have taken a job that involved a member of the Zeron province.

Statesman Klin's dead body stared up at her with doom written all over him. She withdrew her hand from her glove to affirm his death. His neck felt cold when she reached for a pulse, and she knew he'd been dead several hours at least. Slipping her glove back on, she used the wall for support to stand and slid, leaving a bloody handprint on the wall.

Her laser illuminated only small portions of the statesman since her light had to be small in scope, nearly unnoticeable. Moving the light gradually revealed that his throat had been slit, and the hilt of a large knife protruded from his belly.

Seeing his wounds brought home her danger and she trembled in shock, at both his brutal death and her own reasons for being in his study in the first place. Getting caught had always been a danger, since thievery on Mardu was not a lawfully appreciated skill. But now being found would mean certain death, especially with blood on her hands.

Isa wiped her palms on her trousers and flinched when something scraped outside the door from which she'd entered. Her mind whirred and she instinctively sought refuge in a large wooden armoire, contorting her narrow body to fit under several thick blankets.

She breathed deeply to lower her heart rate, slowing her pulse so she could maintain silence and reason out this mess.

"Is she here?" a familiar voice whispered.

Isa's eyes narrowed in concentration.

"Shh, not so loud Daarna."

The man and the woman from the other room.

"Oh bother, Arnath," the woman drawled, though her voice remained a whisper. "The servants are all but gone. It's just you, me, and our murderess." She laughed softly, the tinkle of dark joy sending chills down Isa's spine.

A rustle of cloth sounded. Doors thudded, cabinets were forced open and closed. Isa huddled as far down as she could in the armoire, praying the mountain of clothing on top of her would be sufficient to hide her presence.

The armoire door opened abruptly. She held her breath as something tamped down on the cloth above her.

"Damn it, where is she?" Daarna slammed the armoire shut and Isa gratefully exhaled a quiet breath.

"She's here somewhere. We just have to find her. See the handprint on the wall, the scuff marks on the floor?"

"Perfect." Daarna chuckled with glee. "That print on the wall clearly implicates her. Now we just have to capture her on the premises and it's as good as done."

Arnath's deep voice murmured something Isa couldn't quite make out. Then she blinked in disbelief. They couldn't be ... not in here, not near the dead statesman! Several strained minutes passed.

"More, Arnath, fuck me harder," Daarna cried.

"Yes, yes," he panted. More grunts, then silence. Then, "I'm coming!"

"Wait, let me," she paused and Arnath groaned. "Me too," Daarna keened.

Isa felt sick. The statesman lay dead on the floor in a pool of blood while Daarna and Arnath screwed each other. Had they been watching him while they did it? That thought made her feel truly ill, and she had to force herself to breathe in through her mouth and out through her nose to stifle the nausea.

"That was so good," Daarna purred. "I want to do it again."

*Again? They just had sex in the other room and now in here. Was Daarna in heat?*

"Sure thing, baby. But let's get out of here. We definitely don't want to get caught in here together. And I especially can't be seen until after tomorrow at the House...." his voice trailed into something unintelligible.

Isa's ears buzzed. Something about tomorrow struck a cord, but she just couldn't piece everything together, not when she kept seeing the statesmen's slit throat in a pool of blood. Not when she heard the groans and grunts of two deviants fucking over said man's dead body.

"You're right as always," Daarna murmured. Then a door slid shut and silence settled over the study.

Isa wanted to run from the armoire and the room, but she moved as she'd been taught, with caution. Seeing no one in the room with her, at least, no one *alive*, she hightailed it out of study, only to find herself face to face with a maid.

Thank Flor she'd remembered to wear her mask. Isa shot past the shrieking maid and turned left instead of right when she reached The End of the corridor. For some reason her map of the house and the actual locations of the corridors didn't mesh.

Harron's information on this maze of hidden tunnels had proved remarkably efficient--remarkably efficient as a tool to frame Isa for a murder and theft she hadn't committed.

As she ran to escape, alarms sounded and the low snarl of guard thrells surprised her. One more detail Harron had forgotten to mention. The thrells were gaining as she ran, their six-legged progress and powerful sense of smell quickly diminishing her small lead.

Making a decision, she veered right and leapt into an overly large window frame, narrowly avoiding the gaping jaw of a loose threll barking like mad. Knowing the threll's handler would soon follow, Isa said a brief prayer and jumped out the window into the lake five floors below.

## Chapter Two

Catam's gaze narrowed at the naked woman writhing beneath him. Legs spread wide, her blond curls glistening with dew beckoned him closer. He toyed with her swollen folds, not giving her all of what she needed, his fingers playing her like a finely tuned instrument.

His cock swelled, knowing she was near release. She cried out and came, gushing over his hand while she groaned his name.

"Now me," the woman at his back pleaded, as if she hadn't already experienced two mind-blowing orgasms.

His cock stiffened when she ran her hands over his back, and he turned around to find her on her knees.

"Is this what you want, Sharell?" he asked with a grin, his hand guiding his erection to her lips. As an answer, she engulfed him, her mouth working him like a pump, sucking him deeper, flicking her tongue along his shaft the way he liked.

He allowed his mind to drift, his body absorbing the empty pleasure for what it was, a physical release. Sharell squirmed and moaned as she sucked him, the act making her hotter and wetter.

"Please, Catam, come in my mouth," she begged and sucked harder, deep-throating him as she plucked her clit.

Playing to her fantasy, Catam complied. He thrust deeper into her mouth, faster and faster, until his climax crashed over him. He timed it so that he came when she did, so she received maximum pleasure for her efforts.

He shuddered into her mouth and groaned, satisfied when she swallowed all of him, her mouth tightening and then releasing him as she cried out her orgasm.

"Now me," a third woman's whisper sounded to his left, and he shook his head.

He turned away to don his clothing. "Sorry, ladies, but I'm out of time. I'll try to visit again next month," he promised, and left the three pleasurers pouting and pleading with him to return.

He shook his head as he reentered Nebe6's most crowded pleasure center. Several women shot him come-hither looks that he blithely ignored. Despite his orgasm he felt far from sated. But the hour had struck six and he had a meeting to attend.

To his surprise he saw his brother, Sernal, accompanied Captain Mara and her husband.

Sernal's face lit up when he laid eyes on Catam, the golden gleam of his gaze a familiar feature that never failed to remind Catam of his mother.

"Good to see you, little brother." Sernal's voice rippled through the thick noise of the crowd around them, the sensuality an undercurrent as natural as the thick black hair on his head.

"And you," Catam replied with a broad grin. His grin faded when he noted the serious expressions on everyone's faces. "What did I do now?"

Sernal sighed. "I heard about the incident at Kweg's. Your behavior is bordering on just this side of legal." He gave Catam a stern look.

Catam muttered under his breath and eyed Mara with wounded eyes, an expression guaranteed to make her stand up for him. Unfortunately, her husband Lurin caught the gesture. Though he didn't speak out loud, he must have communicated telepathically, the way his kind often did, for Mara suddenly frowned.

"That's not going to work this time, Catam," she said firmly, while her lips twitched as if fighting a grin.

"What do you mean?"

"She means you've got to stop taking so many chances," Sernal intervened.

"Actually," Lurin corrected, "she means you can't get to her with that wide-eyed, 'feel sorry for me' look anymore. Especially since we both know where you just came from. And sorry is not what you're feeling." Lurin eyed the three pleasurers standing in the hallway from which Catam had recently arrived.

"Not bad," Sernal murmured.

Catam shrugged carelessly and his brother stared at him with concern.

"Actually, Catam," Mara said, "your brother came to us for some help. We're in between jobs, so I've got no problem with you leaving us for a while. And both Set and Nu are beyond pleased to have some time off to, uh, relax," she finished with an attractive blush staining her cheeks.

Lurin gave a wry chuckle and nodded at the Fas brothers, who sat arm in arm with two voluptuous women at the far end of the bar. "You can say it, love. They're happy to be on Nebe6 where they can fu--"

"Lurin!"

Catam rolled his eyes at the happy couple and turned to his brother. "I'm as good as yours. This pair is killing me with so much wedded bliss," he mourned, even as he winked at the lovers.

Lurin grinned and dragged his wife away with him. "Signal if you need anything," he called over his shoulder before disappearing with Mara into the crowd.

Catam watched them go with a wistful smile. Had Mara not found Lurin, he felt sure she would have finally made love with him. Not that he begrudged her any happiness with her mate, but he couldn't help wondering about her prowess in bed. After all, she kept Lurin content, and that man had sexual talents beyond that of "normal" men.

"Hello? Catam?"

"Sorry, Sernal. What exactly do you need help with? I know several women here, and can recommend Sharell, if you want someone with a talented tongue."

A standing family joke, that Catam enjoyed more female companionship than his elder brothers due to his being the "pretty one" in the family, never failed to elicit annoyance from his eldest brother.

Sernal tried to mask his frown by rubbing his forehead. "The day I need help with women is the day I pack up and move to the southern province. Give it up, Catam."

"There has to be some woman here who'll take you. You're only six years older than I am. It's not as if you're an old man or anything," Catam said with a helpful smile.

"Shut up and listen you idiot," Sernal growled. "I have a

situation that requires my attention on Ithra. It's serious enough that I need to leave my current case with someone I trust."

"If you're giving it to me, that means Rafe and Gar are both unavailable, right?"

"Right." Sernal offered no apology, always the practical brother. "Rafe's doing undercover work, and Gar is.... Well, Gar isn't handling Taika's passing very well."

Catam nodded soberly. The second oldest, Gar had wed Taika four years ago. To his regret, Taika and their son had died in an explosion six months past, leaving behind a reclusive, grief-stricken man.

"I haven't seen Gar in months," Sernal continued, "but I talked to Rafe last week. He won't surface--"

"You mean can't surface," Catam interjected.

Sernal nodded. "Can't surface, until his job is done. He told me to tell you not to ruin all the good pleasurers on Nebe6 though."

"Too late," Catam said with a laugh. Despite his recent restlessness, seeing his brother made him feel good.

"Yeah. I'll be sure to tell him when I talk to him next. Now about this mission," Sernal paused and looked around him.

Sensing Sernal's need for privacy, Catam motioned him to follow. He threaded through the masses and found Sharell waiting near a black door.

"Can we use your room for a moment? My brother and I need a place to talk."

Her disappointment that he hadn't returned for her was obvious, but at the mention of a brother her eyes lit on Sernal.

"You can use the room if I can get a thorough introduction to your brother later."

"No problem," Catam said quickly and hustled his brother into the hallway and back toward the room he'd earlier vacated.

"Thanks," Sernal said sarcastically, "but I don't know that I have the time to fuck one of your girlfriends."

"Don't be more of an ass than you have to be," Catam answered in a lighthearted tone, always the tease. "Sharell's a good girl. You'd be lucky to have her."

Sernal sighed. "Maybe later. I've just got too much on my

mind to think about sex now."

Catam could only gape at him. What the hell was Sernal working on that sex could be an almost forgotten occurrence?

"Statesman Klin is dead," Sernal blurted and rubbed his eyes. "But I have an interplanetary dispute to settle, a matter more important to Mardu than dealing with the death of one of our politicians."

"I hate the western province," Catam said automatically. And he did. The west was well known for producing two things, arrogance and deceit, both of which could be found in abundance in Zeron, where Statesman Klin worked.

"Well then, it's a good thing you'll be going north."

"North?"

"Klin died in his home in Voran, a northern territory. His wife found him dead, his throat slit and stabbed in the stomach. Apparently one of the servants saw a masked person fleeing the scene."

"No trace of the assailant?" Catam could feel his blood humming at the possibility of a hunt.

"None. It's been a week and we have nothing more than a brief description of a masked burglar, gender and age unknown, of slight build and possessing both speed and agility."

"So you think it's a burglary gone bad?"

"Well, the safe was open and empty, and the statesman's body was near it."

Catam could almost hear his brother's brain ticking. "But?"

"But something is off about this case. I'm too torn by the incident with planet Aflera to think clearly about Statesman Klin's murder. That's why I need someone I can trust to see to it. I need someone who won't be pressured by the political factions swarming around the death, someone who won't bow to the influence of the rich in the northern province."

"Save the platitudes. Just give me what you've compiled thus far and I'll run with it."

Sernal looked relieved. "Great. Thanks, I really needed your help. You're sure it's no problem with your Captain?"

Catam shook his head. "Family comes first, Sernal. You know that."

"I know. I'm just glad you remember, what with so many women turning your head," he said wryly.

"They don't turn my head." Catam surprised himself with the seriousness of his response. "I don't know why, but none of them do. It's just sex. And after seeing Gar, maybe it's best that it stays that way."

Expecting Sernal to argue with him, Catam was taken aback when his brother nodded. "You may be right."

His brother looked like he wanted to say more, but Sharell returned with a friend on her arm.

"Catam, can your brother play?"

Sernal grinned and took each woman by the arm. "With you on the case, Catam, I suppose I can relax. And since I'm presented with the opportunity, it'd be a shame to ignore such lovely ladies." He winked at them and turned back to Catam. "I've already sent the info you need via mediastream to Mara's ship. It's completely secure, and you know how to reach me if you have any questions."

Sernal was about to walk away with his new friends when Catam asked a question that had been plaguing him. Depending upon the operation, Catam could assume any of a dozen identities.

"Exactly who am I on this one?"

Sernal chuckled. "You're Catam of Mardu, of course, Peacemaker Certified. I'll teleport the badge to you early tomorrow."

Catam stared after Sernal in horror. A peacemaker? After all his trouble with the law, he was now supposed to support it?

Though come to think of it, the badge would help smooth some ruffled feathers if he had to enter those places from which he'd previously been banned. What delicious irony, he thought with a grin, and returned to the ship to inform Mara of his new status.

\* \* \* \*

Two weeks later, Isa still hadn't come any closer to figuring out what the hell really happened the night of Statesman Klin's death.

She nursed a Sour Jack in a dark corner of Shathra's grungiest bar, glad for the comfort the tart drink afforded. She hadn't found ease anywhere else since that fateful night that was turning out to be the worst mistake she'd ever made.

Sighing, she burrowed deeper into her long netters jacket and skulker's cap, grateful for the relative anonymity in the common clothing. She took another sip of her drink and stared moodily at the raucous crowd growing around her.

At least here she might earn a brief respite from the miserable lawmen dogging her heels. By Flor's feet, she was tired of running. Despite the mask she'd been wearing in Statesman Klin's home, her physical description had been posted everywhere. Damn that Harron!

Who else but Harron could have told anyone of her involvement? The bloody handprint she'd stupidly left on the wall had been made wearing a glove, so genetic recovery from the print didn't signify.

More than anything, she wanted to know why. Why had she been set up? Any one of a dozen people might have wanted to murder the statesman. But why do it in his home in Voran, when the streets of Zeron were filled with assassins who normally took care of stray politicians? And why drag Isa into the sordid muddle?

She watched the room warily, idling the time until her source showed. She had succeeded in brokering a deal for information with a nasty little man named Feltang, someone she normally wouldn't step a foot near. But desperate times called for desperate measures, and she nervously awaited his arrival.

She glanced around the bar, noting the majority of this crowd focused on the gaming tables. Few fights broke out here, most of the patrons were involved in illegal gambling. Those not playing the tables engaged in drunken revelry or open fornication with the many pleasurers lingering by the taps.

Finishing her Sour Jack, Isa's gaze panned the room scanning for Feltang. Her eyes passed over a tall figure with dark hair and she froze. He stood with his back to her, talking and laughing with the bartender. There should have been nothing dark or mysterious about a man grabbing a drink, yet something about the dark haired stranger set her teeth on edge.

Her instincts had never failed her, and trusting in her ability to spot trouble, she slowly stood to leave.

"There you are." Feltang sat his wiry frame next to her

with a huff, breathing as if he'd just run a race. "It wasn't easy finding you."

Wanting to leave and yet unwilling to give up this chance for information, Isa reluctantly sat. She glanced back at the bar but the stranger had vanished. Her gaze darted around her, lingering where the dim lighting in the bar failed to reach, but she saw nothing of the man.

"...so I can't stay long. Lady, have you heard a word I've said?"

"Um, no, sorry. Something caught my attention." Still no sign of the stranger. The company nearest her table was a couple fornicating against the wall behind Feltang. She quickly looked back at her companion. "You were saying?"

"First, I want my currency," Feltang demanded and looked around him before reaching out his hand. He reminded her of a port rat, nervous energy and meanness balled into a poorly fed frame.

"Here," Isa grumbled and tossed ten beks at him. "Now the information."

She watched him study the currency in his palm before quickly hiding it in his soiled jacket. Then he leaned toward her and spoke in a low voice. "News from both Zeron and Voran has it that the statesman's consort is offering ten thousand beks for the capture of the person who killed her husband." His rheumy eyes studied her craftily, trying to see beneath the brim of her hat.

Isa swore under her breath. Just what she didn't need. Another group of greedy citizens bent on her capture, as if the law wasn't enough.

"Speculation has it that Klin's assassination was engineered by somebody big, somebody that even the law can't touch," he whispered. "My source tells me they found an Aran blade in the statesman's belly."

Puzzled, Isa could only stare at Feltang. She'd seen The End of the knife protruding from Klin's belly. It had carried none of the ornate sequencing of Aran smith work. No, that blade had been Voranian, or at least designed in Evran, Voran's sister city. The artistry of the handle definitely smacked of northern influence.

Just one more piece of an ever-growing puzzle.

"What did you make from the name Arnath?" she asked. "I know it's fairly common in Voran, but what connection could you tie to Daarna, Lady Klin?"

He shook his head. "There are too many Arnath's to count. At least four work on her estate, and the commonwealth is filled with them."

"Then at least give me a place to start searching for answers. I could have gotten this generalized information without your help," she bluffed in a harsh voice, trying to mask her worry with anger.

She glared at him from under dark lashes, trying to look threatening, subtly reminding him that she had seen him escape from the peacemakers trying to arrest him. One word and he'd see jail time. He didn't need to know the law was the last thing *she* intended to confront.

Feltang swallowed audibly, his gaze trapped under hers like a hunted animal. "I don't know why you give a damn about any of this." She narrowed her stare and he hurried to continue. "Try the western province. Cheltam might know something."

Her glare subsided and his grating voice perked up. "I can tell you something I'm sure you don't already know."

"What?"

"They've brought in someone special to track Klin's murderer."

Her heart raced. "Who?"

"Me," a soft voice rumbled from behind her.

## Chapter Three

At the low growl Feltang fled, disappearing in the hazy mist hanging around the disreputable gaming club. Before she could make her own escape, Isa found herself picked up by her collar and shoved into the shadows.

As her attacker pinned her belly against the wall, his large, hard body pressed against her so firmly that she couldn't move. Hands as quick as lightning flashed over her, removing the twin Zephyr blades and the illegal Melan pistol strapped to her side.

Disarmed, she struggled to free herself but was soon unable to breathe.

"If you stop moving, I'll allow you air." The deep voice smoothed over her, a seductive promise of life.

She immediately stilled and gasped when air rushed into her grateful lungs. He turned her around in his arms, so that her back now touched the wall. His body stood so close to hers that she could feel the rise and fall of his chest as he breathed. Her hat and his proximity blocked her view, so she could see no more of him than a flash of golden skin at the base of his throat.

She innately knew that this man and the dark haired stranger who had earlier alarmed her were one and the same. Her instincts that he was trouble proved correct, and her heart raced with panic.

"Feeling better?" he asked softly, causing her to start in a new feeling of alarm. Amazingly, her body felt as if were not her own, her blood pooling and pulsing in what she surprisingly attributed to lust. She blinked and tried to regain control over her emotions but could do no more than lean into her large captor when he pulled her forward.

"That's a good girl." He purred into her ear. "Now let's see what you look like up close, hmm?" He removed her hat, freeing her long hair from its confines. She refused to look up, not wanting him to see more of her than he already had.

She didn't know how he could see in the first place, considering the veiled darkness of their position, but apparently he could make out enough.

"Very nice," he said, his voice sounding pleasantly surprised.

Isa struggled to hold onto her control as this new threat invaded. His warm mouth blew a caress against her ear, wringing a startled moan from her lips. The patrons in the club didn't give her or her captor a second glance, similar scenes of foreplay occurring all around them.

"What," she began and gasped as his teeth bit softly on her earlobe. His tongue pressed into the sensitive cavern of her ear and her knees buckled. "Wh-what do you want?" She had no idea who this man was. System law would have had her in chains by now, not pressed up against the wall being seduced senseless.

"You have to ask?" he murmured with a hint of humor. "I had no idea such beauty hid underneath that terrible hat."

His lips left her ear to find the pulse beating rapidly at her neck. His tongue swirled over the point before he settled his lips over her soft skin. Sucking lightly, he groaned and ground his pelvis against her.

Isa writhed, caught in the grip of passion beyond her control. With just his mouth, this stranger made her wet and needy.

She gripped the wall for support.

She had come into this less than savory establishment to keep a low profile. Her dealing with Feltang had proved a minor success. This man, however, posed a serious problem. Never before had Isa ever let a small thing like sexuality come between her and a job, let alone her life.

But this unidentified male held her against a grimy wall, stealing her will as he sensuously suckled her neck. She could only assume the Sour Jack had been somehow drugged. She couldn't account for her reaction to this stranger, nor could she fathom why she didn't simply break away from his touch.

He no longer held her captive but caged his hands on either side of her head and leaned against her with his hard body.

Isa tried to turn but he pushed deeper against her as his mouth sampled the tender flesh of her neck, an erogenous zone she hadn't known existed. Stars, she silently cursed as her body responded against her will. She wanted him more than she'd wanted anything in her life, and she had no idea what he looked like! He certainly had height and strength but she knew little more than that.

She closed her eyes, staving off the ecstasy building within her, and called on every ounce of discipline she possessed to resist his heady embrace. Moisture pooled between her thighs and her nipples had pebbled to hard nubs. She felt raw and she ached, and all from his touch. Then she inhaled to get a grip on her body, and she drew in his scent.

She moaned softly, disgusted to find the breathlessness of her tone was not an act. He smelled better than Aflera ambrosia. She wanted to devour him.

As if he sensed her desire, he sucked harder at her neck and moved his hands up under her jacket to caress her full breasts. She could feel the steel of his cock through his trousers, thrusting against her belly, and she desperately wanted to touch him flesh to flesh.

"That feels so good," she rasped and heard his breathing quicken. His hands grew rougher as the want built, and his need fed her own.

Knowing she approached the point of no return, she ignored how much she wanted him to continue his sensual assault. She reached for the one thing determined to cool her ardor, a vision of the dead Statesman Klin. She waited until her captor leaned away from her, one hand leaving the wall, she assumed, to unfasten his trousers.

As soon as his hand reached into his pants, she urgently shoved away from the wall and knocked him aside. She caught a glimpse of golden eyes widening in surprise, of dark hair shaping a sensual face. Then she ran as if her life depended upon it.

She sped through the crowd nimbly, and as she ran, she fought against memories of his touch, forcing herself to hurry. Still, it was a battle to convince herself she didn't want to be caught.

\* \* \* \*

Catam fought to control his breathing, to stifle the wave of heat engulfing his painfully aroused body.

He fastened his trousers and leaned his forehead against his arm, needing the wall for support. He didn't understand what had just happened. One minute he'd been watching the cloaked woman in discourse with that vermin Feltang.

And the next ... he caught her scent, and like a siren she drew him close before decimating his judgment.

Catam was Mardu, and more, he was Xema. His people revered sensuality, simultaneously basking in pleasure while controlling their sexuality from years of steady practice. While he had never disappointed a sexual partner, he had never lost his head with one either.

That the little thief he trailed could have made him forget his discipline astounded him. He breathed deeply, in and out, calming his racing pulse by forcibly ignoring memories of the woman's touch.

His cock still felt uncomfortably hard, and he contemplated one of the many pleasurers near him before deciding against it. Never mind that he enjoyed this particular chase. His brother trusted him to bring in his quarry soon, so play would have to wait.

Then a naughty thought crossed his mind, and his subsiding arousal flared anew.

The thief had started this, with her beckoning scent and delightfully erotic little body. Why not let her finish it? Unlike Sernal, Catam subscribed to no code of conduct. He was no lawman, no matter what his papers said. Catam was Xema, and as such, when it came down to it, he answered to no one but himself.

Smiling darkly, he turned to follow the tantalizing scent of his prey. He moved at a moderate pace, aware that she would be in a frenzy to escape and most likely tire herself out in a few hours.

Catam the hunter stalked swiftly, patiently, and didn't stop until he snared the prize. He never lost his prey. That was what made him so valuable to Captain Mara.

The Fas brothers had strength galore, but Catam possessed speed, agility and a tenacity that made him one of the best in the business. His added sensual charm with the ladies didn't hurt either, he thought as he followed the woman through town.

Too bad his charm had failed with her.

No matter. He would find her and try again. Eventually he would conquer her resistance and bring them both satisfaction that Catam, for one, desperately needed. Unconsciously or not, she had teased him and left him hurting. He could do no less than find her and exact justice, first for himself, then for Klin's family.

Smiling at the thought, he trudged through town, past the stretch of farmland and into the tree line to enter his favorite hunting grounds, the Eron Forest. Night settled over eastern Mardu, and Catam sighed with pleasure, feeling more at home here than he ever did aboard ship.

Under the thick canopy of trees, the Mardu moons may as well have been nonexistent. Wavery, thin streams of light pierced holes in the blanket of leaves, so Catam allowed his extrasensory perception to flare.

Suddenly, the night looked bright and clear. He eyed his quarry's trail with grim satisfaction. In her haste to disappear, she had made no effort to camouflage her escape. Broken vegetation and discernable footprints guided Catam deeper into the forest.

After an hour, he stopped and took note of his direction. The woman moved south, giving her two possible destinations. Either she planned on losing herself in Easfra, another large city in eastern Mardu, or she was headed toward the southern province.

He frowned at thoughts of the south. The southern province had no cities or towns. Inhospitable to all but the most hardened of men and women, the southern jungles of Mardu provided comfort to no one.

Only the crazed or desperate tried to exist in the jungle, where leopards, raptors and kethra, to name just a few, lived to hunt all who invaded their territory.

She couldn't possibly be headed there.

Two hours later he scowled furiously at the trail he followed. He had crossed the Eron Forest and now entered the Fields of Flor. Damn, but she was heading toward the jungle after all. The little idiot was bound to get herself killed in the jungle, if the Fields didn't destroy her first.

Furious that she might come to harm, Catam quickened his pace. He convinced himself his anger stemmed from denied satisfaction. For the alternative was something he didn't understand. How could he care about a person, a thief, he corrected, he had only just met? Hell, he didn't even know her name.

Muttering under his breath, he ran swiftly after her, determined to end this nonsense once and for all.

* * * *

Isa dropped in an exhausted heap onto the blue bed of moss under the overhang. The forest had provided excellent cover, enough for her to lose anyone trying to follow, surely. Besides, night had fallen hours ago, and she'd heard nothing in the dark silence of the Eron Forest.

Exiting the forest had felt dangerous, but in order to reach the southern jungles, she'd had to risk discovery. The tall grasses had helped her feel less exposed, as had the notion that no one was that good a tracker, to have stayed with her for over four hours in total silence and through dark, uncharted forest.

She'd trudged for another two hours before succumbing to fatigue. The small lake and large, hovering rocks provided the perfect place to rest. One of the massive boulders had an inverted L-shape, providing a small ceiling and cover of sorts.

Now resting under the rock, she had a wall of stone at her back and an expanse of water at her front. While Ithra hid behind a cloud, Aran and Sildor shone brightly, illuminating the vegetation on her left and right.

Tall green grasses covered in golden arotrope provided a sweet scent to complement the ripples of clear water in front of her.

Tired beyond measure, Isa settled into the moss bed with ease, her clothes suitable to the temperate climate in the Fields.

She tried to sleep. Her body desperately needed it, but her mind refused to comply. Images of her dark haired seducer bombarded her thoughts. Stars, but he'd been too physically perfect to be real.

Isa preferred dark hair and tall, strong-armed men.

By Flor, she'd gotten her wish with her captor. Black hair teased the nape of his neck, outlining a purely masculine beauty. Dark brows and thick black lashes framed his catlike eyes. And his golden gaze had flamed with carnal appreciation, staring at her with such surprise when she had fled him.

She sighed at those eyes, feeling them even now caressing her. And his lips ... those lips had been both hard and soft, plying her with pleasure while seducing with promises of erotic sensation. She shivered remembering how he had sucked at her neck, a place she'd never thought of as erogenous.

The few times Mathan had tried kissing her neck, she'd laughed and pushed him away, tickled by his raspy beard and amused by the slurping sounds he made. Their coupling had been quick and unsatisfying, far from what she'd experienced with her captor just hours ago despite the fact that they hadn't had sex.

She squirmed to suppress the quickening in her womb, trying to deny the moisture that pooled between her thighs.

She closed her eyes tightly and puzzled over her odd behavior. Never before in her twenty-six years had she *ever* felt so turned on by anyone, and in so brief a time!

She didn't know his name, and she didn't want to know why he chased her. Yet she would have given her soul to feel him deep inside her, to feel him come hard within her body.

She shook her head and opened her eyes. Staring at the narrow rock ceiling above her, she tried to rationalize her feelings.

Perhaps the spontaneity of the moment had caused such a rush? No. She wouldn't be so aroused now if it had only been the moment. Maybe she'd reacted so passionately because it had been so long since she'd had sex. She nodded, thinking that sounded reasonable.

Yet it didn't explain why she could picture him so clearly. She could still feel him touching her, now, several hours and several tree fields away.

She shivered and forced her eyes closed. She would not think of him anymore. She had to focus on the future, and the dangers inherent in her destination.

Visions of the southern province blended into another image of her captor. In this instance, she clearly saw him pressing her against the wall of the bar in Shathra. This time she imagined him releasing his cock from his trousers. And instead of taking her from the front, he'd turn her around and fuck her from behind.

She groaned and turned onto her side, clenching her thighs to prevent the throbbing in her loins from growing.

Damn, but it was all too easy to imagine him taking her that way.

Unable to stop the comparison, she recalled Mathan's feeble attempts at creativity. Since it normally took him no more than a few minutes to climax, he hadn't exactly had the time to try different positions. She frowned. That 'relationship' had lasted barely longer than Mathan's staying time.

Then of course, there was Teve. He'd at least tried to please her. But after experiencing pleasure with professionals, namely her older sisters, he'd declared her cold by comparison.

Oddly enough, memories of Teve didn't bother her like they normally did. Her near-orgasm tonight with the dark stranger must have cured her of her frigidity. Too bad Teve wasn't here to see it.

She rolled onto her back again, feeling a little better about herself. Maybe she did have the Araye pleasurer ability after all. Sex with strangers hadn't appealed to her before, but maybe she was a late bloomer. Maybe she should reject thievery in favor of the sensual arts, like the rest of the females in her family.

But she couldn't help grimacing at thoughts of sex with faceless men, and her ardor cooled. Unfortunately, Isa still didn't have the temperament to *fuck*. She'd *made love* to Mathan and Teve, much to her family's amusement, only to lose them both in The End.

In retrospect she knew losing them was all for the best. And the pain of her sexual failure didn't sting as badly as it normally did.

Perhaps when this situation with the dead statesman cleared, she might find her dark captor and try him on for size. At least then she would know if her one experience with him had been a freak occurrence or a new beginning.

She reached the point where her eyelids refused to stay open without effort, and she blearily gazed at the waxing moons before drifting to sleep, unaware of the hungry eyes watching her from the grass.


Chapter Four

Giving himself a few hours to rest, Catam woke bright-eyed and eager to meet the dawn.

His internal clock had yet to fail him, and he stared in wonder at the colors streaking Mardu's southern sky. Lavender and indigo blended, fighting the horizon's attempt to turn the sky a mild ocher. The moons still glowed, the pale, purple orbs all the more mysterious as their light grazed his quarry hidden under the overhang.

It had taken much control not to waken her with a drugging kiss the minute he'd found her. But Catam was Xema, and Xema men ruled their baser instincts. Strong in both mind and body, he'd ignored his aching cock and forced himself to sleep.

Now, however, he paused in thought and peered over the rock he lay on to stare at the woman lying vulnerably on a bed of moss beneath him.

It was time.

Retreating from the rock, he stretched his frame atop the overhang and nimbly climbed down the outer rock wall. On silent steps he waded through the rock's surrounding grass and entered the woman's shelter, looming over her as if he owned her.

He grinned, a wide, sensual smile that would have spooked her had she been awake.

He did own her.

Her mind, body and soul, until he brought her to Jintak where she'd await trial for the murder of Statesman Klin, belonged to *him*.

Even knowing she may have killed the statesman did nothing to ease the ache in his groin. He knew she was dangerous. The effect she had on his cock told him that.

And in his experience, everyone possessed a hidden well of darkness. So more than likely she had in fact killed the politician.

*What a waste.* He scanned her form, partly hidden behind the long jacket that had parted while she slept. One full, rounded breast rose up and down with each breath she took. He couldn't help staring at perfection, and to his delight her nipple peaked under his regard.

*She's aware of me at least on one level*, he thought with satisfaction. *And soon she'll be extremely aware of me.*

He silently removed everything but his trousers, waiting for her to peel them off, for her to fit her smooth, deft little hands around his cock as she begged him to fill her.

Thoughts of doing so made him thicken, and he was large and throbbing while he stared at her. He stroked himself through his trousers, willing her to rouse.

Pleased when her eyes fluttered, he poised to take full advantage of her confused awakening.

\* \* \* \*

Isa blinked up at an image of the man who wouldn't leave her mind.

"By Flor's dagger, would you just go away already?"

She couldn't believe her imagination could be so clear on his every detail. She hadn't seen his bared upper torso, but she readily anticipated his slim waist, the tight muscles cording his abdomen and the light pelt of hair covering his chest. She could even see his arms rippling with strength, something she had only felt before.

He smiled, flashing bright white teeth between hard, pale pink lips amidst the dark stubble of facial hair. His brows slashed in sardonic amusement and he crossed his arms, drawing her attention to the lean forearms covering his broad chest.

She licked her lips and stared, wanting to pet the silky hair covering his body, wishing that just this once she could control her dreams.

But such was not to be, for her vision shook his head and pursed his lips.

"Woman, you try me, you surely do," he rasped, his eyes focused on her beading nipples. Her jacket had shifted enough to reveal her breasts, clearly visible through the thin shirt she wore. Though black, the shirt was sheer, made of a material light and stretchy enough not to hinder her necessary agility.

Heat swirled through her body the more he stared, and her heartbeat increased rapidly when his image refused to fade.

"You're not going away."

"Take off your clothes." He stood over her like a towering warlord bent on plunder. And if the look he wore was anything to go by, he definitely intended on pillaging *her*.

She could only blink up at him in bafflement, trying desperately to recall just what had transpired last night. Noting the rising sun, she knew not much time had passed in her sleep.

"Did you not hear me?" he asked with an arrogant lift of his brow.

"Okay. You're definitely not a dream." She sat up slowly, aware of the tension radiating through his godlike body.

Subtly glancing at him as she wondered what next to do, her gaze returned swiftly to the heavy bulge in his trousers. He was aroused, and he was huge!

"Yes, sweet, it's all for you."

She gulped and scooted back until she met the wall. Desire flared and she realized she was already wet and aching--for him.

"My name's not sweet. It's Isa." She didn't understand why she needed him to know her name. Nor did she understand why she didn't suddenly break away and run for cover.

"Isa. It suits you." His hands drifted to his hips, affording her a mouthwatering view of his chest. Stars, but he oozed sensuality.

"Who are you?" she asked breathlessly. She cleared her throat and frowned, not liking this strange, needy Isa.

"I am Catam, peacemaker, captor, and soon to be your lover."

His voice rumbled over her like a bolt of silk, soothing and seducing all at once. He knelt down beside her and had her jacket off before she knew what he was about.

"Wait a minute." She tried to resist.

Her boots and socks followed and she sat in her sheer shirt and form-hugging trousers, staring agape at Catam.

His cock seemed to grow before her eyes, straining the taut fabric of his pants.

"I'm done waiting," he promised, his eyes gleaming against the sun.

"Well I'm not ready to have you yet," she challenged, feeling daring and sexual and *very* unlike herself. Her nipples pushed against the fabric of her shirt and she wanted to moan at the sensation.

"If that's the way you want it," he murmured and stood. He stripped out of his trousers without hesitation, giving her an eyeful of temptation. His cock stood squarely at attention, seeming to grow the more she looked at it.

Suddenly he pounced, surprising her with the swiftness of his actions. He had her trousers off and the hem of her shirt in his hands before she knew what had hit her. She barely had a moment to resist before she sat naked before him.

"Beautiful," he whispered with reverence and stroked the underside of her breast. "And so very soft."

"You shouldn't be doing this," she managed in a shaky voice, but made no move to avoid contact with him.

"You're my prisoner," he said with a sly smile. "I can do anything I want with you. Everything I want with you."

He moved in a blur and had her lying flat on her back in her mossy bed. He loomed over her and his cock brushed her stomach.

She gasped at the contact.

"I'm through waiting, Isa," Catam said. His eyes darkened to burnished gold and he lowered his body to hers.

Her curves cushioned him, fitting perfectly against the

rock hard structure of his frame. Isa bit her lip to keep from crying out, but Catam would have none of it.

"Purr for me, little thief. Give me what you promised earlier."

Not understanding his comment, she opened her mouth to question him when his mouth swallowed her words.

He tasted like cream, smooth and warm and so very satisfying. He finessed her mouth, using his lips and tongue to mimic the actions of his body. When he thrust his tongue in her mouth, he ground his erection against her mound.

She groaned and shifted, wanting his cock inside her.

"Not yet," he said huskily, and traced his mouth over her lips to her neck.

He sucked and nipped, leaving stinging pleasure along a trail from her ear to her collarbone. He licked her shoulder and centered himself above her breasts.

"You make me so hard," he breathed and licked her breast slowly, the rasp of his tongue a sensual torment that eased along the pale globe to the nipple aching for his touch.

He rubbed his cock harder against her, and she spread her thighs without thought.

He groaned and she shifted her pelvis so that his cock teased at her swollen nub bathed in the juices he'd created. She wanted him so much. With every thrust of his cock against her, he increased her sensitivity. She was close to orgasm, but not close enough.

His lips finally closed over her nipple and she arched into him, putting the tip of his shaft in direct contact with her clit.

He hissed his pleasure and sucked hard, gently biting her stiffened peak and causing her to cry out her pleasure.

With skilled lips, he made her breasts ache for more, for the touch of his tongue and the scrape of his teeth. His callused hands teased her nipples into hard pebbles of want, and she could feel her arousal pooling around his cock.

"Hell." Catam gritted his teeth and refrained from thrusting deep and hard into her.

He didn't understand this driving need to fuck her so badly. He wanted to bury himself in Isa, so much so that it scared him while it made him crazed with lust.

She shook her head from side to side, needing release that he kept just out of reach. He didn't know why he did it, but he wanted her to come around him. He normally didn't care, seeing to the woman's need before his own. But this time was different.

She arched into him again and he cursed at the effort it took not to come right then. His cock hurt, straining at the effort not to fuck her raw and he finally gave in to his urges.

Teasing her folds, he coated his cock in her moisture and paused, waiting for her to look at him.

She squirmed and stared into his eyes.

"What are you waiting for?" she groaned and reached for his hips.

"For this," he answered and stared at her as he sank deep, sliding through her tight sheath as though he'd done so before.

They both groaned at the joining, at the intense completion the contact wrought. She fit him like a glove, the warmth of her body both welcoming and exciting. He stilled for a moment, letting the feel of him sink into her.

Isa groaned and bucked at his hips, pulling him deeper into her womb.

"Ohh." Her head rolled back and forth, her eyes shut as if in plea for mercy.

Catam would show her none. He withdrew against the strong grip she had on his hips, then rammed into her. She arched and cried out, but he was relentless. Again and again he thrust, harder and deeper, always changing the friction against her clit.

The frustration and need that had built since their encounter in the bar increased until he could bear it no longer.

"Catam, please," she begged and locked her ankles around his waist. "I need more."

Gritting his teeth, he pressed against her clit and rode her hard. It didn't take much before she came, screaming his name as she tightened around him. And Catam, a skilled Xema used to making women beg to love him, was helpless to follow her into bliss.

Her contractions heightened the feeling in his cock and he tensed, the pleasure overwhelming. Ecstasy consumed him, blacking out his vision as he spurted inside her. Isa continued to come, groaning and tensing around him. Her body milked him, prolonging the pleasure until he sank onto her, drained and sated.

He rolled to his side, remaining joined with her while keeping from crushing her. She lay in his arms, her breathing harsh, her heartbeat thumping loudly in the silence of the new morn.

Catam sighed and hugged her close. She smelled of sex, of him, and the hint of wildness that had attracted him in the first place.

"Gods, woman, I think you've killed me."

He heard a small chuckle followed by a groan, and he knew he'd never before felt so alive after sex. Though sated, his mind remained clear, his body felt weightless, and his spirits were ready for anything. He had reached *wainu*--that spiritual place where perfection rested.

Wanting to thank her for sharing such peace, he opened his mouth and froze.

*What the hell had just happened?*

Only a select few Xema and Thesha--the System's lone sensually gifted races--could reach *wainu*. And to Catam's knowledge, no other System inhabitant even knew about such a state. How then had Catam experienced such bliss in the arms of a common thief?

She must have felt his tension for she drew apart from his embrace enough to look up at him.

"Catam?" she asked hesitantly.

Shit. Panic replaced the contentment he'd been feeling, and he wanted to both curse and thank her for taking him to perfection.

"Who exactly are you?" He withdrew from her, putting a necessary distance between them. He'd just come so hard he'd seen black, yet the minute he looked at her his ardor rose, strong and solid.

Her eyes fell on his stiffening cock, but she didn't comment on it. "I told you already." She looked uncomfortable, but more than that, she looked ... like she wanted to cry?

Dread filled him. Catam preferred to face a hundred barbarians rather than a woman's tears. And the fact that she tried to hide her sorrow shook him to the bone.

"What's wrong?" he asked quietly, deliberately releasing his tension as he soothed her with his voice.

She subtly wiped at her eyes and turned her gaze to the lake beside them. "Why are you so angry with me? Wasn't it good for you?"

He stared at her, wondering at her game. "Good for me? Hell, woman! I came for more than a minute! You're wet with my seed. Of course it was good for me!"

His angry tone should have insulted her. Instead she slowly smiled. "It was really good, wasn't it?" She seemed inordinately pleased with herself. "I was hot, wasn't I?"

Catam's easy nature reasserted itself as humor at her bragging stole through him. "You were scorching."

"You're hard again." She pointed to his groin and licked her lips. She blinked and reached down, slipping her fingers through her dark curls, making his cock swell.

"I want you again. I should be too tired, too sensitive, but I want you again, right now."

She looked wondrous at the revelation, and some of Catam's concern faded. If Isa was surprised by her body's response, she couldn't possibly have any idea what she'd done for him.

For a man who prized control, Catam should have been more upset over her revelation. He had no idea what had happened, and obviously neither did she.

Her fingers dove deeper, fingering her clit while she stared at him in invitation.

Without another word, he rejoined her on the ground. Wanting her again, he decided to take her fast this time. He quickly mounted her and thrust deep. He sealed his mouth to hers and mated with her tongue, pulling her deeper into his thrall.

As their coupling continued, he lost track of his control, of who was really in charge. Her slick heat stole his thoughts and he reacted to her urgings unconsciously. He sucked her tongue and grazed her breasts with his chest, knowing she liked the way his silken hair teased her nipples.

She arched into him, gripping his buttocks to pull him deeper, and his patience snapped.

His hips like a piston, he pumped in and out, driving her into another orgasm before he spilled into her with a harsh cry. His cock pulsed within her tight pussy, and he had to grit his teeth to keep from keening aloud.

The aftershocks faded after a time and he drifted into *wainu* without thought. Oddly enough, this time perfection wore Isa's face.

Chapter Five

Isa's body ached in strange places. She sat up, confused at first that she wore no clothing and that moisture pooled between her legs. Then she blushed, recalling Catam's ardent lovemaking.

By Flor's dagger, she wasn't frigid after all!

She wanted to shout with joy, to run to her family and share with them the news that she had in fact inherited the Araye gift of sensuality. She liked being a thief, truly, but the option had never before been present to be anything but. Now she could enter the world of the pleasurer, if she so chose.

She frowned, wondering why the thought of sex with others felt so distasteful. And then her answer appeared from around the corner of the rock face.

Catam strolled toward her with both arrogance and possession stamped on his sensual face. His lips quirked at her nudity and she realized she'd been grasping her jacket to her breasts.

"No need for that," he drawled and pulled the jacket from her.

Whereas she'd before been unconcerned about her nakedness, now she felt vulnerable, and a tad ... ashamed? Disappointment filled her as she realized she may have disproved her frigidity, but she still didn't have the mindset to become a pleasurer.

"I can see you're having doubts," Catam murmured. He took one last lingering look at her and sighed. "We'd best save this conversation for when you're dressed. You might as well make use of the lake to clean up."

He glanced again at her body, seeming pleased to see evidence of his seed smeared on her thighs.

"I'll be a minute," she mumbled and hurried into the water, ignoring the deep chuckle that followed her.

She quickly washed herself clean and exited the water, only to have Catam staring at her as if she were his last drink of water in the desert.

"Maybe I'll wait behind the rock," he said in a gritty voice and disappeared.

Breathing a sigh of relief, Isa did her best to dry herself with her coat before donning her clothing. She couldn't help that her shirt and trousers stuck even tighter to her as a result of her wet body. With a shrug, she dropped her jacket to the ground and sought out Catam.

He lounged on top of the massive rock like a lazy cat, swinging one leg over the side while he gazed at the sky.

Common sense told Isa she'd be better off running than facing Catam. Despite the incredible, mind-shattering sex, she was still a thief, and he was still a peacemaker intent on bringing her to justice. Yet she couldn't make herself leave without trying to seek some understanding.

"We need to talk," he said, and she jumped. He continued to stare at the sky, and she hadn't realized he'd known she stood there.

He rose and stretched, then gracefully joined her on the ground.

"I've got a dilemma," he admitted and leaned back against the rock to stare at her. "If it were up to me, I'd spend the next few weeks fucking your brains out."

She blushed dark red at his crude language and he laughed. "Sorry, sweet, but it's true. Even now, after the incredible session we shared, I want you again."

She glanced at the bulge in his trousers and shook her head in disbelief. She felt too sated and relaxed to want sex just yet. Was the man for real? He certainly looked too good to be true, and his sexual prowess ... maybe he was one of those new pleasure droids?

"Isa?" He looked puzzled and she scrutinized him from head to toe.

"You are flesh and blood, aren't you?"

He flashed her a grin. "I am. If you want to blame something, blame yourself. I'm not usually this, ah, stimulated."

"Well then." She had no idea what to say to that. She was still having a hard time acknowledging that she could respond to a male sexually with anything other than:

"Maybe I'll come next time. Don't worry about it."

"If I was a normal peacemaker, this would be much easier," he said and took a deep breath.

"What do you mean *a normal peacemaker*?" Alarm flared as she realized for all Catam's seeming safety, he might be working for the real killers.

"What I mean is that I'm not normally a peacemaker."

She relaxed hearing that he did indeed wear the badge.

"So you're normally what then? A pleasurer?"

He snorted. "I wish. No, I'm a bounty hunter currently on leave to help my brother. Sernal's the peacemaker, but he's got too many responsibilities just now."

He stared at her, making her uncomfortable with his scrutiny.

"What?" She crossed her arms belligerently, hiding her nervousness with anger.

"I just don't see it." He shook his head and walked around her, studying her from different angles. "You're gorgeous. You have a body to kill for. And you're a thief."

*A body to kill for? Gorgeous?* She could really grow to like Catam if he continued to say things like that.

"I don't get why you'd murder a statesman, for Stars sake. Don't you have a brain in that pretty head?"

Suddenly his compliments didn't sound so wonderful.

"I do have a brain, you drun. If you'd use what small intellect Flor granted you, you'd realize I'm being set up." She glared at him, her arms akimbo.

Her black hair curled around her face, her eyes flashed like green danstone, and Catam wanted to lay her flat on her back and take her again.

Scowling at his lascivious thoughts, he focused on her combative stance and glowered at her when he realized what she'd called him.

"You know, sweet," he gritted through his teeth, "if you're trying to get on my good side, try not insulting me. I don't like it."

"*You* don't like it?" She looked incredulous. "*I* don't like having the law on my tail. I don't like being accused of a crime I haven't committed!"

"So you weren't in Statesman Klin's home the night he was murdered?" Disappointment settled in his belly. If he had a bek for every time one of his bounties protested his or her innocence, he'd be a rich man.

"I didn't say that." She shook her head and her cheeks glowed with passion.

*Down boy*, he ordered his cock.

"I was there that night," she explained.

"But?"

"He was dead before I arrived."

"Sure." He grimaced. That was the best she could do? The sex must have muddled his brain. He'd actually convinced himself she might be innocent. No one who'd murdered another in cold blood could have taken him to wainu. At least, he hadn't thought so.

"Catam, listen to me," she urged. "I should never have taken a contract from Harron, but I did, and it was a mistake.

"He sent me to Klin's home in Voran. I was supposed to steal a priceless heirloom Klin had stashed in his wall safe, along with anything else I could get my hands on. Unfortunately, I missed my first opportunity to enter the study when a rather amorous couple surprised me in the wife's bedroom."

"Go on." The story had a lot of details. He'd see if she could keep them straight. One fact, however, held a ring of truth.

Catam knew of Harron. The slimy bastard had once tried to cheat a friend out of a priceless antique. Luckily, Sernal had found out and put a stop to his pawn brokering days. It appeared, however, that Harron might have taken to brokering other things, like theft and murder.

"I heard the man groan "Daarna" before he and she, uh, climaxed."

Catam wanted to grin. She sounded so embarrassed, and after the intimacies they had shared. Then her words struck him. "Wait a minute. You heard him say Daarna?" *Klin's wife?*

Isa nodded. "I managed to sneak into Klin's study while they were occupied. But instead of the wall safe, I found Klin lying dead. His throat had been slit and he'd been stabbed in the belly." She scowled. "And he'd been stabbed with a Voranian knife, not by an Aran dagger."

"So you're telling me you never saw the statesman alive. What about the safe?"

"It had been opened and emptied before I arrived. I found Klin by tripping over him." She frowned. "Contrary to what you might think, I'm a damned good thief. I wear a mask and gloves, and my handprint was found on his wall because I slipped in his blood trying to get up from a fall."

Catam stared at her, thinking. It had bothered him that the thief had left a handprint, especially since the lab had determined a gloved hand left the print. Why would a thief be smart enough to wear gloves but not wipe up a handprint left in blood?

"I barely had enough time to hide before Daarna and her beau Arnath entered."

He didn't like where his thoughts took him. "Did you see Daarna and Arnath?"

"I saw the back of Daarna's body, and I can tell you she had dark, curly brown hair. I didn't see Arnath, though."

Daarna had to be Klin's consort. But Arnath?

Isa continued. "They made me sick when they started screwing each other right by Klin's dead body. There was blood all over the floor! They would have kept at it if Arnath hadn't cautioned Daarna to be careful."

She paused before she added, "He said something about not wanting to be seen together before tomorrow. I had assumed he meant he didn't want to be seen at her house when Klin had just been murdered. Now I'm not so sure."

"The elections began the following day," Catam said more to himself than to her. "Arnath Bedenzi beat out the minor competition since his greatest opponent, Statesman Klin, had just died."

Catam's thoughts flew, the ramifications of such a discovery hard to swallow. "You said you wore a mask?" That last detail still bothered him.

She nodded. "I always do. So how could the maid who saw me leave the study know it was me? And since the print I left was virtually useless, how did the law immediately know to look for me?"

"Harron sold you out."

"Exactly." Isa's voice thickened with anger. "But Harron doesn't do anything for free. He had to have gotten orders from someone else to set me up. Problem is, I just don't have that many enemies. I honestly don't think anyone I know committed the crime."

"No. Daarna and Arnath could have used Harron for that." He stood staring at Isa, deep in thought.

What if some other peacekeeper had been sent to capture Isa? No one would believe her story. It was just too awful and unbelievable to be true. And yet ... according to Sernal's notes, Daarna had a penchant for pretty baubles, and pretty men, none of them hers. The woman had clever hands and an insatiable sex drive, making Klin's life hell trying to keep her out of the public eye.

"Isa," he said slowly. "Did anything else about that night at Klin's make you suspicious? In addition to the heirloom, Harron's boss gave you permission to take anything else you wanted. Why didn't you?"

"I told you, Catam. The safe was empty. And finding Klin dead...."

"But you had to have cased the study before seeing Klin. He lay behind a large desk that would have blocked your view upon entering the study."

Isa pursed her lips. "To tell you the truth," she paused in thought, "I don't remember seeing much of value to take. Why do you ask?"

Catam nodded. The lack of expensive items in the study fit with the suppositions in Sernal's notes. "Apparently Daarna likes to steal from her husband."

Isa's eyes widened, and she said the next thing on his mind. "I wonder who she uses to pawn the goods?"

"Harron," they both answered.

After a moment, Isa's lips curved. "So I take it this means you believe me?"

"It's getting hard not to. Too many pieces just don't add up. But you're still wanted by the law, and with Daarna's public sympathy garnering her power and Arnath's new political fame, we're going to have a hell of a time proving this."

"At least they don't know I overheard them talking. If they did, they wouldn't have sent a peacemaker to collect me. They'd have sent an assassin."

Catam's nerves frazzled at thoughts of Isa in real danger. "They still might. Arnath is an extremely ambitious man. Recently voted into office, he'll do anything he can to keep his position."

"I'm a loose end." She voiced quietly.

"Yes, you are. And you know what that means?"

"He's going to kill me?" She swallowed, and he saw her bravado faltering.

"No," he answered firmly, denying the possibility. "It means we have to go back to Voran to find some answers. And the sooner the better, before Arnath decides to place the Ari on you."

Ari--the assassin's mark of death. Isa smiled sickly and Catam wanted to hold her, but he could see the effort it took her to maintain a fearless front.

She inhaled deeply and pasted an overly sweet smile on her face. "Voran, here we come."

\* \* \* \*

*Four Days Later*

"Take your payment and remove yourself from this house before someone recognizes you," Daarna Klin whispered furiously, looking over her shoulders as she shoved a small pouch into his hands.

Harron clutched the silken purse in a claw like grip and scowled. "It wasn't my idea to come here, my lady. I only did it as a favor to our newest statesman. Believe me, I have no desire to be implicated in any of this."

So saying, he nervously backed away and strode as quickly as his bulky frame would take him from the outer gardens.

Daarna watched until he disappeared beyond a cluster of catha lilies. What could he have been thinking to show up here, and now of all times? Hosting Arnath's welcome celebration had been postponed due to Klin's untimely death. But politics lived on in Voran, regardless of its dying constituents.

Still in supposed mourning, Daarna put on a good face and generously offered to stake the new statesman, backing him not only with her newly inherited and considerable wealth, but also with her personal vote of support by hosting this dinner party.

The sounds of guests arriving filtered through the house and the open doors of the back patio. Turning to encounter the throng of curious well-wishers, she took a step inside the house before a large hand settled on her shoulder.

"Good evening, Lady Klin." Arnath's deep voice flowed

over her like warm rain and she shivered, the cultured sound of his greeting making her wet with remembrance.

She cleared her throat, her tone courteous. "Good evening, Sir." Several staff passed by, scurrying to finish the dinner arrangement. "I trust you are satisfied with the preparations?"

"Hmm." He shrugged.

"I'm sorry?"

He turned his attention to one of his aides. "I'll join you shortly. Keep the guests occupied for a moment, will you?" His aide nodded and Arnath's polite façade held. "Lady Klin, I did have one or two concerns you might be able to help me with. If you would, please?"

He gestured for her to precede him back outside toward the patio's treasure, a vast gazebo shaded from prying eyes by the massive hedges cut in a maze-like pattern surrounding it.

Once they reached the gazebo, Daarna frowned. The servants had yet to light the area and due to the clouds covering the moons, she could barely see under the gazebo's roof.

"I'm sorry, Statesman. This should have been seen to--"

He yanked her under the gazebo's roof. "It should have," he rumbled and she heard the rustle of fabric. Then his hand closed over hers in a tight grip. "This festivity is far from satisfying," he whispered harshly. His grip tightened until she cried out in both pain and excitement.

"What can I do to make things right?" she asked, nearly on her knees due to the sheer pressure he placed on her wrist.

"You know what to do," he rasped and brought her hand to his groin. She could feel his heat and the shock of his naked flesh meeting her hand caused her to gasp.

Kneeling before him, she could hear his heavy breath above her, could feel his gaze directed at the top of her head.

He released her wrist and she rubbed it absently, aware that Arnath's flesh strained and bobbed just a breath from her lips.

"Do it," he ordered, his voice thick.

She slowly neared his erection, her hesitancy exciting him for she heard his breathing quicken.

"In your mouth, whore," he panted, and groaned when her lips slid over his cock, her mouth swallowing him all the way to his velvety sack.

Daarna worked him hard, her mouth sucking and releasing, building a pressure that agonized with promise. She found a rhythm that brought muffled moans to his mouth and she fingered her clit, excited beyond measure when Arnath's fist gripped her hair to press her closer.

"More, Daarna," he gasped and began pumping into her, no longer still.

"How much more?" she teased, withdrawing her mouth enough to speak around his cock. Her lips grazed his shaft and she nipped lightly with her teeth, making him surge deeper.

She brought a hand up to toy with his skin-soft sack straining for release, while her mouth lightly sucked him, taking him in only so far.

"Fuck," he cursed and rammed his cock deep into her mouth, almost to her throat. His hand maintained a vice-like grip on her hair, shoving her face into his groin so that she could barely breathe.

She controlled the urge to gag, only barely, and in just enough time to swallow the cum that filled her mouth.

"Fuck, yes," he whispered as he continued to pump, his seed shooting down her throat like thick, milky ambrosia. He released the tangle-hold on her hair and his fingers rubbed small circles against her scalp.

Daarna swallowed all of him, licking the remains from his pulsing shaft. The stinging pain in her scalp felt oh, so good.

"That's right, baby," he breathed and stroked her hair.

"You taste delicious," she flirted, wishing she could see him. "Not that I'm complaining, but why fuck now, with so much to lose if we're caught?"

"Because I needed it," he said roughly. "Besides, we won't get caught, that's why Harron was here." His voice suddenly sounded close to her ear and she realized he knelt next to her. He forced her to her feet, keeping his face very close to her belly.

"What?" she gasped when his hands traced her legs beneath the gown she wore.

"Hold this and listen," he ordered in a gritty voice,

shoving the fall of her dress into her hands, effectively baring her mound to the fresh air. "Harron was here to finish the job."

He licked at her folds, unerringly finding her nub that plumped as he suckled.

She wanted to shriek but did her best to keep quiet. The low rumble of guests grew louder, signifying definite danger of exposure. The risk only made her wetter and she squirmed against his probing tongue and fingers.

"I'm so close," she moaned.

"Shh, careful sweet." Arnath backed off, letting his fingers slide in and out of her dripping pussy. "Harron is going to set up the Ari for your housebreaker. She's one risk I'm not willing to take. Now let's see how quiet you can be while I finish what I started."

Imagining the death of Isa Araye, brutal and bloody, in addition to Arnath's questing tongue made her shatter into a thousand pieces, and only her hand over her mouth prevented her from alerting all to their presence.

"Now, Daarna," Arnath whispered in a smug voice, "sneak away to fix yourself. Despite the fact that I can't see you, I'm sure you look like you've just been fucked. And we can't have people saying that Klin's surviving mate isn't as pure as they like to think."

Daarna chuckled and escaped the gazebo through the rear, darkened section of the garden. If only Arnath knew ... she had fucked many of the more influential members of the crowd here tonight. How else would her husband have gotten elected?

She shook her head and entered a hidden passage leading to her dressing room. With Klin dead and Arnath under her control, she was right where she wanted to be.

She shivered again, thinking of the Ari. If only she could be present when that bitch-thief met her demise. Daarna sighed. The sacrifices she made in the name of politics.


Chapter Six

Isa grimaced and stared with disdain at the legion of

politicians and their lackeys mulling through the Klin estate.

"I thought this was a bad idea before, but now I think you're trying to get me killed."

Catam's bright smile flashed against the black backdrop of sky. "Such a naysayer. Really, Isa, this is just your style. Wealth and stupidity together in one place? Aren't your little hands sweating to steal something from one of those idiots?" He gestured to Daarna Klin's partygoers.

Isa blinked and stared thoughtfully at what she could see of Catam. "You really aren't a peacemaker, are you? I think your opinion of the western provincials is worse than mine."

"It is. Just be thankful we didn't have to go west to gather information. I'd be worse than a raptor with all my shrieking and complaining."

Isa shook her head, a grin twisting her lips.

It was hard to be in a bad mood around Catam. He saw the humor in everything. The past four-day journey north had been both invigorating and enlightening.

Catam's sexual appetite notwithstanding, he seemed laidback about the entire legal issue with Isa. He didn't try to tie her up, nor did he seem to worry she might run. He paced them both, his stamina a thing of beauty. And he had an agility that rivaled hers.

He continued to make love with her at every available opportunity, and though she knew she was getting in too deep, she didn't have it in her to refuse. Sex with Catam felt too damned good.

Sweat broke out on her forehead as she remembered Catam taking her upright, against a tree with no preparation on her part. Surprisingly, her body had accepted him without reservation. They'd come in a conflagration of need and desire, a heady mix that brought emotion too close to the fray for comfort.

Isa sighed and stared at the crowd that continued to grow at the Klin estate.

"A thousand beks for your thoughts," Catam teased, a familiar rumble in his voice that hinted at sexual play.

"They're worth more than that," she countered, and tried to focus on anything but Catam's nearness.

His dark clothing blended with the night sky, so he should

have been invisible. But hell, Isa couldn't stop remembering what he looked like without his clothes.

"I can smell your need, sweet," Catam murmured and pressed against her.

Sure enough, his erection burned into the small of her back.

"Catam, not now," she protested halfheartedly. "We have to be alert in case Klin's security approaches."

"Shh, I'll hear them." He yanked her trousers down to her knees and fumbled with his pants. Within moments she felt his cock burning along her buttocks, sliding between her cheeks like pure silk.

"Catam," she groaned softly and reached up behind her to grasp his head.

He moved into her hands and pressed wet, carnal kisses to her throat while his fingers spread her wet need along her folds.

"Your smell, it's like a drug," he whispered and circled his thumb around her clit, sensitizing the hard nub until she wanted to cry out with frustration.

She pressed back against him, aware he wanted her as much as she wanted him. His cock strained and he groaned with every sway of her backside.

"If you keep that up I'll come right now," he threatened in a growl. "I've been thinking about this all afternoon."

"You're insatiable," she said on a breath and bent forward, bracing her hands against a nearby tree. She sighed with relief when he finally entered her.

From this position, he seemed to fill her tighter than he had before. His shaft slid deep into her womb, and he stayed like that for a moment, as if savoring the connection.

Isa marveled again at how perfectly he fit, at how right it felt to be with him. He knew exactly where to touch her, had from the first moment they'd made love.

Catam shifted, pulling out before sinking back inside.

She bit her lip and closed her eyes, reveling in his touch. He began thrusting and she met his pounding rhythm, her patience worn thin, her need too great to stave.

"I have to come inside you," he uttered in a harsh whisper. "I have to feel you surrounding me, milking me dry."

He groaned and his fingers quickened over her flesh as he

pistoned his hips. "Wainu," he groaned and stilled inside her, coming hard in shudders that refused to let her go.

Knowing she had brought him satisfaction increased her own pleasure, and with one more glide of his thumb over her clitoris, she came, exacerbating his orgasm. His fingers shifted and bit at her hip to hold her still, all the while her inner walls clamped down on his pulsing cock.

Breathing hard, Isa felt as weightless as a feather. She wanted no more than to bury herself in Catam's arms, content in the warm safety of his hold.

She hadn't forgotten his reason for finding her, but his actions contradicted his orders. His every thought and deed since finding her had been protective, not punishing. And he seemed to want to get to the bottom of Klin's mysterious murder as much as she did, despite the fact that his orders were to bring her to Jintak and nothing more.

A soft kiss pressed into her neck and she shivered. She could feel his seed dripping down her leg, could feel the cool night wind blowing across her naked groin. And she didn't care.

"How do you do this to me, time and time again?" she wanted to know, as much teasing as she was genuinely curious. "Before I met you, I'd had sex. But nothing on your scale. Nothing even came close."

She felt his lips curl into a smile against her neck. "But I'm from Mardu, Isa."

"I am too. From one of Mardu's moons that is."

"Aran, yes. I find it interesting a woman with your looks and sensuality didn't find herself immersed in the sex trade." He gently disentangled himself and she redressed. "Why is that?"

She didn't want to admit her failures to Catam, a man with whom she could be the sensual woman she'd always wanted to be. If he knew how others--hell, how *she'd* always perceived herself, would he think less of her? Curiosity over his reaction swelled.

"Isa?"

"I was frigid," she blurted, waiting to see how quickly he would distance himself from her. Frigidity was a condition unheard of and unaccepted among her people.

Catam knew she couldn't see him through the darkness, so he felt no need to hide his shock as he fastened his trousers. Frigid? She had to be kidding. And just how had she come to such an asinine conclusion?

The Xema believed in sexual pleasure, for both men and women. Yet the thought of Isa with other men made Catam uncomfortably possessive. He blinked, surprised to feel jealousy. He'd never felt that before, not in regards to a woman.

The closest he'd come to feeling jealousy had been the envy he experienced when he saw the intimacy between his captain and her husband. He'd thought about it a lot and had come to the conclusion that Mara's joy coincided with his recent dissatisfaction with his life.

He sure as hell wasn't in love with Mara, so what did his dissatisfaction mean?

"Catam?"

Isa sounded stiff, probably worried, and he hastened to alleviate her concern.

"Sorry, sweet. I'm just stunned you could think yourself frigid. You're the most sensual woman I've ever met, and I know what I'm talking about."

She paused. "I'm sure you do."

He wanted to laugh despite his confusing affection for the beautiful thief. She sounded as jealous as he'd been feeling.

A man's voice interrupted his thoughts, and he and Isa grew silent. "These damned politicians." Feeling his hunter's instinct surge, a powerful energy that sizzled through the contentment his climax had brought, Catam released the hold on his Xema abilities.

He used his heightened senses, ignoring Isa's gasp of surprise.

With his acute vision and hearing intact, he could plainly see their intruder. A lone security guard visited the tree line near their position, relieving himself.

Catam waited with Isa until the guard returned to his post.

She poked him in the chest. "Your eyes, they're glowing! How--"

"Later." He shushed her with a firm response. "Right now we need to get closer to that party before the clouds shift from the moons. As soon as the guests depart, in another few hours I hope, we'll enter the estate."

She nodded. "I was about to suggest that myself, until you distracted me." Her eyes gleamed with pleasure and Catam felt masculine pride swell.

Pleasing Isa pleased him. Unlike time spent with other women, Catam didn't have the ability to maintain control with Isa. With her he was helpless to do more than react.

His body stirred at thoughts of Isa melting around him, and he cursed his unruly cock to behave. He couldn't understand how he could remain in a state of sexual readiness, considering he'd just come deep inside of her.

That thought brought a primal satisfaction that sharply reminded him to watch his step.

Already he felt far more than was healthy for his little thief. Despite the shady circumstances surrounding her case, he and she lived in two different worlds.

He hunted the System's wanted inhabitants, and she regularly broke the law.

His jaw tightened at thoughts of the inevitable separation between them, and he squelched the reminder of reality.

"See that copse of furen trees near the rear of the garden?" he asked to refocus his thoughts.

Her eyes narrowed and she nodded.

"Follow me."

Impressed by her stealth, he didn't feel the need to constantly check on her progress. When they reached the copse of trees, he felt her at his back though he hadn't heard her so much as step on a loose branch during the brief trip.

"I told you I'm good," she whispered.

"Cocky too."

He heard a small chuckle and then an unspoken silence settled over the two of them as they waited for the party to clear.

Catam rested his back against a tree stump while he watched Daarna's guests through the hanging vines framing his view of the estate.

Arnath appeared near Daarna every time she stepped foot on the back patio. When she entered the house, Arnath subtly followed.

Had Catam not known of the pair's connection, he might not have noticed how smoothly they moved together.

Just one more detail to prove Isa's story true.

Catam had been a bounty hunter for more than a decade. And in that time, he'd seen plenty from the seedier side of life. He usually had little trouble reading the criminals he brought to justice. And he maintained a sharp nose for the truth.

He had a hard time reading Isa though, and that surprised him. Perhaps her innate sensuality threw him, or maybe his rampaging hormones when around her screwed with his judgment. Whatever the reason, he had distrusted her story from the very beginning, both because it sounded unbelievable, and because he didn't trust his reaction to her.

Hell, one out of every six men in the western province was named "Arnath." And though "Daarna" wasn't as common a name, anyone who'd visited the northern province even once would recognize Daarna Klin's name. The woman and her husband had more currency than the Mornian mints.

Watching Arnath and Daarna, however, clearly illustrated something deeper existed between the two. They brushed against one another "accidentally" for the *fifth time.*

Catam couldn't tell from this distance, but he'd bet his next pay-credit that Daarna's smile suggested more than a simple show of support. No, he'd wager she stared at Arnath like a wanton, hungry for sex.

She and Arnath disappeared again to mingle with the last lingering guests. An hour, feeling more like two, passed.

Catam waited calmly while Isa twitched, nervous and impatient. The last pair of voices faded and he shot to full attention. He heard a transport fire up and depart.

"The last guest just left," he informed Isa, and she sat up, peering through the vines.

Daarna and Arnath reappeared on the patio and moved deeper into the garden, both looking pleased with themselves. Moonlight chose that moment to shine over the estate, illuminating everything but the deepest recesses of the maze and its center.

"We did it, love," Daarna crowed and toyed with Arnath's neckpiece. She unraveled the blue silk from his throat and wrapped it around her fist.

"Yes, I did," Arnath said arrogantly. He bent his head to Daarna and brushed a kiss over her lips. "You did a wonderful job showing your support, Lady Klin." He bowed and Daarna smiled, though Catam thought her eyes looked hard. Apparently she hadn't cared for Arnath's "I did" comment.

Trouble in paradise? Isa could only be so lucky. But at least the kiss confirmed her story, that Arnath and Daarna were in fact lovers.

"What's my reward to be then, Statesman Bedenzi?"

Arnath opened his mouth to answer but closed it in a snap when a young man joined them.

"What is it, Mirk?"

Oblivious to the sexual undercurrents in the garden, Mirk rattled off a slew of compliments and after-action notes Arnath needed to follow come the next morning. Daarna looked irritated. Arnath's annoyance, however, faded at the glowing descriptions of himself.

Once Mirk took a breath, Daarna spoke in a queenly voice. "Well, gentlemen, I've had a long day. I thank you for your assistance tonight, Mirk. I don't know what the statesman would have done without your help."

Mirk beamed.

"No, thank *you*, Lady Klin." Arnath bowed and placed a chaste kiss on her hand. "You have been instrumental in guiding me through this first and most difficult phase of adjustment. Your husband's contacts will assuredly improve my success in the district."

Daarna nodded.

"Now, Mirk, please go and get some rest. Lady Klin? Might I take a final look at your late husband's file on the Border properties? I promise, that's the last I'll ask of you this night."

Mirk smiled and bid them goodnight. Once he left the garden, Arnath escorted Daarna into the house with a polite but much more aloof manner.

"We're not the only ones still awake out here," Isa commented in a low voice. "I know this household. Once those two head inside, the servants will spend another few hours cleaning up this mess and straightening the house before tomorrow. My bet is that by quarter morn, we should be okay to break into the house."

Catam agreed. "Sounds like a plan. Until then, let's get some rest. I'll take first watch."

As he studied her, he couldn't help comparing her to the pampered women of Nebe6. He couldn't imagine Sharell traipsing through the Eron Forest or hiding out in the shadows of the northern province.

"What?" Isa shot him a wary look.

"It just amazes me that someone as beautiful and sexy as you makes a living breaking into people's homes. It's dangerous work, when you could be doing something much more *pleasurable* and making hand over fist doing it."

She blushed, understanding "pleasurable" to mean sex sharing, as he'd intended.

"But I realize why you don't work flat on your back, so to speak." He grinned. "You might not be frigid, Isa, but you're sure as hell not pleasurer material." Her face fell and he continued. "You're too warmhearted for that."

She stared at him in surprise and opened her mouth as if to speak, then shook her head and lay back, closing her eyes.

"Wake me to take watch," she mumbled and drifted into a light sleep.

Curiosity burned. He wanted to know what she would have said, but she didn't move, her breathing slow and even.

Chapter Seven

Catam sat back against a tree, nestled with Isa in the comforting shelter of the furen thicket. Using his acute senses of smell and hearing, he remained attuned to their surroundings while gazing at Isa's peaceful features.

She had some issues with her sensuality, not a surprise considering how awkward she would feel among the Aran people. Arans prized sexuality. They practiced sex with multiple partners, gender and race nonspecific.

A respected trade, pleasuring was considered an art form on Aran. And though not all Aran women necessarily became pleasurers, an Aran woman uncomfortable with her sexuality would be unique indeed.

For his part, Catam rarely had the chance to visit Mardu's pleasure moon. On those days when Mara let her crew "relieve some stress," as she liked to call it, they frequented

Nebe6. For one thing, the pleasure planet sat in the center of the System, and for another, the Fas brothers loved the place.

Keeping Raggas happy took precedence over a lowly Mardu. His lips curled. He had speed and agility, but Set and Nu definitely had the edge in the strength department. Rockheads, the both of them, he thought with warm amusement.

Shipmates easily became family when one spent as much time with them as Catam did, and he genuinely liked his crewmates.

Thinking of his crew turned his thoughts to his real family, in particular his brother Sernal.

Catam had last reported to Sernal two days ago. He briefly mentioned Isa's capture and added a vague excuse of some "planetary-related delays." If Sernal knew why Catam hadn't yet brought Isa to justice, he'd pitch a fit.

Sernal always played by the rules, a fact that both amused and appalled Catam, the most rebellious member of his family.

No, Sernal would definitely not approve of Catam's intimacies with Isa, no matter how right they felt. And this "investigation" Catam pressed would not be appreciated either.

Reminders of his rebellion made him content enough to sit idly, waiting for the estate to settle. Isa's breathing hitched and he placed a comforting hand on her cheek to soothe her worries.

"Soon, sweet," he whispered and leaned down to place a kiss on her forehead. "Soon we'll have some answers, and if we're lucky, they'll be the right ones."

He ignored the sudden pain he felt at thoughts of Isa leaving him to undertake another job, or worse, Isa imprisoned in Jintak. Instead he focused on the sounds of servants scurrying inside the house.

But much as he wanted, he couldn't stop pondering the future. Once they found the answers Isa needed, he would return to the life he knew aboard Mara's ship. Bounty hunting was his calling, and he accepted it.

Why then did the thought depress him?

And Isa, well, if she didn't see the inside of a prison cell because of her "part" in Klin's death, she would most likely return to a life of crime.

With her given profession, it was only a matter of time before the law caught her. Sooner or later, she would visit Jintak's prisons.

Terrible things happened in prison. Images of her future jailers mistreating, perhaps raping her, had him seeing red. And what if the next peacemaker on her tail believed in death over imprisonment, a common problem among Mardu's lawmen? What if one of those more enthusiastic peacekeepers felt forced to kill her in the name of justice?

His thoughts grew steadily darker and he cursed his rabid imagination.

What was wrong with him?

He forced himself to remember that his world normally rotated on a "happily ever after" axis. Mentally listing the positives, he noted that the restlessness he faced daily had been nothing more than a phase. Since taking Sernal's place and meeting Isa, his boredom had faded altogether.

Another positive: incredible sex. The sex with Isa was on a scale beyond anything he'd ever experienced. Finding wainu with her definitely put him on a higher plain toward happiness.

Why then, when he'd recently attained a level closer to true joy, did thoughts of a future without Isa leave him feeling miserable? He scoffed at the notion she might be more important than this mission for Sernal. So they'd had sex, what of it?

*He* controlled his world and those he allowed close. *He* would choose a woman to be his mate, someday in the *far, far* future.

Mate? He shook his head. Where had these deep thoughts come from? He still had a mission to complete, and a woman's future to decide. He glanced down at Isa shifting restlessly under his regard. Sleep troubled her, and he wondered what she dreamed.

The more time he spent with Isa, the more he liked her. Sure, she had a sensuality that made him see stars with very little effort. More than that, Isa's quick wits impressed him. Her ability to push herself beyond her fear earned his respect.

He thought about those qualities and finally had to admit what he'd been thinking for the past few days.

"Shit. You didn't kill him, did you?" he asked quietly of her sleeping form. She hadn't killed anyone, and that meant the two of them were in for a world of trouble once the estate finally quieted.

*Trouble.* He had to laugh. *Trouble* should have been his middle name. He lived for it, borrowed it, and occasionally personified it with a capital "T," much like his sleeping quarry.

He studied Isa's full lips that suddenly curved into a small smile as she slept. It looked like they might very well have more in common than he'd first thought.

\* \* \* \*

Isa woke with a headache and an urge to wipe that sexy grin off Catam's mouth. By Flor's heart, did the man ever find anything less than amusing?

For the past four days he'd teased, tantalized and made her near crazed with lust and laughter. She'd never had such pleasure in a man's company, both in and out of her clothing.

Now, however, was not the time for amusement. While he might see the humor in everything, awareness of their dire situation had overwhelmed her subconscious, lending to less than pleasant dreams.

She felt more tired now than before her nap. Behind closed lids, images vacillated between eternal imprisonment in Jintak and Catam, naked and aroused.

In one scene, dead Statesman Klin pointed a finger at her, his throat slit and his belly gushing blood as he presided over her judgment. Inevitably, a biased jury of politicians would sentence her to jail, where she'd suffer hideous torment forever.

In the next scenario, Catam made love to her with an intensity that left her breathless. His catlike eyes would glow with sensual fervor as he licked her from head to toe. And his cock would strain against her mound before penetrating her, salving the wounds of aloneness and a lacking sexuality that too often lived within her.

"Isa?" His deep voice soothed and he leaned over to help her to her feet. "Bad dreams?"

She wanted to laugh out loud at his uncanny ability to read her, but managed a tight nod. If she started laughing, she'd probably never stop.

"The estate seems at rest. I thought we should go in now."

She frowned. "Why didn't you wake me to take watch?"

"You looked like you needed the rest." He shrugged and his full mouth tilted at the corners. "Besides, I like watching the rise and fall of your breasts in sleep."

She wanted to chastise him for saying so, but the warm glint in his eyes finally penetrated her morose mood and she found herself smiling. "You're impossible."

"I aim to please." He bowed. "Since you're familiar with the land, I'll follow you." He pretended to peer around her and wiggled his eyes at the vicinity of her backside.

Isa shook her head and choked back a laugh. Once again he lightened her state of mind with his mere presence.

She crept through the garden, keeping to the shadows, her mind half on the task at hand while the remainder of her thoughts dwelled on the sensual man at her heels.

As she snuck through a window left ajar and entered the house, she wondered how different this situation might have turned out had Catam not been the one seeking her.

Most peacemakers would have brought her to justice immediately, or worse, brought her to Lady Klin, her accuser, before taking her to Jintak. Though a common policy to bring together accuser and accused prior to trial, peacemaker "justice" normally spelled trouble for the one under investigation. And in Isa's case, she felt sure death would have been waiting.

"Now what?" Catam asked, and Isa realized she'd been standing behind the floor-to-ceiling draperies in the hallway outside the hidden corridor that led to the study.

How eerily familiar.

She took a deep breath and turned down the corridor. Pointing to the first door they passed, she informed him, "This is the room where I hid, where I accidentally overheard Daarna and Arnath having sex."

He nodded and eyed the room as they continued down the seldom-used hall past several other rooms. The hallway ended at a large red door.

"And this leads to the study where I found Klin." She swallowed nervously, not wanting to reenter the dead man's last resting place.

Catam cocked his head and his eyes blazed. She still couldn't wait to hear his explanation for that. "It sounds quiet. The room's empty. Let's go."

Isa slowly turned the doorknob. Thankfully it was locked, reassuring her what Catam said was true. She skillfully unlocked the door using a set of tools that never left her side, then entered the room without making a sound. Catam quietly closed the door behind them, enshrouding them in darkness.

Completely black, the room felt more like a tomb than a study. Isa cautiously eased her way toward the desk when a light snapped on, blinding her. She froze in fear of discovery, and cursed Catam and his entire lineage to blazes when she saw him near a desk lamp.

"It's okay. I made sure both doors are locked. I'll hear anyone that comes near enough to either door to discover us," he tried to reassure her.

She clenched her jaw and managed to hit him in the stomach only once. "Next time, warn me first."

He choked and rubbed his belly, giving her a hard glare for her efforts.

Oddly enough, his soured mood restored hers enough to smirk. "Right then. I'll look through his desk to see if I can find anything. You check the rest of the room."

They began searching the study, looking for anything to link Daarna or Arnath to the statesman's murder. Isa didn't believe either suspect stupid enough to leave the evidence in plain sight, much as she might hope otherwise.

"My brother left me a file on this case," Catam said quietly as he searched. "The information I have on Daarna looks quite damning, especially when paired with what you told me."

Isa stopped and stared at him. "So you do believe me?"

"I wouldn't be in here otherwise."

Warmth unfurled within her. Finally, someone actually believed in her innocence! Even her own family hadn't trusted her enough to let her hide with them on Aran.

"What exactly led you to believe I didn't do it?" She wanted to know what Catam saw that her own flesh and blood missed.

He stopped searching the statesman's bookshelves and stared at her with an intensity that made her uncomfortable. "There's just something about you, Isa, that makes me believe in you."

A moment of silence descended on the study, and the two stared at each another with puzzled fascination.

"Thank you." She bit her lower lip, wanting to say more.

Catam's eyes blazed and focused on her lips. Before she could say anything, his expression froze, his eyes turning from sensuous to wary. "Someone's coming. Move, quickly."

He doused the lights and dragged her to the opposite door from which they'd entered. She didn't hear anyone but trusted his instincts. After turning through several corridors to dodge random servants, they entered into a dimly lit hallway.

He dragged her to a halt and ran a hand through his hair in frustration. "Do you know where we are?"

She nodded. "This should be the guest wing, according to Harron's iffy map. I didn't get a chance to see it in detail before, because I was running for my life from the thrells. Speaking of which," she murmured uneasily and looked around her.

"They're not here. Obviously Daarna wasn't expecting us tonight." His teeth gleamed in the shadows.

"Funny. Why don't we--"

He clapped a hand over her mouth and shoved her inside a nearby door that was, thankfully, unlocked. Then he dragged her to a large closet and threw them both inside, cracking the door almost to a close before the door to the bedroom opened.

"What the hell is taking her so long?" Arnath muttered to himself as he turned on a lamp and began undressing.

"It's Arnath," Isa whispered.

"I know. Shush."

Isa glared at the breath brushing her cheek. The closet, though narrow, held enough space for the two of them to comfortably stand one behind the other. Isa stood in front of Catam, able to peer through the narrow crack between the door and frame. She could feel him pressing against her back as he tried to peer over her head into the room.

"Why do you think he's still up?" she whispered again, ignoring Catam's order to be quiet.

"I have a bad feeling we're soon going to find out."

Sure enough, Daarna Klin entered the room and locked the door behind her. Arnath removed the last article of his clothing and stood completely nude. Much as Isa hated to admit it, he made an impressive vision of lean muscle with a full, heavy arousal.

"Oh no," Isa groaned. "Not again."

"What?" Catam whispered.

"The last time I was here I had to wait hours until these two finished coupling. What is it with my timing?"

She felt his body shake with laughter. She didn't see anything the least bit humorous about being trapped in the closet. In fact, the more she thought about it, the more she realized how foolish she had been to enter Klin's home in the first place. She should never have trusted Harron to begin with.

Catam interrupted her self-castigation, jolting her body to awareness. He nuzzled her neck and nipped her ear, sending a shiver of heat straight to her loins.

"Do you like Arnath's cock?" he murmured in a sexy rumble, shocking her with his question.

"What?"

"Look at him, Isa. And look at Daarna."

Daarna slowly disrobed and stood facing Arnath, her hands circling her lush breasts.

"We have all night, love," Daarna teased Arnath and placed one hand over her mound, sliding her fingers through her dark brown curls. He groaned his approval and began stroking himself, urging her to continue.

Isa's breath caught. Before, watching Daarna and Arnath play hadn't been the least arousing. But now, with Catam breathing down her neck, his warmth flush against her, every action Daarna and Arnath shared seemed like foreplay between her and Catam.

"Watch how she touches herself." Catam licked her neck. "See how Arnath's cock swells? That's what you do to me, sweet."

She could feel evidence of Catam's arousal thrusting against her hip.

"Catam?" she whispered. Much as it should have disgusted her, she couldn't help feeling turned on by Arnath and Daarna's sexuality, especially since it sparked Catam's arousal.

"Shh. Just watch. And feel," he ordered.

Arnath let go of his thick cock to caress Daarna's breasts.

He grew rougher in his handling and Daarna cried out, begging for more. He answered by suddenly lifting her in his arms and striding to the bed. He dropped her there and spread her legs wide.

Isa's breath raced at the erotic image, coupled with Catam's roaming hands. With nimble fingers he eased her shirt free from her trousers, and within moments covered one breast in his callused palm.

She bit her lip and arched into his hand, silently begging his fingers to tug on the nipple that tightened with need. Instead he teased her, letting the full weight of her globe rest in his palm.

In the room, Arnath buried his face in Daarna's pussy, causing the woman to cry out her delight. Arnath lifted his head to shush her, and Isa felt Catam's smile against her neck.

"You women are so loud," he teased before unfastening her trousers. "Try to keep quiet while I get a better feel for your needs."

She heard him chuckle but felt some small satisfaction when he found her wet and needy, for he groaned. He began stroking her clit, his fingers no longer teasing but hard and pressing with intent.

"Catam, it's too much," she forced herself to whisper and again bit her lip to keep from crying out loud.

"No sweet," he rasped and removed his hand, only to free his cock from its confines. His other hand left her breast and then he was positioning her, bracing her hands against the doorframe. "It's not enough."

## Chapter Eight

Catam clenched his jaw and called on his last reserve of patience. He wanted nothing more than to ram his cock into Isa's wet little sheath. Instead he slowly filled her, pressing deeper and deeper until he could go no further.

In this position he could clearly see Arnath eating Daarna's pussy like a last meal, and the image further aroused him. He all too easily imagined licking Isa's sweet cream with as much enthusiasm.

Isa gasped at their contact and he tugged her hips against his, flexing within her.

"Yes," he hissed when she unconsciously pressed harder against him, taking him in even further. Her tight, hot pussy tensed around him and he fought the urge to come right then. "Isa, sweet, I want to fuck you so hard," he admitted in a groan and began moving.

He slowly withdrew, the friction incredibly erotic, before plunging hard and fast. He could see her hands gripping the doorframe in the darkness and he in turn clutched her hips, controlling her movements.

She fought to grind against him, but he would not allow it. He needed to make his claim, to mark her as irrevocably as she had marked him.

Pants and groans from the bedroom filled the silence and Catam felt safe allowing Isa's small moans, muffled by the door and Daarna's loud responses.

"More, Arnath! I need your cock, now!"

Isa seemed to echo the cry by lifting her hips to take Catam deeper. Her pussy clenched around his cock, and he knew he wouldn't last much longer.

"I'm going to give it to you, Isa. No more waiting," he whispered and licked at her ear. She shivered and his satisfaction rose another notch. Flor, but she responded so openly to his every touch.

One of his hands released her hip and sought her hard nub burning for release. He rolled her clit, pinched the sodden flesh between his thumb and forefinger, wishing he could lick her without breaking stride.

He continued to fuck her, Daarna's cries and Arnath's grunts spurring him on. He saw Arnath mount Daarna, his politician-white ass humping while he fucked Klin's widow. Then Catam closed his eyes and saw no more, fully enthralled with Isa's delectable body.

Her pussy gripped his cock and she strained against his fingers, desperate to come. Her arousal pushed his own, until he could feel his balls draw up, hardening to the point of pain. He was so close to release....

Daarna screamed, shattering the sounds of pleasure around them. Arnath soon followed, his scream shrill and surprisingly effeminate.

Catam noted this while continuing to pump, determined to distract his pleasure until he'd seen to Isa's. He didn't have long to wait.

He pinched her clit harder, the pressure pushing her past her limits. She stiffened and let out a gasp as her body tensed.

She clenched around him like a vise and he thrust faster, deeper. "Fuck," he gasped, unable to stop himself. "I'm coming, sweet. Oh yes." His breath left him as he shot hard, drenching her womb.

They remained locked like that for a moment, oblivious to Daarna and Arnath, to the world around them.

Catam basked in wainu, and more, he basked in Isa's very presence. Her scent, the sweet, untamed spice of sex and wildness, wrapped around him in a mantle of affection. He felt closer to her at this moment than ever before, and he struggled through the wearying contentment of wainu to understand why.

The danger of exposure, the risk of mating with a woman who could bring him to bliss so easily, the life-threatening circumstances surrounding their relationship, perhaps those factors enhanced the bonds between them rather than a true and honest affection.

Yet, he couldn't quite let go of the fact that he wanted her again, now. He wanted her spread before him. He wanted to lick her sweet pussy, to taste her spice and his mixed together. Even now the scent of their lovemaking overwhelmed him, and his softening cock stirred again.

"Oh, Catam," she murmured throatily. "You feel so good inside me."

Her words made him hard as stone and he breathed deeply, aware that Isa needed time to recover from the explosive orgasm he'd given her.

"You're still hard." She chuckled softly and tilted her hips, then pushed back against him.

Catam bit back a curse and stilled her movements, his hands fastened to her hips.

"Don't move, Isa, or I'll fuck you so hard you won't be able to sit for a week."

"I doubt I'll be able to sit now," she complained, her voice throaty. "I'm completely satisfied."

Her words frustrated him, but Catam reminded himself

his kind were unlike others. He withdrew from her body, still achingly hard. He didn't know why he felt such disappointment that Isa didn't want him right now. Hell, he shouldn't want her again so soon either, despite his Xema heritage. But she did something to him.

"What are you doing?" he asked when she suddenly turned around to face him.

"Brace your hands on the doorframe and be very, very quiet."

He tensed, confused and half-hoping she might actually want him again now.

"Relax, Catam," she teased, her voice sounding from the vantage of his naval, and moving steadily lower. "Watch Daarna and Arnath. Who knows? Maybe you'll learn a thing or two."

"Witch," he growled, and groaned when her mouth closed over him.

The feel of her lips around his cock felt like pure, unadulterated bliss. She tasted him with her tongue, and he knew she tasted herself as well. Up and down her tongue stroked, her lips suctioned to his shaft. She slid her mouth around him, testing his girth as it continued to grow.

By Flor's heart, he was near to bursting.

As if she could sense his desire, she paused and whispered, "Tell me what they're doing."

It took Catam a moment to recall that he and Isa were not alone, so far under her spell was he. He blinked and fisted one hand in Isa's silken hair, needing the contact to keep him focused. The urge to thrust deep, to feel her throat on the head of his prick, consumed him.

"They're cleaning each other," he began, his voice harsh with desire. "He's taking a rag over her pussy, thrusting it deep to clean out his seed."

Catam gasped and closed his eyes for strength when she sucked incredibly hard. Far from painful, it aroused him almost beyond measure.

"Continue," Isa ordered, enjoyment clearly on her mind as she licked his pulsing shaft.

"She," Catam swallowed when her tongue grazed his sack. "She's saying something I can't understand." With effort, he watched the naked couple chattering to themselves. Isa engulfed him again, sucking him deep.

He couldn't help himself. He tightened his hold on her hair and thrust further into her mouth.

She clenched his hips and forced him out, then drew him back inside her mouth, pulling his buttocks until the head of his shaft brushed her throat.

He cursed softly in four languages, determined to last.

"What are they doing now?" she asked around his cock.

"I want to see you," Catam whispered aloud his desire, lost to anything but Isa. "I want to see your lips closed around my cock. I want to see you when I come, to see you swallow all of me."

She groaned, a soft sound that reverberated around his cock, stimulating the already sensitive nerves to the point of pain.

He nearly begged her to end it. A Xema begging a woman, of all things!

"Arnath just stuck his dick in Daarna's mouth," he rasped, saying anything to regain a measure of control. "He's fucking her mouth now, in and out," he said as his own body followed his words. "She's swallowing him, all of him," he breathed.

Isa clutched his buttocks tighter and drew him inexorably deep.

Panting with the effort to keep from ramming into her throat, he tried to resist her pull when her tongue stroked the underside of his shaft just under the head.

Unable to stop, he thrust once, then twice, and finally came. She swallowed him greedily as his hands burrowed into her hair, holding her to him. Her lips robbed him of speech, and he almost collapsed on top of her, so satisfied he felt weak.

Groans and grunts sounded through the door, finding Catam's ears as he finally returned to his surroundings.

Isa remained on her knees, gradually letting his cock slide from her mouth. She licked him gently and let him fall limply against his groin before she straightened.

Standing so close to him, she couldn't help but notice his still ragged breathing. She smiled with satisfaction. Her thighs slid together as she fought for balance. Pleasuring Catam had made her wet, the taste and touch of his cock an aphrodisiac to her senses.

The man did something to her, something that made her

lose all reason. She should have been upset making love in a closet, in a *murderer's closet*, to be precise. But she could only feel contentment. She knew Catam had experienced the ultimate bliss.

His sweet cream had slid down her throat with ease, his taste the raw essence of him that she would never in her lifetime forget.

"Isa," Catam said in a low voice. She waited with curiosity for him to speak. He said nothing, however, and grabbed her in his arms, hugging her to him in a tight, secure grip.

Her heart melted. She would curse herself and her inability to separate the man from his job later. Right now she intended to revel in his affection. She hugged him back and smiled to herself when his hold tightened.

She had no memories like this to compare. With the other men in her life, she'd had disappointing sex, and always felt as though she'd missed something grander, more meaningful. Though she'd been lectured time and again by her mother that women didn't need orgasms to have good sex, Isa had never felt replete.

She did now.

Giving Catam back the pleasure he'd given her had been a wonderful gift, both for him and for herself. She'd been too sensitive after her orgasm for another one right away, but she'd felt Catam's hardness still within her. Pleasuring him had made her wet all over again.

Still, she felt just as connected with him now as she had after sharing mutual intercourse.

She sighed and glanced through the closet crack at the bedroom bathed in light, unfortunately aware that they had company and would for the better part of the night.

"I wish it weren't so tight in here," she whispered against his chest.

"I don't know," Catam drawled, satisfaction and humor lacing his words. "I kind of like the close quarters."

She told herself she wouldn't ask. She knew he'd enjoyed himself. "You liked it?"

"If I'd liked it anymore, I would have shouted down the house."

She let out a soft breath of relief and pulled back from his embrace, eager to change the subject. "Believe it or not, this waiting is exactly what happened to me the last time I paid this house a visit. Don't worry. We won't be here all night."

An hour later she crept out of the closet with Catam hard on her heels. They left the room as silently as they'd entered, Arnath and Daarna asleep and snoring.

"Lightweights," Catam muttered as they moved swiftly down the corridor away from the room.

"Lightweights? What? You could have gone another round?"

"Isa, despite the closet, if we'd had more time, I'd be fucking that sweet pussy of yours right now. Better yet, I'd be eating you, savoring every drop."

Isa blushed bright red and increased her pace.

He chuckled. "What? Too honest for you?"

She glanced back to find his gaze bright and engaging, a contented smirk lingering on his full lips and a swagger to his gait.

"That's my one regret about this job," he said.

"What?" She stopped and stared at him. He regretted being with her?

"I regret that I have yet to taste you. For all that we've done, we've yet to make love leisurely in a bed, where I can take my time licking you until you cream all over my lips."

His words made it hard to focus on anything but having Catam inside her again. Then footsteps sounded near and she started to awareness.

"Ah," she cleared her throat, "we'll have to do something about that then. Later." He chuckled. "Now stop distracting me. We need to get out of here before we're found. I think I know where to go to get the answers we need."

Catam nodded. "Fine. Then lead on, sweet."

His voice sounded gritty, and she knew he'd aroused not only her, but himself as well with his sex talk.

She grinned and increased her pace. There around the bend should be a servants' exit. Harron couldn't have sabotaged this entire map. She'd checked a clean copy of the Klin estate blueprints during her two week run from the law, and had found only one or two inconsistencies between the real map and Harron's.

They found the servants' exit and Isa heard Catam

mumble a thank you to Flor for seeing them out safely.

"Catam, never thank Flor until the job's done," she whispered. "You'll jinx us."

"Too late." Catam cursed and threw her through the exit door. "At least four thrells are coming, and they sound angry."

Isa and Catam broke into a run, snarls and grunts following them along the paved pathway around the house.

"We can't keep to the path," Isa gasped as Catam passed her. "Security will be waiting for us."

They turned a corner and not surprisingly, six men armed with phasers stood menacingly in the garden patio.

Catam slowed and stopped, his arms up in surrender.

"We're unarmed. Before you do anything, call off the thrells."

One of the men gave a shrill whistle and the thrells gaining on Isa and Catam broke off chase and joined the head handler.

He ordered all four beasts inside and left, leaving five men to guard Isa and Catam.

"Let's talk about this," Catam tried in an easy voice.

"Silence, thief," one of the men barked. "Uron, inform Lady Klin we've found the housebreakers. Keep it quiet. We don't want Statesman Bedenzi to know we have trouble here."

*As if Arnath won't know when they find him with Daarna,* Isa thought with a huff. She swallowed her alarm when the guards motioned for Catam and her to draw nearer.

Forced to move, they did so, until Catam stopped a few feet from them.

"I'm a peacekeeper. Check my papers." He opened his jacket slowly and nodded to an inside pocket.

One of the men laughed out loud. "Sure."

"No, really. I followed her," he nodded at Isa, "inside the house and had just captured her when someone released the thrells. Please, check my papers."

The lead guard nodded but kept a wary eye on Catam. "Sherf, search him."

Sherf found Catam's peacemaker papers and looked disappointed as he handed them to the lead guard.

"Catam of Mardu?" the lead asked.

"Yeah."

"I know your brother, Sernal. I didn't realize you had two peacemakers in the family."

"Why am I not surprised you know Sernal?" Catam distanced himself from Isa, lowering his hands as he walked calmly toward the guards.

They accepted him and Isa felt very much alone.

Catam chuckled at something one of the men mumbled and turned to leer at her.

"Sherf, much as I agree with you, I can't have you saying it out loud."

In the blink of an eye Catam laid Sherf out flat on his back, unconscious.

"Catam!" Isa cried worriedly. What was he thinking? He would get himself killed!

The lead guard gaped and redirected his phaser. "You traitor!" He began blasting.

Catam narrowly avoided a phaser pulse by ducking behind a nearby stone fountain. Then the attention turned back to Isa. She dove for cover too late to avoid a burning wound across her shoulder. "Catam, what are you doing?"

He laughed nearby, ducking when a shot would have struck him. "Saving your ass?"

She wanted to blister his hide for scaring her when he did it again. His lack of communication skills not withstanding, he could at least warn her to prepare for his stupidity.

She watched the man she'd made love with for the past several days turn into someone she didn't know in the slightest. His eyes became twin orbs of fire before he began to shimmer, fading from sight only to reappear a far distance away.

The guards fired at random all around, hoping to hit one of the 'Catams' dancing just out of reach. He laughed, an arrogant chortle that sent worry down Isa's spine.

One guard suddenly toppled to the ground. Isa blinked when his phaser found its way into her hands, *out of thin air*. She felt a brush against her cheek.

"Be careful," Catam whispered then vanished again.

Another guard fell, then another, until only the lead guard remained.

"Damn you," the guard shouted and fired haphazardly around him. "Show yourself."

"Okay." Catam shimmered to visibility behind the guard's

back and struck him in the neck. He caught the man and gently led him to the ground. "He's a friend of Sernal's. It'd be rude to let him drop to the rough ground," he explained in Isa's direction. "He might hurt himself."

Isa could only stare. Catam's eyes glowed, but no longer with the burning intensity he'd worn before he'd set storm to the guards. He looked positively thrilled, excited and pleased with himself all at once.

Isa clenched her jaw. "Let's get out of here. And don't think you're not going to explain this. You're in a lot of trouble, *Peacemaker*." She ignored the wounded look he shot her and stalked past the garden, back the way they'd come.

*It was a good thing he hadn't been killed. She wanted that job for herself.*


Chapter Nine

They spent the next few hours in silence, putting a healthy distance between Voran and Tekar, the northern territory where Isa hoped to find Cheltam. According to Feltang, Cheltam was her best hope for information.

Right now, however, she wanted anything but information. She wanted Catam's stupid, prideful, macho head on a platter. She jerked at a low-lying branch and grimaced at the pain that shot through her arm.

Her shoulder throbbed. The blood pooling from the wound had matted onto her jacket, and the fabric now clung to her arm. Fortunately, the jacket masked the wound, leaving no blood trail to their escape--an escape that almost hadn't occurred because someone thought he was invincible.

Unable to keep silent any longer, she swiftly turned and found Catam's gaze warm and full of humor.

"What the hell is wrong with you?" she seethed.

He looked shocked at her outburst. "What? What did I do?"

"What didn't you do? You didn't tell me what you were planning. You didn't use a lick of sense when you attacked a guard--in plain view of the others! You didn't seek cover until after they started shooting."

She opened her mouth to continue but Catam quickly bridged the distance between them and covered her lips with his hand.

"If I lift my hand will you stop harping already?"

He sounded exasperated, and she couldn't believe how dense he acted.

She bit his palm and he cursed, whipping his hand away. Her eyes bright, she admitted, "I was worried, you drun!"

His eyes narrowed and his lips thinned in displeasure.

"You could have been killed," she continued. "They fired everywhere, and only by Flor's grace did you escape unscathed. What the hell was that, anyway? I want my explanation, and I want it *now*!"

His gaze warmed. His golden eyes filled with an emotion she couldn't quite name, and he stared at her for a moment before his expression sobered.

"I'm sorry I worried you."

Tears threatened and Isa blinked rapidly to maintain some dignity. She'd be damned if she'd cry for the halfwit.

"I'm sorry, sweet," he repeated and embraced her in a tight hug.

The movement, thought comforting, brushed her shoulder and she couldn't contain a gasp of pain.

He quickly sat her back and held fast to her forearms, studying her. "Isa?" His eyes glowed and she knew he used that odd sense he possessed to enhance his vision. His gaze lingered on her shoulder and he cursed, loudly and creatively. "Why the hell didn't you tell me you'd been wounded?"

He sounded panicked, completely opposite of the arrogant warrior who battled and defeated five security guards. "Isa? I need to see the wound."

He handled her with the utmost gentleness, but still she shrieked when he peeled the jacket from her arm. No longer encrusted with blood, the wound oozed and throbbed painfully.

"Isa, this has the beginnings of an infection." His voice calm, Catam worked to force the worry from his tone. Her arm didn't look healthy, and the wound held a distinct stench of decay that his keen senses detected. Only two hours had passed since she'd received the laceration, but every second in their less than sanitary surroundings counted.

He needed to take her to a physician. But they had at least another few hours before they reached civilization. And considering the incident with the guards at the Klin estate, by now he, along with Isa, had a bounty on his head.

By Flor's dagger! He fumed as he studied her arm and knew it had to hurt.

"I wish you had told me about this earlier," he muttered as he studied the deep blast. The phaser should have seared the wound, burning any infection. But he recalled Isa rolling on the ground in her haste to duck the guards, and who knew what now contaminated her blood?

"It'll be fine. Leave it." She tried to take her arm back but Catam refused to let go.

Worry gnawed at him, an unfamiliar emotion he'd only recently experienced with his brother Gar. Gar, he reasoned, just needed time to deal with his grief. But if Catam didn't do something for Isa, he feared she might not have the time to deal with her troubles.

Coming to a decision, one he prayed he wouldn't regret, he decided to turn to those he trusted. He reached into his jacket and retrieved his com device.

"What are you doing?" Isa asked.

He ignored her and waited for someone to answer his signal.

"*Mara's Light*," Lurin Vez's voice returned over the com device. "How may I help you?"

"Lurin, it's Catam." He ignored Isa's whispered oath to disconnect. "I have a situation here and I need some help, some *discreet* help." He paused and nodded at Lurin's suggestion. "Fine. I know the place. We'll be there as soon as possible." He hung up to find Isa looking livid.

"How could you do that? I'm wanted by everyone in Mardu. I'm worth ten thousand beks to anyone who brings me in! Do you really think your friends won't succumb to that kind of temptation?"

Catam grinned. "Sweet, you have no idea the temptation Lurin lives with on a daily basis. Captain Mara is, well ... you'll see when you meet her."

"*Captain Mara?*" Isa's eyes shot green fire and Catam

delighted in the possessive streak curling her fingers into tight fists.

"Relax Isa, she's my boss, my real boss."

Isa's eyes flared to a darker green and she cursed him to eternal impotence. He flinched at the thought.

"You're bringing bounty hunters to help us? You must be crazy!" she continued to rage when he dragged her in a new direction.

*Yeah, crazy*, he thought glumly as he toted the screeching woman, *crazy in love*.

* * * *

Nu, Set and Lurin stared with approval at Isa marching stiffly in front of Catam, a long jacket folded over his arm. When she saw the three men waiting by a shuttle outside the pleasure club, she turned and colorfully cursed the Mardu to eternal damnation.

"I like her already," Nu murmured, earning a grin from his brother.

"She's got a mouth on her as nice as that body," Set commented with a sly wink.

Catam's head shot up, surprising Lurin that at such a distance the Mardu heard the comment. Catam glared at them and dragged the woman the rest of the distance to meet them.

"She sure looks tasty," Lurin drawled and felt a surge of furious possession emanating from Catam, as the Mardu shifted to stand protectively between the men and his "gracious" companion.

"Thanks for coming," Catam said in a growl. His voice sounded harsh, but his hands were gentle on the woman. "This is Isa, and she needs some help."

"I need my head examined, traveling with you," she grumbled.

"We can arrange that too," Lurin said, choking back laughter at Catam's glare.

"That's Nu and Set, and this is Lurin, my captain's husband," Catam introduced them casually, a curious emphasis on Lurin's relation to Mara.

Lurin laughed, pleased with Catam's jealousy. He clapped the man on the back and with Nu and Set, led the escapees to the shuttle. "You're in luck, Isa. We happened to bring along a physician friend of my wife's."

"I don't know why we need the help. My arm's not that bad."

Lurin sensed her pain and would have merged to ease some of it if Catam hadn't proven so prickly over the female. Lurin's kind, the Thesha, could control the female mind. But sensing to do so would push Catam in a direction the Mardu wasn't ready to go, Lurin left the woman alone.

"Actually your arm looks infected," Set remarked and drew nearer to study it.

Nu closed the shuttle doors behind them and within moments the shuttle left Mardu behind and entered space. Lurin watched as Catam glared Set away from the woman, then led her to the physician waiting with her kit in the back of the craft.

While the doctor fixed Isa's shoulder, Lurin pulled Catam aside to learn more about the situation. The stubborn Mardu turned to face him, but refused to budge more than an arm's length from the woman.

"So Catam, is there some specific reason you called on us instead of your brother for help? Not that we mind, but this was his mission in the first place."

Catam sighed. "I didn't want to call you at all. But Isa's arm needs attention. I can't contact Sernal because I'm already late bringing her in." He paused and glanced behind him at Isa.

"And?" Lurin's eyes narrowed as he studied Catam's face. "I know when you're holding back. Let's have all of it. What else is going on that we should know about?"

"Nothing--"

"And don't tell me nothing because Mara specifically told me not to return to the ship without answers."

"You don't really take orders from your own wife, do you?" Catam scoffed.

Lurin raised one brow in answer. "You know Mara. You've taken orders from her for years. What do you think?" Lurin recalled the last set of orders he'd taken from his wife involving strips of silk and a jar of sylvan sweets.

"You've got that look on your face." Catam grimaced. "Forget I asked."

Lurin crossed his arms and waited.

"Fine. You win." Catam bit his lip. "But you cannot pass this to Sernal."

"Agreed."

"Lurin, you're new to the bounty hunting business but even you can see that life isn't always black and white."

"Tell me about it. I distinctly recall telling you and the others I was innocent. Yet you still put me in chains and imprisoned me aboard your ship."

"Exactly my point," Catam emphasized. "Certain evidence pointed to your guilt, yet Mara and myself sensed your innocence."

"Mara and *you*?" Annoyance crept over Lurin at memories of the harrowing experience. "My wife was the one who believed in my innocence. I don't recall your help until the very end."

Catam waved that aside and replied in low voice so as not to be overheard, "You Thesha have always been too sure of yourselves. Hell, I knew what you were the moment we picked you up. Had the ship not been hijacked, I'd have set the captain on the right trail to freeing you, and without giving away your secret."

"It's a moot point now." Mara knew firsthand the gifts of the Thesha. Lurin didn't worry she would ever betray him. He trusted her completely. For the most part he trusted Catam to be as trustworthy. It helped that the Mardu now needed *his* help, cementing their bond even further.

"Yeah, well, I'm digressing." Catam blew out a breath. "The point is, your situation and Isa's are very similar. Just as you were falsely accused, so was she. And Sernal isn't in a position as a peacemaker to open a new investigation, not without going through the proper channels. By the time he can get through those channels, Isa will be dead."

Catam sobered after uttering those words, and Lurin saw how very much the thought bothered him. Interesting.

For the past year, working with Mara's crew had been an eye-opening experience. The Fas brothers proved amusing and tenacious, strong in resolve and in physical toughness. He'd enjoyed watching them work. The Raggas normally brought their bounties in through sheer force alone.

Catam of Mardu, on the other hand, worked in a completely different manner. Using innate charm and a keen sense of wit, he cajoled and convinced his bounties to turn themselves in. His affable nature often caused others to overlook his fighting skills. When charm didn't work, however, as in the case of Rantak Borsham, Catam stalked his prey like an ancient Xema warrior. Lurin thought the man's abilities were truly a wonder to behold.

Lurin had seen the Xema train, but he'd never actually seen a Xema warrior in battle. Unlike the Raggas, the Xema relied on their stealth, on their agility and extraordinarily quick reactions. The blurring, distorting techniques Catam often used to confuse his quarry were astonishing.

"Lurin?"

Lurin realized he'd been staring at Catam long enough to cause questions. "Sorry. You were saying?"

"Dammit, pay attention here." Catam's eyes narrowed in anger, an odd occurrence for the normally even-tempered Mardu. "Isa's life is on the line. She's being framed for a murder she didn't commit."

Lurin scowled. He knew that scenario only too well. "Sernal copied us on the file. If Isa didn't kill the statesman, then who did?"

"Lady Klin and Arnath Bedenzi," Isa answered in a loud voice. Her eyes burned with anger and a hint of fever.

Lurin thought the fever explained her incredible accusation. "You're kidding, right?"

"No, she's not." Catam shook his head. Then he turned and ran a finger over the blue, shiny material covering her shoulder. "Does it still hurt?"

"No. Meyrna gave me something for the pain. She said the quer bandage should heal the wound by tomorrow."

"Good." Catam's face relaxed in relief, and Lurin couldn't help smirking at how the mighty Mardu had fallen.

"What are you grinning at?" Catam asked, puzzled.

"Not a thing. I just think it's quite a coincidence how alike my situation is to Isa's." He turned to Isa. "That's how I met my wife, you know. She captured me and never let me go."

Lurin looked directly from Isa to Catam and waited for his meaning to sink in. Not soon after he spoke, Isa blushed and refused to look at Catam.

"I, uh, I need to ask Meyrna a few more questions." She deliberately pulled the physician a good distance away.

Catam waited until she was out of earshot. "What the hell was that about?"

"You really don't know?" Lurin waited for Catam to refute him, but he didn't. The Mardu looked thoughtful, then he frowned.

"Things are complicated, Lurin. It's not as easy as admitting the words."

"It's a start." Lurin leaned closer. "Don't make the mistake I made. I almost waited too late to see the truth. Open yourself to the possibilities, Catam."

"But my life is on *Mara's Light*. I'm a bounty hunter. That's what I do."

"Why?"

"Why?" Catam sputtered. "Because I was bred to track, to hunt. I'm not like my brothers. I'm no peacemaker."

"Fine. But why can't you and Isa have a future?"

"She's a criminal, Lurin. Sooner or later she'll have a bounty hunter after her. And it can't always be me. Or worse, she'll have another peacemaker on her tail."

Lurin saw the hurt cross his face before Catam cleared his expression. "Catam, you're not thinking clearly."

"Unfortunately, I am. Look, I appreciate the help, Lurin. Now I need to check on Isa," he said and quickly joined her by the physician.

Lurin sighed and shook his head. Catam had seemed an intelligent man. Why was it the moment a woman entered the picture, rational thought suddenly vanished? Ah love, he thought as he studied the pair standing close together. True love's path might cross and even diverge, but The End state would eventually be the same.

Lurin stared hard at the woman and tempted her to *see* him. She continued to nod at the physician, her leg brushing Catam's. She didn't react at all to his mental probe.

Interesting. Very interesting.

## Chapter Ten

Four hours later, Catam and Isa stood in Isa's new room on board *Mara's Light*.

"It was really nice of my captain to lend you a room while

you're recuperating," Catam said calmly, willing Isa to stop her nervous pacing.

She frowned at him and continued to walk around the room, checking for listening devices, hidden monitors and anything else that might turn a dark light on his crewmates.

He sighed with exasperation. "By Flor's dagger, Isa! It's been several hours already. Don't you think if they meant to get a bounty from you, we'd have drifted closer to Jintak in the west, instead of hovering over the north?" He nodded pointedly toward the portal.

She glanced over her shoulder and stared at the outline of the northern province against Mardu's ocean.

"I'll grant you the room is nice," she said with a brief glance at the bed. "But I'd much rather be in Tekar talking to Cheltam right now."

"Instead of being cooped up in a bedroom with me?" he asked with his usual charm. He kept his tone lighthearted, but his body thrummed at thoughts of Isa and a bed.

For the past week he'd taken her in the forest, against a tree, and in a closet. Having a bed available conjured delightful thoughts of Isa naked, thighs spread wide to surrender her sweetest offering.

His cock swelled at the thought.

"I'm still waiting to hear your explanation about what happened in the garden yesterday." She cleared her throat, her voice not as angry as he might have expected. That she strove to maintain eye contact told him she'd noticed his arousal.

*Good. Let the anticipation build until she's dripping wet for me.*

He loosened his shirt and her eyes widened. Sitting on a nearby chair, he waited until she stopped pacing to begin. She sat on the bed and he wanted to grin with satisfaction.

"I told you I'm Mardu," he began, "specifically I'm Xema."

"And that means...?"

"That means I can do what other men can't." His gaze lingered over her breasts, pleased when her nipples perked through her shirt. His eyes rose to see her blush and he smiled. "I have an ability, through heavy training and my bloodline, to enhance my senses. My sight, hearing and sense of smell are magnified when I 'turn on,' for lack of a better term, my abilities."

"The glowing eyes thing?"

He nodded. "Yes. My training also accounts for the blurring, that near-invisible trick I pulled on those guards at the Klin estate." He stared at her, serious now. "I wasn't taking on more than I could handle, Isa."

"Five men at once? With phasers?" She seemed incredulous.

"Five men with phasers," he affirmed. "My kind live for the challenge, the thrill of the hunt. That's why I make such a good bounty hunter. It's my nature, Isa. The guards at the estate became a challenge, and while I admit I enjoyed the skirmish, I should never have put you in harm's way." He stared down at his feet before letting her see the guilt in his eyes. "I'm so very sorry you were injured. I should have moved you out of the way before I attacked."

Her posture relaxed and he thought her anger might have abated. "But *you* were in harm's way."

"No. I'm completely aware of my limitations." He stood, finished discussing, finished explaining. "And I'm also aware of my skills in certain areas."

"What areas?" she asked in a breathy voice. Her eyes deepened to forest green, reminding him of the moss bed where he'd first made love to her.

"Oh," he said as he approached her, "I'm a skilled tracker." He removed his shirt and toyed with the collar of hers. "I move quickly." With nimble fingers he removed her shirt and stared down hungrily at her flushed breasts. "And I never stop going after what I want."

He undressed in a hurry and removed the rest of her clothing. Then he startled a gasp from her with the quickness of his sensual attack. One minute he stood in front of her, the next he had her flat on her back in the bed.

"You're fast." She welcomed him into her arms.

"Not always," he murmured with a grin and bent to kiss her.

The shock of oneness he felt when his lips touched hers no longer surprised him, and he reveled in their intimacy. Heat burned where they touched. She lit a fire in his belly, a need that went far beyond the physical. When she arched into his questing hands and greedily welcomed his tongue in her mouth, he couldn't help longing for the moment to last.

He teased her tongue, caressing her flesh until she moaned and arched into him, wanting more. While he feasted on her mouth, he ran his palms along the sides of her body. Her curves fascinated him, soft and womanly, yet hard with muscle beneath. The body of a talented and lovely thief, one who'd stolen his heart.

He slipped his hands over her breasts and palmed their fullness, tweaking her nipples until they felt hard, burning into his chest and scoring twin paths of desire wherever they touched.

She moaned and twisted beneath him, and his shaft met moist warmth through her nest of curls.

"Please," she gasped and bucked, trying to force him inside her.

He ignored her plea and moved down her body, trailing his mouth over the heated flesh with a skill that left her moaning his name. He sucked and licked, leaving lovebites that were more pleasure than pain.

He laved her breasts, feasting on the rich mounds. Her nipples were like ripe berries, and he wanted to suck the fruits, to taste her sweet juice. He bit gently at the turgid peaks and blew to arouse her further, aroused in turn when she pleaded for more.

Every brush of his cock against her body sent his pulse skyrocketing. He could feel a wave of desire building as he nudged down her breasts to her navel.

Her smooth, ivory skin was tight and begged for his touch. Yet it was her scent that drew him further down.

He continued to kiss her belly while his hands slipped from her breasts to her hips, and lower. His slid his hands from her hips to the front of her thighs and back, running his palms around to cup her buttocks.

Then he slid his fingers further, between her taut cheeks to the wetness between her thighs. She moaned and spread her thighs wide.

"Yes, love, I'm going to give you what you need," he whispered, fascinated with her feminine perfume. The more he scented, the harder he grew. Already he felt harder than a pike, her every brush against his cock a measure of sweet pain.

Yet the scent of her, her very essence drew him. With a

prodding finger he slid past her buttocks to the wet core dripping with desire. He toyed and tested the extent of her need, pleased and further aroused when she coated his finger easily.

"Catam, I need you," she breathed and pressed harder on his finger.

He gave her what she desired and thrust the digit into her, delighting in her moan. Then he could wait no longer.

With his finger inside her and his other hand beneath her buttocks to lift her pelvis, he nosed through the dark 'v' of hair protecting her woman's fruit and found the sweet treasure he'd been searching for.

He closed his eyes and with a deliberate and full stroke, tasted what he'd been longing to find forever. She sobbed his name and pressed into his mouth, and he knew he'd found that heavenly plane without wainu.

His tongue lapped her cream, devouring her essence, and he grew drunk on the taste of her. Her ecstatic cries only added to his high and he began thrusting his finger in and out of her as he suckled her clitoris, nibbling at the hard nub.

"Catam, I'm going to come," she moaned and thrust against his tongue, arching uncontrollably into his touch.

"Yes," he rasped. "Come for me, love, let me taste you. You're so sweet, so spicy sweet." He groaned, unable to stop from pressing his sensitive cock against the bed.

Not wanting to come unless deep inside of her, he rose to his knees to free his cock from any touch but air. He buried his face in her pussy and licked her again and again, not getting enough of her.

He pleasured her clit until he knew she could take no more. Then he sucked hard, one long, last time, and she came.

She spasmed and cried out, and he felt a wash of sweetness hit his mouth. Moaning, he continued to lick until he could wait no longer.

On the edge, he grasped his cock lightly, only enough to guide into her. With one deep thrust he joined her. Her contractions, her scent, and her taste merged to drive him mad.

He pumped mindlessly, enraptured in her soft texture, and then he came, exploding into her with a force that made him dizzy. Pleasure washed over him as she continued to come, milking him of everything.

He poured everything into her, crushing her under him and unable to stop himself. But she didn't seem to mind. She clenched his hips with her thighs and wrapped her ankles around his waist.

When he could, he looked down and saw her eyes shut tight, heard her breathing as labored as his. One final contraction pulsed around him and then she relaxed.

"Oh, baby," she gasped. Her arms and legs fell to her sides, and she lay limp, completely drained.

Feeling the same, Catam rolled onto his back beside her and sighed, awash in the rapture only Isa could provide.

"Your taste," he paused to lick his lips, "is ambrosia. Sweet and spicy." He turned his head to see her smile, her eyes closed. "I'm afraid it's going to be addicting."

She chuckled, a weak sound that hinted at sleep. "I hope so. I've never experienced that before, but I want to do it again."

"Never?" He stared at her in surprise.

She kept her eyes closed and he saw a blush stain her cheeks. "Never. I can't believe what I was missing."

"With me it only gets better," he teased, well aware he meant "only with me."

"We'll do it again, then. As soon as I wake up," she slurred before her breath evened and she fell asleep.

Catam turned to face her, tracing her features with his eyes. In repose she looked like an angel, a perfect woman with which to share the rest of his life.

Hovering in wainu, the thought didn't scare him. A life with Isa seemed predestined, and more, attainable. A dozen thoughts and possibilities presented themselves while he drifted in a haze of joy, until the possibilities became a plan of sorts.

He curled an arm around her, pleased when she turned and curled her backside into his groin. His cock stirred at the silken feel of her buttocks, but the immense pleasure in sex had taken its toll. He fell asleep holding her in his arms, dreams of the future and the past mixed into a blissful present.

\* \* \* \*

Isa snuggled deeper into the warmth surrounding her.

Catam's smell lingered and she inhaled, as if to take him into her lungs and spread him throughout the rest of her body.

She blinked at the light they'd forgotten to turn down and wondered how much time had passed. She felt remarkably relaxed, her arm didn't throb and her mind felt clear of worry or care.

Catam mumbled something against her neck and pulled her closer to him. She felt his erection brushing her bottom and smiled, remembering how amazing it felt to be kissed and caressed down there.

By Flor's heart, she'd never be able to look at Catam's mouth again without remembering how it felt against her folds, how that raspy tongue felt stroking her clit.

She squirmed at the remembrance and Catam surprised her by easing his stiff shaft inside her. The position was something she hadn't tried before, but thoughts left her as he began to pump. With one hand he pinched her nipples, and she closed her eyes, wanting to simply feel.

His breathing harsh against her neck, he thrust again and again while his fingers danced magic between her thighs. She came scant seconds before he did. Her body stiffened around his, and she could feel him pulse inside her. He came in great spurts and groaned her name before he finally relaxed.

"I can't get enough of you," he admitted in a gravelly voice. He nuzzled her neck and thrust one final time before withdrawing. "You get so wet for me."

She blushed, aware of how responsive she was and how needy that made her seem.

"And I love the way you blush." He chuckled. "Didn't I tell you before that if I had my way, I'd be fucking you every chance I could get?"

"You said something to that effect," she answered, embarrassed to feel so much loss once he pulled out.

How did he make her so needy? The more she had him, the more she wanted him. What did that mean?

"I can see your mind racing. What's wrong? Didn't I pleasure you enough?" he asked, sounding concerned.

"Enough?" She had to laugh. "Any more and I'd be unconscious. No," she lied, "just thoughts of Lady Klin and Statesman Bedenzi that won't go away."

He kissed her on the shoulder. "I talked to Lurin about that. I'm going to arrange a meet with Cheltam for us. Lurin said they'll drop us in Tekar. At least we'll be able to avoid Voran authorities for a while." He paused. "But it's only a matter of time before Sernal becomes agitated."

"Agitated?"

"My brother is a stickler for the rules. And on this mission I've bent more than my fair share."

Knowing he'd done so for her, she felt guilty. "I'm sorry if I've caused you trouble with your family."

He laughed, surprising her. "Isa, you're the first person I've met that causes as much trouble as me. No wonder I can't keep my hands off you." His smile turned into a grimace and he groaned. "Speaking of trouble, I was supposed to introduce you to Mara before we got so involved. Shit. I hope she's in a better mood than when we boarded."

Isa both dreaded and wanted to meet the woman Catam spoke about with such respect. Knowing the woman was married to Lurin, a man any woman would covet, should have put Mara beyond Isa's jealousy. Unfortunately, Isa's heart and mind conflicted over Catam's captain.

She and Catam dressed and left the room. They stopped first at the galley for a meal. While they walked, Isa envisioned a plain, stern woman that had somehow captured Lurin's eye. The woman captained a bounty ship, after all. How feminine could she be? Those thoughts made her feel progressively better ... until they entered the galley.

"Well, well. Catam. It's about damned time." A husky voice growled the less than pleasant greeting from behind them.

"Captain Mara," Catam began, oozing charm. "I was just telling Isa about you.

The woman snorted. "I'll bet." Then she grabbed a plate of food and waited for them to join her.

Isa's stomach soured as she stared at the sensual dynamo. Tall and lithe, with dark brown eyes that sparkled, Mara could easily make a killing as a pleasurer on Aran or Nebe6, for that matter. That Catam seemed beside himself to please the woman only irritated Isa further.

"So you're Isa Araye," Mara said before biting into a small blue fruit.

Damn. She had all her teeth too. "I am."

Isa's blunt words raised the captain's brow. Isa kept her gaze on her plate, not wanting Catam to see the jealousy tugging at her heart. Let him think she had an aversion to bounty hunters in general, as she'd more or less already told him.

"You seem to have caused everyone a lot of trouble lately. Though my husband seems to like you."

Isa heard what sounded like a muttered curse. She turned to see Catam as intent on his food as she pretended to be, and dismissed the noise.

"Lurin seems pleasant enough, for a bounty hunter," Isa responded. She needed to remain pleasant. The captain was, after all, giving them a free ride, when she could have collected on Isa as a legitimate bounty.

Mara stared at both Isa and Catam, her eyes narrowed in study. She surprised Isa by suddenly laughing.

"What?" Isa and Catam asked simultaneously, garnering more laughter from the woman.

"Nothing," Mara said with a shake of her head. "I'm just sorry we had to meet under such circumstances."

Her brown eyes shone with mirth and Isa found it hard to hang on to her envy. Nothing in the way Mara acted seemed proprietary concerning Catam, nor did she seem bothered by Isa's presence on the ship.

"I'm sorry to put your ship in jeopardy," Isa conceded. "Should anyone know you're helping me, you could be in a lot of trouble."

Mara waved her words away. "I've been in plenty of trouble before. You should ask Lurin about our "courtship" before we married. What a nightmare. But I wouldn't trade it for anything."

She glanced at Catam and smiled, though her words had a distinct bite. "And speaking of nightmares, your brother Sernal is worse than a rash." Catam choked on a mouthful of food. "I thought he had an interplanetary dispute to settle. How the hell does he have the time to signal me every few hours?"

"I'll talk to him," Catam offered quickly.

"You do that." Her voice and expression suggested he do so, and quickly. "And you're going to owe me some pretty long watch hours when you come back."

A buzzer sounded, interrupting her, and she thrust her com unit at Catam. "Damn. That's probably him again. Stall him or join him, but don't let him board this ship yet. I've got a few things I don't want to have to explain to a peacekeeper. And you know what I'm talking about." She stood to leave. "Isa, glad to meet you. I'm sure we'll have a chance to talk when this mess you're in clears."

Mara smiled and winked at her, turned a no-nonsense look on Catam, then left the galley.

They sat in silence before Isa exhaled a deep breath. "Wow. That's some captain you've got there."

"I know." He looked glum. "She's great to have on your side, and a royal pain in the ass when it comes to handing out watch assignments."

Isa couldn't help but grin at his dejection. "Look at the bright side. She didn't tell you not to come back, and she actually thinks this mess I'm in will clear up for the better."

"You mean this mess *we're* in." The com unit buzzed again. "And if you think I'm not involved, wait until you hear Sernal. He'll tell you how screwed up we both are, but in a lot more colorful terms."

## Chapter Eleven

After several minutes of one-sided conversation, Catam interrupted his brother by disconnecting.

"Was that wise?" Isa asked, looking decidedly uneasy.

He sighed. "Probably not, but I couldn't take much more. He's been like that since childhood. All lecture and no fun. Don't worry, as soon as he's done throwing things, he'll call back."

Sure enough, they had time to finish their meal before the com unit sounded.

Catam rolled his eyes and hastily swallowed his last bite. "Hello?"

"If you hang up on me again, I swear I'll come down on you so hard you won't see the sun for at least three months. Brother or not, I'll slam you in Jintak's holding tank and lose the digi-data until you grovel like a threll."

Catam knew his brother had reached the limits of his patience. "Sorry for disconnecting, but you wouldn't let me explain a thing."

"Talk," Sernal ordered curtly.

Catam hurriedly explained Daarna and Arnath's involvement in Klin's death and detailed the skirmish with the guards at Klin's estate.

"Okay," Sernal said slowly. "But you still haven't explained why it's taken you so long to report, or why the suspect isn't in custody in Jintak. You could have furthered the investigation after you completed the mission. I wouldn't have objected."

"You don't understand." Catam ran a frustrated hand through his hair and deliberately kept his back to Isa as he lowered his voice. "If they haven't already, Arnath and Daarna will put out the Ari on your suspect. She'd no doubt be dead right now if I hadn't altered the plan."

He heard silence while Sernal digested his justification.

"So you did what was best for the suspect to keep her alive? All in the interest of justice, I assume? I'm sure she's not attractive. And I know you didn't have sex with her. Tell me you didn't."

"Ah, well, that's a little more complicated." He held the com unit from his ear to avoid going deaf. He glanced at Isa and saw her blanch at some of Sernal's loud and obscene phrases.

After a short pause, Catam put the unit to his ear again. "Are you through?"

"You and I are long overdue for a talk, Catam," Sernal seethed. "But in the meantime, I'm working to smooth over Statesman Bedenzi's indignation over the situation with the guards. With any luck I can convince him not to press charges against you.

"You have two more days. Get me the evidence to clear Isa Araye or I'll find her and bring her to Jintak myself. Understand?"

Catam reluctantly agreed. "Understood."

"And you call me with a progress report first thing tomorrow, upon Aran's rise."

That didn't leave Catam much time, but he and Isa would have to make the best of it. With their allies running short, he didn't want to chance bringing Sernal's wrath down on them too.

"I'll call you. I promise," Catam growled at another of Sernal's threats and disconnected.

"That went well." Isa's sarcasm chafed what little remained of Catam's pride. Nothing like having your older brother make you feel like a child again, only to have your lover turn around and do the same.

"I did the best I could." He glared at her, realizing he directed his frustration at the wrong person, but was unable to stop himself. "Maybe now you'll take a hard look at thieving. Keep this up and you'll be living in Jintak, as sure as Klin's dead. Is it worth it? Stealing for mere currency?" he added with disgust. "Is it worth your freedom, your life?"

"It's worth my dignity," she answered in a quiet voice. "It's worth my self-respect. So don't lecture me about thievery. If I could apply my talents elsewhere, don't you think I would have? But on Aran, there's little choice for a daughter, and less so for a fourth daughter."

She gave a short laugh, devoid of humor, and he knew he'd hurt her. "Be glad I'm not a pleasurer, or you'd owe me thousands for the sexual favors you've taken during our short acquaintance." She deliberately made light of their relationship, reducing their intimacies to the physical, and shamed Catam at once.

"Now why don't you let me finish my meal in peace while you contact Cheltam, hmm?" she turned to her food, successfully ignoring him as he stood there, wondering what to say.

A short 'I'm sorry' seemed too trite and since he couldn't think of anything better, he left the galley in search of the control room.

He'd wanted to talk to Isa about her choice of profession for some time, but not like that. He could almost see the trust and openness between them fading as she withdrew into herself.

Hadn't he speculated on her difficulties growing up on Aran? Why hadn't he allowed his brother's anger to simply roll off him, instead of reacting with an unasked-for sermon? *Hell*, he thought with a scowl, *I sounded just like Sernal.*

He stalked into the control room and ignored everyone.

He sat at a locator station and punched in all known facts concerning Cheltam. Having worked with the information specialist before, always via mediastream, Catam knew how to reach him, but not necessarily where to reach him.

Half an hour later, after speaking with several of his contacts in Tekar, Catam located Cheltam. The man currently resided in an upscale neighborhood within the gambling district.

"Captain Mara?" Catam asked after disconnecting his call. "Can you set us down northeast of Qalteh's club in Tekar?"

She nodded. "No problem. Nu, set course for Qalteh's, and before you ask, no, we're not setting down for more than the time it takes to drop Catam and Isa. I swear, you Raggas live to gamble," she muttered. When Catam headed for the door, she stopped him. "A moment of your time?"

He nodded and chanced a brief glance at Lurin before he left. The Thesha mouthed "good luck," making Catam groan. He didn't need another lecture. Not now.

Mara led him to her personal library and closed the door behind them.

"We'll be there in a few minutes. I should inform Isa." He tried to sound earnest, and not as if he was trying to escape.

"She can wait," Mara murmured. She sat on the edge of her desk and waited until he sat across from her, where she could look down at him. "Catam, why have you been so depressed lately?"

"Depressed? I haven't been depressed."

"Not since you met Isa." She pursed her lips. "Ever since Lurin joined us I've noticed a change in you. This past year, you've turned from a lighthearted rogue into a moody, thrill-seeking danger-trap."

"I like Lurin," he protested, uncomfortable with her insight.

"I know you do," she said softly and her eyes warmed. "But something isn't right and you know it. Oh, you're still funny and pleasant to be around, but when you think no one's looking, you seem to sink into yourself. And lately you've been volunteering for one dangerous assignment after the other. You try working alone, as if Set, Nu and Lurin don't exist."

"I'm sorry. I didn't realize I was such a liability," he said stiffly.

"Don't freeze me out," she ordered. "You know it's true. Tell me, Catam. We've been together for more than six years. I'm your captain yes, but I'm also your friend."

The sincerity in her voice and in her eyes made him rethink his caustic comment. "I don't know what's wrong with me," he admitted on a sigh. "I was glad to have Lurin aboard, still am. But seeing you and him together, I don't know. It made me start questioning my choices. I mean, is this my life? Hunting the scum of System and visiting a new woman in a new port between jobs?"

"It's funny, but I didn't see a problem with my life until Lurin forced me to take a second look," Mara mused. "Now you're taking a second look, and you don't like what you see." She paused. "Or do you? Isa's a beautiful woman."

Catam grimaced. "She's beautiful, intelligent, and trouble. She's a thief, Mara. And we track those people down and hand them to the law."

"People change, Catam. Star's sake, you can change too. It's not set in stone that you live life as a bounty hunter--not that I'm recommending you change career paths."

"Change isn't as easy for some as it is for others."

"Meaning?"

He shrugged. "My people don't like change, and neither do Isa's. The Mardu are expected to play when we're young, then chose a profession and follow it until we're no longer able to work."

"But why?" She stared at him in surprise.

"That's the way the Mardu are. That Isa comes from Aran, one of our moons, doesn't make her less Mardu. It's a sorry trait, I know, but not everyone is as flexible as you are."

"You're more flexible than you know." She watched him with appreciation. "I've never seen you lose a bounty. Ever. And rumor has it you've never lost anything you really want."

"I am the best," he bragged to lighten the mood.

"Well if you want more out of life, then take it. If you want what Lurin and I have, be brave enough to accept it when it's thrust under your nose, or in your case, placed in your custody."

"You and Lurin love each other. I didn't say I was in love

with Isa."

Mara rolled her eyes. "You didn't have to. I know you better than you think. The entire time she's been on the ship, you haven't left her side except when absolutely necessary. You completely disregarded Sernal's orders. And I know that while you hate the peacekeeper mission, you would never deliberately foil your brother unless you had a very important reason."

"Tell him that," he muttered.

"And most important," she continued, ignoring him, "when you gaze at Isa, you have that look."

"What look?"

"The same look Lurin wears when he looks at me." She nodded and winked. "When a Thesha swears off all other women, you know it's true love."

Catam had to agree. In the past year, he'd never seen a man so completely besotted with one woman. And for a Thesha, a man that could have any woman he wanted with little effort, "besotted" translated to "in love."

Conscious that he felt as if a weight had fallen off his shoulders, Catam stood. Opening up to Mara had made him feel worlds better. It was as if the fog confusing the real issues disappeared, leaving him a clear path toward the future.

"Thanks, Mara." He hugged her, not surprised to feel a mental push to disengage. He let her go, already planning his next meeting with Isa.

"Sorry." Mara's face heated. "Lurin and I have a tendency to stay connected." She tapped her head.

"He's a lucky man." Catam smiled, glad that Mara finally had someone to love her as she deserved.

"I know. I'm constantly reminding him."

He laughed. "Would you mind postponing our landing another hour? I need some time with Isa."

"Not a problem. Good luck."

He left Mara to find Isa where he'd left her, in the galley.

She nodded politely when he entered, but gave him no more welcome than that. Knowing she had a right to her anger, he strove for patience.

"We'll be approaching Tekar soon."

She didn't respond.

"Mara wants us in our room prior to landing."

She frowned up at him. "Why?"

He shrugged. "Something about doing an emergency landing for practice. Since this isn't a regular stop, she's trying to make good use of the trip, I guess."

Isa stared at him suspiciously before she stood and preceded him to the room.

*Not a bad lie*, he congratulated himself. Just a little further.... She entered ahead of him and he refrained from rubbing his hands greedily. He discreetly set the lock using his personal ID and turned to face Isa.

"What did you just do?"

He knew his little thief would take note of every detail. "I just locked us in."

"Why?" She sneered at him. "So you can fuck me again? Well this time it's not free, Catam. It'll cost you." Her chest heaved with emotion, anger and hurt lacing her words.

"I'm willing to pay any price," he said softly and shortened the distance between them. "I'm sorry I sounded judgmental earlier. I'm not really. I respect what you do, even if it worries me."

She looked confused. "What?"

"I shouldn't have taken my anger at my brother out on you."

"No, you shouldn't have." She seemed slightly mollified.

"And I shouldn't have lectured you about your life's work."

"Agreed." She nodded, relaxing.

"I just need to show you there's more you're capable of, much more."

Without giving her a chance to respond, he sealed her mouth with his own.

With preternatural speed he disrobed her, caressing and kissing her as he found bare skin along the way.

"Catam, wait," she breathlessly protested, her eyes glazed with passion.

But he wouldn't stop. He couldn't. He lifted her in his arms and set her on the bed, following her to prevent her escape.

"Let me show you what you can do," he whispered and ran his lips down her body. His hands toyed with her breasts while he hurried to taste her, needing to experience Isa's essence in its truest form.

His mouth immediately centered over her mound and he kissed the thatch of silky hair, satisfied at the shiver that shook her. Her scent enveloped him and he nuzzled her mound, seeking the source of the spice that beckoned him forth. Moving lower to the soft folds protecting her treasure, he licked them and groaned when he tasted the moisture that flowed between her thighs.

"Catam, please," she moaned, squirming beneath him.

"For you, love," he answered, "anything." He plunged his tongue between her folds, lapping at the honeyed fluid. He dipped his tongue into her sheath and closed his eyes, feeling her arousal seep into his.

He gripped her thighs to steady himself, when all he really wanted was to fuck her senseless, long and hard. He wanted to come inside of her, wanted to feel her pussy gripping him tight.

But the soft mews and hungry motions her body made kept him firmly ensconced between her thighs. *So sweet*, sounded like a mantra in his head as he licked the evidence of her desire. She tilted her pelvis and cried out, releasing another gush of want, and her clitoris commanded his attention.

He lifted his head to stare down at her, spreading her legs further apart to better see her beauty. Red and flushed, her clitoris looked like a ripe fruit. Smiling at his analogy, he bent down and bit her gently.

"Catam," she cried and convulsed, stiffening beneath him. Her orgasm consumed her for more than a minute while he continued to lave her with his mouth.

When she stilled, he stopped and rose above her.

"You are amazing," she gasped. Her eyes were hazed with pleasure, her soft skin flushed with passion, and he thought she had never looked as beautiful as she did then. Her black hair spread around her like a bed of night, illuminating the golden vision of pure sensuality lying in naked glory.

"I can't be mad at you when you do that," she pouted. Her full lips, stung from his loving, curled into a smile and he knew she'd forgiven him.

"If I'm not inside of you in two seconds, I might die," he groaned.

"But I don't think you're truly sorry yet," she said and her breathing accelerated.

"Hmm?"

"Stand over there," she ordered as she left the bed. "Turn around."

He turned and found her staring at him. Her gaze traveled from the top of his head to rest on his swollen cock.

"Very nice," she purred. She walked up to and around him, and it killed him when her breasts touched his back. Her arms encircled his waist, and her hands teased the hard planes of his abdomen.

He drew in his breath when her fingers teased his pubic hair.

"Please," he begged, needing her hands around him. Already his dick felt like it would explode. He could smell her on his tongue and on his lips, and the scent made him wild to have her.

"Tell me again how sorry you are," she said and trailed one glorious finger over his throbbing shaft.

He closed his eyes and prayed for a quick end.

"I'm so very, very sorry," he said thickly, but kept his hands to his sides. This was Isa's show, and he'd be damned if he'd do anything to interrupt her now.

Her hand fisted around his cock and he groaned her name.

"Now I'm going to give you what you really deserve," she said and began pumping his shaft.


## Chapter Twelve

Isa felt heady with power when Catam's head rolled back on his neck and his body trembled. She quickened and slowed her pace around his cock, wanting to bring him to the edge without letting him go over.

As much as she'd already come, she wanted him again. Teasing Catam made her wet with desire, and she wanted him out of control and insane with lust. She wanted power over him, as he'd wielded the power to hurt her with his thoughtless words earlier.

She suddenly let go of his shaft and circled to his front. He panted like an animal and she smiled, a feline grin that made him swear.

"Tell me what you want," she whispered and lowered to her knees. "Tell me exactly what you want."

Catam's hands were clenched so tightly she thought he'd leave marks in his palms.

"Isa," he stopped and shook when her tongue licked the side of his shaft.

"Isa what?" She blew on the head of his cock and licked the fluid that sobbed to be released.

"Suck me, Isa," he breathed, his golden eyes glowing as they glittered at her. "Take me in your mouth. Swallow me, love, swallow all of me."

She opened her mouth and took him in an inch at a time. His knees shook and she sucked him, hard. He shouted and thrust, unable to stop himself. And she sucked harder.

She swiftly created a rhythm that brought him closer to relief, and then she grazed his velvet sack with her hands.

"Isa, love, I'm going to come," he groaned as she cupped him.

She increased her rhythm and continued to caress him. His thrusts grew stronger and she let him pulse, needing him to come. She wanted him to be as powerless in her hands as she was in his.

"Sweet," he whispered on a strangled moan before he shot into her. His cum slid down her throat like honeyed cream, thick and rich. He pulsed and pulsed, his hands clenching her shoulders for support when he began to tremble.

Finally spent, he eased down beside her on his knees and took her in his arms. He hugged her to him as if he'd never let her go, and something shifted inside of her.

The hurt and the self-doubt disappeared. She had brought Catam, a legendary lover, to his knees. She had done this. And he had reveled in it. By all rights she should have been imprisoned, and he had risked everything to help her.

She hugged him back and closed her eyes, basking in his warmth. She could taste him, salty sweet, all man and yet more than that.

"It'll all work out, love," he whispered against her hair. "You'll see."

How long they remained like that she couldn't say, but it took an intercom warning to break them apart.

"Fifteen minutes to Tekar."

"Already?" she asked in astonishment.

"Unfortunately so." He sighed and patted her on the butt. "You'd better get dressed unless you want the crew seeing you like that." He frowned and she knew the thought disturbed him.

A ball of pleasure warmed her belly at the thought that Catam might feel jealousy over her. As she dressed, she mulled over what his jealousy might mean.

"Isa?" He spoke her name with a tenderness that had her blinking to see if it was real. "Thank you, love." He took her limp hand and kissed her palm. "I owe you more than you know."

"What--"

"Catam and Isa to the boarding platform. Now," Mara's voice commanded through the overhead speaker.

He kissed Isa quickly and once they both dressed, pulled her after him to the second deck of the ship, to the boarding platform.

"I found Cheltam and he's willing to meet with us. I get the feeling he doesn't exactly like Harron."

"Not many do," Isa admitted, adding her name to the list.

Lurin and Mara joined them on the platform.

"Good luck," Lurin said as he shook Catam's hand. He grabbed Isa's hand in his and heat burned at the contact.

"Although I don't think you're going to need it," he said to Catam through a wide grin.

Catam nodded. "Thank you. I'm borrowing a com unit so I can contact Sernal tomorrow."

"Thank the Stars," Mara muttered.

"He won't bother you again."

"Yeah, well, it might not be a bad idea to keep us in the loop too," Lurin offered. "Just in case you need any help."

Catam opened his mouth in protest, Isa was sure. The man had an aversion to receiving assistance. "We will," she said firmly and nudged Catam to answer in kind.

"We will," he said quickly.

She contained a grin, pleased that he still seemed willing to do anything to stay on her good side.

Mara gave her a conspiratorial wink and stepped back with Lurin when the ship landed.

The outer hull opened to allow their exit, and they left armed with two phasers, a com unit, and a small bag of provisions to see them through the next few days. Flor willing, they'd only need to get through tomorrow. With luck, Cheltam would show them just how to beat Harron at his own game.

\* \* \* \*

Qalteh's was a surprise. Isa had assumed the gaming club would be much like the filthy bar where she'd met Feltang in Shathra. Qalteh's, however, was anything but.

The premier gaming establishment in Tekar, and in the entire northern province, according to ads surrounding the town, Qalteh's catered to a higher clientele. Isa noted a few statesmen mingling with the high and middle classes, all with avarice gleaming in their eyes.

Highborn or not, those in Qalteh's came for serious gambling or serious pleasure. Like the bar in Shathra, open fornication surrounded the gaming tables. Pleasurers by the dozen loitered near high-stakes tables offering solace to the losers bent on drinking themselves into oblivion.

Unlike the bar in Shathra, however, these pleasurers were handsome creatures, and watching them perform was akin to watching art.

Isa couldn't help staring at two male pleasurers servicing a fashionably half-dressed woman.

"You don't need two when you have me," Catam growled in her ear.

"I'm just surprised at the quality here. I didn't expect as much."

"I know." He nodded and looked around them. "This place sits in the slumpits of Tekar. Only the invited are allowed entry, and only if they pay the required fee."

She glanced up at him in surprise.

"Cheltam was interested when I mentioned Harron," he explained, "so he arranged for us to enter on his tab."

"How much are we talking here?" she asked uneasily. Catam might not understand the rules of the "underground," but she knew accepting favor from someone meant having to return it later at a much higher price.

"Don't worry. Cheltam owes me more than just one lousy entrance fee."

She wondered at his and Cheltam's relationship when a large man with a scar running down his face approached.

Catam tensed until the man bowed and asked them, politely, to follow him.

Keeping himself between Isa and their guide, Catam seemed tense as he subtly looked all around them. Isa didn't understand the sense of threat. The club wasn't that crowded, and those that mingled seemed far too intent on gaming and sex to even look their way.

She gave Catam an inquiring glance.

"The Ari," he said under his breath and she stilled.

She'd forgotten, or chosen to forget, that small, significant detail. How could she have dismissed a possible assassination on her life? She stared at Catam. *Great sex, that's how I forgot about it.*

She didn't relax until they reached a private table in the corner lined with drapes. From here she'd be able to put her back to the wall, facing any coming threat.

"Welcome friends," a soft voice hummed from inside the drapes. The scarred man pulled back the partition to show a lone man sitting in the shadows.

"Cheltam?" Isa asked, quelling her nerves. She glanced at Catam and saw him make the oddest face.

He looked stunned, completely shocked at Cheltam's presence. Then he caught her staring at him and muttered, "No one else could command this corner save our enterprising host." His tone grim, Catam answered with a warning glance at the man patiently waiting. Then he reluctantly sat across from Cheltam and nodded for Isa to do the same.

Isa sat and the scarred man left them, dropping the drapes to surround the small table. A lone candle's flicker lent the small alcove a cozy feel, and had Cheltam not been present, she might have enjoyed the intimate setting with Catam.

"So, we meet at last," the informant whispered, the sound like the patter of raindrops on glass. "Isa Araye, in the flesh."

Isa studied the man, surprised at what she found. He sat straight and tall, his dark brown hair cut to his shoulders and tied in a fastidious sweep at the base of his neck. Amber eyes studied her with a keen intelligence as he tapped a graceful, long-fingered hand on the table.

"So you're Cheltam. Feltang mentioned you, and you're not what I expected," she said bluntly.

"I'm sure you expected someone as filthy and nervous as Feltang," Cheltam responded with dry humor. "I hope you're not disappointed."

"She's not," Catam interrupted. "We're here to talk about Harron."

Isa felt Catam's hand under the table curl around her thigh and she swallowed audibly. Heat flared where he touched her, and the possession in his grip thrilled her. She had to focus on Cheltam to control her desire, and she felt a flush darken her cheeks when she saw Cheltam's knowing grin.

"Harron, hmm," Cheltam paused. A decanter of purple liquid suddenly appeared in the center of the table surrounded by three glasses.

"Cheltam," Catam warned.

"Hold a minute, Mardu." The inflection in the informant's voice didn't change, but she could tell Catam had irritated him. "In celebration of Harron's certain and unavoidable demise, I ordered Chelfont 2040." He nodded to the purple liquid.

"You have expensive tastes," Isa murmured.

"But I so deserve it."

Catam sighed and squeezed Isa's thigh. "First you drink it, then I will."

Cheltam muttered something under his breath but he took a sip before pouring Catam a glass. After Catam swished the liquid in his mouth, he nodded and released her leg.

Cheltam poured Isa a glass. "See? It's vintage wine, something even you can appreciate, Mardu."

Catam rolled his eyes at the veiled insult and Isa chuckled. There was something about Cheltam she liked, though she couldn't put her finger on it.

"Now tell me about Harron," Cheltam said softly.

Isa explained her job for Harron, leaving out nothing in the details concerning Daarna or Arnath. The informant listened in silence.

"Well?" Catam said to dispel the quiet. "What do you know?"

Cheltam finished his wine, refusing to be hurried. His arrogance spoke volumes and Isa wished she felt as easy.

"We don't have all day," Catam growled.

Isa glared at him. They couldn't afford to scare Cheltam off, not at this point.

"How do you put up with him, my dear?" Cheltam sighed and pushed away his now empty glass. "Very well. Harron has been working for Daarna Klin for the past five years. Statesman Klin was in office for eight years, and the last five were spent keeping his wife in line."

"So he did know about her affairs," Catam said, as if confirming what he already knew.

Cheltam nodded. "But he didn't know this past year she had an ongoing affair with his fiercest rival, Arnath Bedenzi."

"That makes sense," Isa said. "But where does Harron come in?" She didn't understand. Klin had been wealthy, so Daarna shouldn't have wanted for anything. Why steal from her husband? And why use Harron to pawn her own goods?

"At first Daarna stole from her husband to finance her gambling habit. That's how she met Arnath in the first place," Cheltam explained.

"He was blackmailing her?" Catam toyed with his glass. "That sounds like his style."

"Yes," Cheltam agreed. "She began pawning her jewelry and antiques to finance Arnath's campaign against her husband. Apparently once he won Klin's seat, Daarna would be off the hook."

"She isn't," Isa said with a frown.

"Ah, but that's because she has him right where she wants him." Cheltam smiled. "It was her idea to use Harron in the first place. He came up with your name, Isa, because you refused to work with him on so many other jobs. Why did you concede this time?"

Isa shook her head. "I wasn't thinking straight." No, Teve had dumped her and she'd desperately needed to escape.

Catam frowned. "You sure as hell weren't." She glared at him and he coughed. "I mean, it's too bad about the whole situation."

Cheltam stared at him strangely before continuing. "Yes, well, in any case, Daarna decided to murder her husband, steal his wealth, and place the blame on a thief from Aran. The blade used to stab Klin was Voranian. Arnath's father made it, and Harron just happens to have it in his private safe."

"How do you know this?" Isa asked, amazed at what

Cheltam knew.

He shrugged. "Information is my game. It's what I do." He acted nonchalant, but she could see him preening.

Catam saw it too, for he muttered, "Peacock."

"All I need to do then, is steal it back from Harron and we've got the evidence to support my story."

Catam looked thoughtful. "It seems almost too easy."

"It is." Cheltam smiled, and his affability faded under a predatory grin. "It so happens I acquired the knife from Harron. You can have it, for a price."

Catam stilled, menace filling his frame. His eyes glowed and Isa wanted to warn Cheltam to tread carefully. Catam would only be pushed so far.

"You owe me," Catam reminded him through clenched teeth.

"I think not. I don't owe you a thing," Cheltam answered calmly.

"Damn it, you--"

Isa cut off Catam's roar by "accidentally" spilling wine on his lap. He looked shocked and had she not been so desperate to salvage the situation, she would have laughed.

"Look, Cheltam, I need that knife. Just tell us what you want."

Cheltam's gaze remained on Catam when he answered in a cool voice, "I want you, Isa. Just you."

## Chapter Thirteen

"You bastard," Catam said and lunged over the table.

Cheltam surprised them all, dodging the attack and pinning Catam to the wall with one hand on his throat and another holding a phaser.

"Don't move, my dear," he said quietly, "or I'll put your lover to sleep for a long, long time."

Isa stopped in her tracks, just a foot away from smashing Cheltam in the head with the carafe.

"Put it down," he said without looking at her.

She placed the glass decanter on the table and stared angrily at the back of his head, wishing him to hell.

"That's right, everyone calm down." Cheltam released Catam who snarled angrily. The informant wisely kept his phaser sighted on Catam's chest. "Both of you sit back down and listen.

"I want Isa, and I want her to accompany me, tonight, back to my home. If she's as good as I imagine," he said, his eyes blazing with a sudden heat, "I'll give her the knife and a thank you."

Isa's jaw dropped. She'd never before had anyone blackmail her for ... sex? Maybe Catam had done something to her that made her seem sexy to the male species. Her sisters had men fall all over themselves for their attention. But not Isa. Not until Catam, and now apparently Cheltam.

"Let me get this straight," she said for clarification. "You want me to go home with you and have sex with you. That's what you want in exchange for the knife?"

Cheltam grinned, and for the first time Isa noted how handsome he was. He shouldn't need blackmail to get a woman. Why this, and why her?

"Cheltam," Catam growled, "this is the most asinine thing--"

"I figure this way I'll be enjoying Isa while you deal with the Ari on her head. This is as good a place as any to start searching."

His words doused Catam's anger and made Isa puzzle with worry. Cheltam knew about the Ari? If she indeed had an Ari over her, the smart thing would be to avoid her, not bring her home. What was Cheltam thinking? Then again, as she'd often heard said, men tended to think with their cocks or not at all. It seemed Cheltam wasn't as intelligent as she'd originally thought.

Catam cleared his throat. "Okay."

Isa turned an incredulous gaze on him. "Okay?"

He looked uncomfortable as he avoided her glare. He did, however, radiate frustrated anger as he cursed Cheltam. "When this is over, I'm going to peel your lips from your face, you piece of drun."

"*Okay?*" Isa repeated, in shock.

"Cheltam, give us some privacy, if you can manage that, you back-stabbing bastard."

Cheltam nodded and stood, ever calm, ever polite. "Of

course. I'll wait by the bar. Drekk, the man with the scar, will escort you to my conveyance when you're ready to leave," he said with a bow to Isa.

The minute he departed, Isa turned to Catam in a rage. "Okay? As if you have any right to turn me over to him! There's no way I'm going to have sex with Cheltam to get that knife back! Hell, give me a few hours and I'll steal it from him."

"Isa, calm down. I have to take care of the Ari. Much as you don't want to admit, until the Ari disappears, your life is forfeit. And I can't defeat them if you're with me, distracting me."

"But to have sex with Cheltam?"

"You will not fuck Cheltam," he said evenly, spacing out each word. "Stall him, lead him on, whatever, just keep him busy 'til I join you again. Despite that he's an ass, he won't hurt you. He won't force himself on you ... unless you want him to."

His gaze held a touch of hurt, as if he'd seen her attraction to Cheltam, and she blushed.

"He's an attractive man. Excuse me for noticing. But I'm no way in hell going to have sex with him!"

Catam stared searchingly into her eyes. He must have found what he sought for he sighed and hugged her close. "I'm sorry. I don't know what's come over me. I just see red imagining you and him together, alone."

Isa watched him grow angry all over again.

"Catam, trust me. I'll be waiting for you with my clothes on and my ears open." The thought of him facing the Ari, for her, was the deciding factor in telling him the truth. "Please be careful," she said and hugged him to her. "I love you."

\* \* \* \*

I love you.

What kind of words were 'I love you' before a woman left her man to 'have sex' with her man's brother?

What the hell was Rafe doing posing as Cheltam? Some undercover work! When Catam first spied his older brother sitting pretty as you please in the corner, his blood had boiled.

All this time Catam had been receiving tips from his contact Cheltam, tips that led to one successful bounty after another. And those tips had been given to him by his law-loving, peacemaker brother?

He shouldn't have been surprised Sernal kept the truth of Rafe's identity from him, if Sernal even knew the truth.

Catam frowned.

Rafe could be one unruly bastard. It was possible Sernal didn't know about 'Cheltam,' or what Rafe had planned tonight. Then again, Sernal normally seemed to know everything, an irritating trait that made getting away with anything nearly impossible.

Cheltam, a.k.a., Rafe of Mardu, had been right warning him about the Ari though. Catam would be better able to fight the assassins without worry for Isa clouding his focus.

As long as Rafe kept his Flor-damned hands off Catam's woman.

Mentally castrating his brother, Catam seethed and left the table in search of the assassins. Rafe's, "This is as good a place as any to start searching" comment clearly indicated the assassins had trailed them to Qalteh's. But if what Rafe said about Harron was true, then Rafe had the evidence pointing to Isa's innocence--unless he'd lied to ensure Isa's compliance.

Damn. All this second-guessing was giving Catam a headache. Grumbling under his breath, he opened his senses and proceeded to "sniff out" those involved in the Ari.

\* \* \* \*

The ride to Cheltam's home had been uncomfortable. The man said nothing, simply stared at her profile the entire way back.

He politely escorted her inside a massive structure in Tekar's wealthy sector, then left her in his study while he changed into something "more comfortable."

She immediately began a search of the study. She didn't imagine Cheltam foolish enough to leave her in a room hiding anything important, but she might find something useful before he returned.

His bookcases held classic volumes of Mardu poetry and Sildorian prose, an eclectic mix of musical disks, from the conventional to the hottest trends in today's clubs, and myriad holograms of landscapes, presumably places he'd visited or hoped to visit.

Not surprisingly, she found no family portraits or evidence of ties with another living soul. From the little she knew of Cheltam's reputation, he brokered information. He never divulged his sources and always proved reliable. Descriptions of the man always varied considerably, and she wondered if he had in fact worn a disguise at Qalteh's.

If so, she figured he'd stay in character. She only hoped his level of "comfort" matched hers.

"You like Mardu poetry?" his smooth voice called to her from the open doorway.

She hastily set down a volume she'd been holding. It had looked out of place so she'd taken the book from the stack hoping to unlock a hidden compartment. No such luck. Turning, she opened her mouth to respond and froze in shock.

His dark brown hair was slicked back from his head, his hair wet from a recent wash. He wore simple gray trousers that though loose, clung to his frame when he moved. His shirt lay unfastened over a brawny chest, his skin a smooth, golden brown.

She couldn't stop staring at his male beauty. Hell, he reminded her of Catam. The look in his golden gaze told her he was aware of her attraction, and the satisfaction that glinted there warned her to be wary.

As he strode toward her, she noted absently his lack of footwear. That he wore only the outward trappings of civility made her want to run and not look back.

"Like what you see?" he teased and stopped a breath from her. He tugged on a lock of her hair. "I do."

As he bent his head for what she assumed was a kiss, she narrowly avoided his lips and took a hurried step back.

*Catam, think of Catam*, she mentally repeated, not understanding how this man could seem so attractive. Making love with Catam had convinced her she could never be a pleasurer. Before Cheltam, the thought of sex with another male made her shudder. But now, this golden-eyed stranger made her stomach quiver and her heart race. A distressing situation all around.

"So," he paused and sat in a formal chair to watch her, "how long have you known Catam?"

"Long enough," she muttered and stepped away, putting his desk between them. Not caring how inappropriate it might be to sit behind his desk, she nevertheless plunked into the comfortable seat and remained on her toes, ready to flee should he make a move toward her.

"It's funny," Cheltam drawled, "but I've never known the bounty hunter to be so particular about his women." She mentally grimaced. As if she needed reminders Catam had a life beyond that which she knew. "I've never known him to be so possessive."

"Really?" she tried to sound bored.

"Really," he said with a smile. He crossed his legs and for a moment she saw a hard bulge between his thighs. "So how close are you two?" he asked in a low voice.

"Very close."

"I know he's fucked you. He may not be the brightest, but he's not that stupid."

"He's an extremely intelligent man," she defended with a cool voice. "He found you, didn't he?"

Cheltam chuckled and relaxed in his seat. "That he did. And he found you. But he didn't get his hands on the evidence you want so badly, did he? I have it in my safe, the one you haven't yet found."

"Is it in here?" She had to know. Her hands were itching to go over the study again.

"Alas, no. It's in another room. And no, I won't tell you where. That would be foolish, considering how very well you do your job."

The compliment both pleased and disturbed her.

"You're familiar with my work, then?"

"Of course. The minute I came into possession of the knife, I did a thorough check into your history." He steepled his fingers and stared at her. "Funny you aren't more amenable to sex with me. From what I gathered, your family runs one of the most popular pleasuring establishments on Aran."

"Well, if you're so smart," she said through her teeth, "you should know I'm not a part of that business. Why the hell would I be involved in this mess if I was so successful on Aran?"

He laughed. "Good point." He uncrossed his legs and stood, his erection impossible to miss. "Now that the necessary small talk is out of the way, let's get started with our trade."

He moved around the desk in a flash and she blinked, not sure how he could be standing over her when a second ago he'd been seated.

"Cheltam?"

He lifted her to her feet, none too gently, and caged her in his arms. He smelled like spiced areesia, a rare plant on Mardu known for its sensual effects. She tried hard not to inhale too deeply and pushed at him. His arms felt hard under her protesting hands, as she gripped his biceps to keep him at bay.

"Ah," he murmured and leaned down to lick the pulse in her neck. "You want to play the unwilling maiden, eh? Funny, I wouldn't have pegged you as a coward."

Heat shot through her, a combination of lust and anger. "I'm not a coward," she seethed. "I simply don't want to have sex with a man I don't know, don't respect, and frankly don't like."

"Ah." He smirked and drew her protesting form closer, so that her breasts pressed through her thin shirt onto his bare chest. "You may think you don't like me, but your body knows the truth."

He glanced down and she followed his gaze, embarrassed to see her nipples hard, raking his chest like twin beacons of desire.

"And I'd wager your pussy is wet and waiting for me." He closed his eyes and inhaled. "Hmm. I bet you taste like sweet hazel cream."

He held her tightly in his arms and ground his pelvis against hers. She felt his erection burn through her trousers, and damned her body for turning traitor. The hell of it was, she couldn't help her responses.

*I'll just play him until Catam arrives. Surely I can resist him until then.*

"Look, Cheltam," she said in a less antagonistic tone. She would respond to him gradually, to make her actions more believable. "I want that knife. Let me see it, hell, put it on the desk out of my reach if you have to, and I'll do whatever you want." She licked her lips suggestively, like she'd seen her sisters do, and saw Cheltam follow the movement like a raptor.

"Anything?" he asked in a deep voice and pressed his cock closer.

She swallowed loudly and he groaned. A feeling of pure feminine power washed over her and she blinked, surprised that now, of all times and places, she should finally find her sexual confidence.

"Wait right here," he ordered in a gritty voice and left the study.

She sagged in relief and focused to cool her ardor. In retrospect, she felt whole. Much as her body might respond to Cheltam, her mind and heart belonged to Catam. Thoughts of him made her worry, and she prayed to Flor to guide him in his quest against the Ari.

If anyone could break the Ari, Catam could. His skills and understanding of the criminal classes would be to his benefit. Besides, as close as they had become, she would know if something happened to him. And so far, she only felt nervous and angered thanks to Cheltam.

He returned and she studied him, wondering just what it was about the man that made him so sexy. He didn't have Catam's beautiful hair or amazing looks, but he had something.

He stood a head taller than Catam, had deeper golden eyes, and a degree of calm that seemed missing in her lover. His body was similar to Catam's though, muscular to reflect his strength, but not meaty like a Ragga.

His face, surprisingly, reflected character. He had a strong chin and sharp nose, clearly delineated cheekbones and cat-shaped eyes that gave him an exotic quality. Yet his eyes were hard--measuring and unforgiving. Despite the heat in his gaze when he looked at her, something about his perusal seemed judgmental.

"What? You're still clothed?"

"Let me see it," she ordered. His lips crooked and he glanced down at himself. "The dagger," she emphasized.

He sighed and placed it on the desk. She was careful not to touch it, glad the evidence lay in a sealed bag to protect it from contamination. She looked closely to find the familiar hilt, the Voranian design stained with blood, and nodded.

"That's it."

"Of course it is," he sounded offended. "I didn't set out to cheat you. I'm an information broker, not a thief." He paused. "No offense intended."

"None taken," she said wryly, aware their interaction now seemed less based on lust and more on business. She felt comfortable instead of threatened, and wondered how he would feel knowing that.

His erection had faded, she noted subtly, and wondered about that too.

"I was thinking about that 'anything' you mentioned earlier," he said softly, immediately drawing her attention.

"What about it?" *Come on Catam. I need you here, love.*

His cock stiffened noticeably and she couldn't help but groan.

"Never fear, sweet," he said with a chuckle. "I'm always ready for a lovely woman. And you're lovelier than most. Those lips of yours look plump and soft." He grazed his erection with his hand, pulling her gaze to the long shaft and heavy globes outlined by his thin trousers. "I'll bet you've sucked Catam dry more than once."

Mention of Catam strengthened her resolve. She could feel herself getting wet and ignored the sensation. "Why so much interest in Catam?"

He shrugged and sat down in his formal chair, this time with his legs splayed wide. "What can I say? I'm curious as to why you'd sleep with a peacemaker. I think of you as one of my kind, the kind that detests the law. Had Harron not been involved, I wouldn't have offered one iota of assistance." He stroked himself lazily, his eyes glittering with lust as they focused on her breasts, and he continued.

"Did you think sleeping with him would lower his guard? Perhaps you've already traded sex. Sex for freedom? Catam doesn't usually play by the rules, so I can see him using your pussy as payment. Wonderful peacemaker," he scoffed. "He has no integrity when it comes to sustaining the law."

She let his insulting remarks roll off her back until he impugned Catam. "You don't know what you're talking about. And if you're smart, you'll shut up."

"Have I offended you?" He acted surprised, but the glint in his eyes told her he had intended such.

"Just tell me what you want me to do." She crossed her arms over her chest, wanting more than anything to leave.

"I want you to suck me like you do Catam," he said slowly, eyeing her response.

She sauntered to stand between his thighs and stared down at the outline of his cock with a measuring look. It swelled under her regard and she curled her lip.

"Impressive. You look rather large," she commented evenly, "but I could never treat you the way I do Catam." Kneeling between his thighs, she put her palm flat on his cock and he sucked in his breath. She began stroking him, easing beneath his guard with her touch, and he closed his eyes in pleasure.

His breath hissed when she fondled the sack beneath his shaft and she smiled, a sharp twist to her lips that had he seen, would have scared the hell out of him.

"Don't you want to know why I could never suck you like I do Catam?" she asked and began priming his cock, fisting her hand around his girth, sliding her palm over the soft fabric encasing his shaft.

"Why?" he groaned on a breath.

"Because I love Catam. You on the other hand," she said sweetly and tightened her hold on his dick, "you I don't like so much."

The sigh on his lips quickly turned into a gasp of pain, and her smile turned to one of sincere joy.

## Chapter Fourteen

"What the hell is going on here?" Catam shouted as he entered Rafe's study. From a side vantage, he saw his brother sitting in a chair, his eyes closed in bliss as Isa knelt between his thighs with her hand buried in his crotch.

"Catam!" she cried and leapt to greet him.

His brother, however, merely groaned and tumbled out of his chair to a heap on the floor, clutching himself in pain.

"Isa, what's going on?" Catam repeated, tension leaving him when he realized pleasure was the furthest thing from his brother's mind.

"This drun had the nerve to tell me to 'suck him the way I do you,' can you believe that?"

Catam glared at his writhing brother. "No, I can't. I think he got what he deserves for trying to seduce my woman."

Isa stared at him slack-jawed. "Your what?"

"My woman." Catam smiled. "Haven't you realized yet where you belong?"

"I, wh-what about the Ari?"

"I took care of it," he said firmly, not wanting to detail his victory over four assassins. Isa tended to worry when he was outnumbered.

"But Catam, we barely know each other," she stalled. He could see the pleasure battling the worry in her eyes.

"It's over, love, don't you see? My brother has the evidence to free you. It's just a matter of officially declaring Arnath and Daarna the guilty party and arresting Harron."

She frowned. "Sernal has the dagger?" She stared over her shoulder at the desk. "Then what's that?"

"That," Rafe said in hoarse voice, "is the evidence he's talking about. And I'm his brother."

"My not-long-in-this-world brother," Catam growled. When he saw the abject pain in Rafe's face, he relaxed some. "She gave it to you good, didn't she? Damn I love you," he told Isa and kissed her full on the mouth.

"Your brother?" She stared from Rafe to Catam with narrow eyes. Then her eyes flew wide open. "You love me?"

"Is it so hard to believe?" he asked, his mood sobering.

"I'm outta here," Rafe grumbled and limped toward the doorway. "Call me when it's safe to come back," he added over his shoulder and shut the door behind him.

Silence descended over them as they regarded each other. Catam wanted to kiss her, to wipe Rafe's memory from her mind. He wanted to claim her, mark her as his own.

He only hoped she wanted the same.

"You say you love me," she said slowly, "but you don't really know me."

"I know you're a beautiful, courageous woman whom I respect. You're a thief, and I'll admit I don't like what you do, but it's not who you are. In a choice between indiscriminate sex and stealing from the wealthy, I agree with the choice you made.

"But Isa, it doesn't have to continue that way. I love you," he said, willing her to believe it. A spark of hope lit her eyes, but underlying the hope was fear. "I hate change as much as you. We're both of the Mardu mindset. But together we can do anything."

"What if I told you I hated that you're a bounty hunter?" she asked quietly. "Would you change for me?"

"To choose between my profession and you is no contest. I choose you, every time. If you don't like what I do, I'll do something else. Isa, I want to spend my life with you."

"But don't you want to be sure I love you too?" she asked, a grin curling her lips. "I was worried when I told you I loved you at Qalteh's. Maybe it was just the heat of the moment."

"I know you love me," he said arrogantly, pleased when her eyes shot sparks of green fire. "You could never make love the way you do if you didn't love me."

He grabbed her and kissed her breathless. "I'll show you."

He disrobed her while he distracted her with his mouth, then he quickly shed his own clothing.

When they were both naked, he pulled her with him to the chair his brother had recently vacated and sat her in his lap. "I don't want you remembering my brother in this chair," he said in a gritty voice. "That you had your hand on his cock at all is something he'll pay for, dearly."

"Well, it was kind of arousing," she teased and slid her moisture over him. His cock parted her folds and he groaned at the contact. "But I never did this with him."

He leaned forward and caught one breast in his mouth. He sucked hard, loving the deep moan she gave as she leaned into his mouth. The motion put her above his penis, and with little effort he slid into her welcoming warmth.

"Catam," she breathed and closed her eyes as she sank over him.

"Yes, sweet," he said thickly, "think only of how much I fill you. Ride me, love; take me deep inside you."

He put his hands on her hips to guide her, but she caught a rhythm that all too soon had him gasping for release.

Up and down, she moved. Her pace quickened before she deliberately slowed, driving him out of his mind. She paused above him, maintaining the slightest contact with her pussy at the head of his shaft.

"Fuck me, now," he ordered and shoved her down, making them both groan at the exquisite feeling of fullness. She wrapped around him, squeezing him with her slick walls, and the rapture nearly undid him.

He quickly lowered his touch to pinch and pull her clit, massaging her mound and whispering words of sex and passion that had her increasing her pace in a hurry.

"Yes, harder," he gasped and shut his eyes, lost in the sensations, an image of her naked and on top of him firmed in his mind's eye.

She rose and sank hard, gripping his shaft between her thighs, and he saw bright lights behind closed eyelids.

"Yes," she cried and tightened, her clit hard and bursting as he caressed it with her cream. She came, slicking around him, and her walls squeezed him into ecstasy.

He gripped her thighs hard enough to leave bruises and thrust up into her, coming in great shudders.

On and on their climax lasted, until Isa sobbed with contentment, "I love you so much," and collapsed against his chest, still straddling him.

"And I love you," he rasped and flexed his cock once more, groaning when she pulled him deeper. "I love everything about you Isa. And if you really need to thieve for a living, I'll stand by you. I'll probably worry myself to death," he muttered, "but it's better than living without you."

She smiled against his chest. "I'm a damned good thief, and I'll be damned good at whatever else the future holds."

"How about as my future wife, and mother of my children?"

"Really?" she peeked up at him, her eyes glowing with happiness.

"Really. You are the best of thieves, love. You stole my heart and I expect you to keep it, forever and longer."

Wainu settled over them both, a step closer to true joy. And given future years spent with Isa, Catam knew they'd find their bliss together.

\* \* \* \*

An hour later, Rafe knocked on the door. "May I come in now? After all, it is my house," they heard him murmur.

"Hold on," Catam shoved Isa into her clothes and was finishing pulling on his shirt when Rafe entered.

"I hope you're feeling better," Isa said, and studiously avoided looking at his groin.

"I am, thank you," Rafe answered politely.

"And if you think we're not going to talk about whatever the hell you were trying to pull with her, think again," Catam growled.

Rafe sighed and walked, no longer limping, to his chair and sat. "Sernal told me how much trouble you were digging for yourself, so I decided to help." He favored Isa with a smile before continuing. "According to Sernal, you were falling fast for an Aran thief. I had to know her position concerning my baby brother."

"Baby brother?" Isa stared at Catam, startled to see him flush.

"They're always trying to tell me what to do," he grumbled like a little boy.

Isa laughed, understanding more about Catam's family dynamics. She couldn't really fault Rafe for wanting to protect his brother. But he could have handled it another way.

"So are you Xema too?" she wanted to know.

He inclined his head. "I am so blessed."

"Well that explains it, then," she said more to herself than Catam, relieved to know the attraction had to do with genetics.

"Explains what?" Catam asked with suspicion.

"The fact that he reminded me so much of you," she answered glibly, and after a moment Catam relaxed.

"Sernal and I look more alike, but Rafe and Gar could be twins."

"Speaking of Gar," Rafe added, "I'm pulling the recluse out of hiding to join the living again. I'm tired of playing Cheltam, so I think I'll let him do it for a while."

"So there is no real Cheltam," Isa said.

"I'm as real as he gets. There's always a need for a good source, and it keeps me 'in the know' as far as intelligence in the criminal world. Sorry I couldn't tell you, Catam, but I was never sure how solid your com security was."

"Yeah, whatever. I'm just glad you're bringing Gar back. He's really worried me." He offered Isa a quick explanation about Gar's situation.

"How sad," she said, knowing if Catam died, she'd feel absolutely lifeless.

"Grieving needs to run its course, but not at the cost of one's life," Rafe said quietly. He cleared his throat and continued. "On another note, I conferred with Sernal while you two were in here making all kinds of noise," he said with rebuke.

Isa blushed while Catam grinned widely.

"I'll teleport the knife to Sernal as soon as we're done here. As we speak, Sernal is rounding up Harron, Daarna and Arnath. I wouldn't want to be Arnath around those hotheaded northerners. I wouldn't put it past one of them to put an Ari on Arnath the minute he leaves the House meeting."

Isa breathed a sigh of relief. "So it's finally over?"

"I'd say it's just beginning," Rafe said with a grin. He stood and approached them. "How about a hug from my newest sister?" Ignoring Catam, he gave Isa a massive hug and a warm kiss on the mouth that had Catam growling.

"Hey, after the pain she put me through, I deserve something nice, don't I?"

Isa laughed.

"You think I'm bad," Rafe warned, "wait until you meet Sernal. He's a royal--"

"Pain in the ass," Catam finished with a sigh. "But he's my brother and I love him."

Rafe laughed, the golden light in his eyes a mirror for Catam's. "So what do you two have planned for the future?"

Catam stared at Isa with a naughty grin. "We plan on making all kinds of noise," he quoted his brother. "So either give up your study for the night, or show us a room with a nice, wide bed."

Rafe rolled his eyes. "I had to ask."


Epilogue

One Year Later

"That's another forty you owe me," Nu said and collected his beks from his cursing brother.

"I really hate that Mardu," Set muttered, glaring at Catam's grinning face.

"Can I help it you bet on the wrong person? I told you Isa

would get us that shipment under priced."

"Yeah, but the way you aggravated Murson after capturing his brother, I felt sure he'd sooner cut off his arm than deal with us."

Mara laughed. "You should know by now that Isa can procure anything we need, and at half the price. I can't believe you never thought of logistical procurement before, Isa. It's as if you were born to it."

"Well," Isa said with a modest grin, "it seems to me it's just thieving of another sort. And speaking of which, your husband owes me fifty beks. He bet on Murson too."

Lurin shrugged apologetically to his wife. "You didn't see the way Catam treated Murson's brother. Honestly, Mara, it was painful to watch!"

Mara turned a disapproving glare on Catam, who sat innocently next to Isa.

"What could I do? He made some disparaging comments about my captain. What should I have done?"

Mara appeared to think about it. "Look, next time try to be friendly with those we might trade with in the future. It'll make Isa's job that much easier."

Catam shared a grin with his wife. "But Mara, without a little challenge to keep us occupied, we're sure to find trouble out there."

"That's the truth," Set murmured and turned back to his console, grumbling.

Lurin chuckled and shook his head. "He's right love. And unfortunately, Isa's as bad as he is. Trouble with a capital T."

Isa leaned toward Catam and murmured in a low voice, "Speaking of trouble," she said and stroked her belly.

His eyes widened. "You mean...."

She nodded.

"By Flor's Heart! I'm going to be a father!" he yelled to everyone in the room. Then he grabbed Isa and dragged her to their quarters.

"On no," Set groaned dramatically. "More trouble on the horizon."

Lurin laughed. He sat frozen for a moment while the others returned to work. His eyes blazed bright blue before he turned to Mara with a funny grin.

He whispered, "I just 'snuck a peek' at Isa's belly. Make

that, double trouble."

## The End

Printed in the United States
36835LVS00002B/139-513